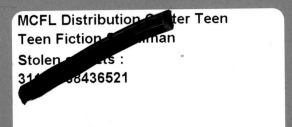

STOLEN SECRETS

L. B. SCHULMAN

BOYDS MILLS PRESS
AN IMPRINT OF HIGHLIGHTS
Honesdale, Pennsylvania

For information about permission to reproduce selections from this book,
please contact permissions@highlights.com.

Boyds Mills Press
An Imprint of Highlights
815 Church Street
Honesdale, Pennsylvania 18431
Printed in the United States of America

ISBN: 978-1-62979-722-9 (hc) • 978-1-62979-919-3 (e-book)
Library of Congress Control Number: 2017937877

First edition

10 9 8 7 6 5 4 3 2 1
Designed by Barbara Grzeslo
Text set in Janson

To my children, who were born
when this was a seed of an idea
and helped give it life
so many years later

APRIL 1945, BERGEN-BELSEN CONCENTRATION CAMP

The naked limbs of the dead blocked her path. She tried to step over them, but the disease had weakened her knees, and she buckled to the ground like an enemy plane shot from the sky. Her gaze landed on the vacant stare of a prisoner, bony arm extended as if to invite her into death. That's when she noticed she'd ripped off her own dress in a fit of fever. All she had left was an envelope, crushed in the grip of her hand. She thought to herself: Hold tight! No one must have it!

Later she woke to a ruckus. Soldiers swarmed the yard. The one with a beret clasped a cloth to his nose. A Brit folded over his gun and vomited. She didn't comprehend, couldn't tell her enemies from her saviors.

The soldiers searched for movement among the still, dragging life from the remains.

Save me! she longed to shout. Can't you see I'm alive? My skin holds the blush of fever! Her mouth was too parched to speak. The words held captive in her head.

With tremendous effort, she raised one hand from the ground, cradling the envelope to her chest with the other. Over here! Her fingers waved like grass in the breeze, except there was no grass in this place. No plants at all. No colors of spring. Only the murky gray of crushed rock and waxy skin under an unremarkable sky.

Darkness bled through her vision. Then God, in an unexpected act of mercy, swaddled her in silence.

ONE

THE FLOORBOARD UNDER MY FEET RATTLED AS IF THE truck was going to disintegrate.

"Mom, slow down." My fingernails were deep in the faux leather seat of the U-Haul.

A sign welcomed us to Sacramento. I told myself that after a week on the road, I could handle two more hours.

Mom swerved around a car and then pulled back into the lane. I waved my fingers in front of the rearview mirror, hoping the driver could see my apology in the dim light. According to *Road & Travel Magazine*, 37 percent of aggressive driving incidents involve firearms.

"This truck has a blind spot bigger than Montana," I told her. "You should look over your shoulder."

"Sorry, got lost in my thoughts."

She'd said the same thing yesterday, after heading twenty miles in the wrong direction on Route 257.

Last week she'd been bouncing around the house, chatting about the joys of city life, the thrill of change, new adventure. Now she seemed untethered. I knew she had a big job interview in a few days, but unlike me, Mom wasn't the anxious type.

I know you're upset about the move, Liv, Mom's AA sponsor had told me as we'd heaved the last box into the van. *Try to be supportive of your mom, at least until she finds her people.*

Tom was worried about Mom drinking again, I knew it. She'd been sober for five years. I guess it was his job to point out the rocks in her path so she didn't stumble.

I tapped my jeans pocket, checking that the list of Bay Area AA meetings was still there. "If this interview thing doesn't pan out, do you think we can go back to Vermont?"

Several seconds passed before Mom said, "San Francisco's a culinary hot spot, Liv. I could throw a dart and land a job."

I sighed. She didn't care that I'd left behind friends I'd had since preschool. Wherever I'd gone, a hand had waved me over. My social life really took off when I started dating the only boy who'd ever liked me back. In May, Sean was voted Hottest Guy in the sophomore class. By association, I ranked top ten. Higher than I deserved—and meaningless, really—but it still made me happy.

"I miss Candace and Audrey. I *really* miss Sean," I said now.

"Long-distance relationships don't usually work out, hon."

Her cavalier comment was like a whirlpool, sucking me under. It took the screech of brakes to shoot me back to the surface. Our truck had stopped less than a foot behind a minivan with stick-family decals on the back windshield. Cat and dog, too. Mom took her hands off the wheel to stretch her arms behind her head. "Oops," she said.

"I can take over if you need a break," I said. The moon blanched in the brightening sky. It was almost dawn. Good thing, because I hadn't practiced night driving yet.

She shook her head, unbrushed hair settling like tumbleweed on her shoulders. "You just got your learner's permit, Liv." Letting go of the wheel again, she transferred a ponytail holder from her wrist to her hair. Our van veered to the left. She adjusted back with her thigh.

I turned to the window. Hill after hill flashed past, carpeted in sun-fried grass. We passed a sign: *Capitol Inn, Affordable Comfort at $54.99*. According to the bank app, we had three thousand dollars left after giving our new landlord first and last month's rent with deposit. I knew we couldn't afford a motel—especially not this close to our destination.

"Maybe we should get some sleep," I said anyway.

Mom drove past the exit without comment. The eyes of an opossum caught our headlights. "Watch out!" I called.

Too late. She'd flattened it.

"Already dead," she said with a shrug. "You know, you're going to like San Francisco, Liv. There's a farmer's market on every corner. Everyone's vegan there."

Out of 837,000 people, none of them ate meat? It made me crazy when Mom made up stuff, but with an hour and twenty-nine minutes left, I let it go.

"I need coffee," she announced.

This was her seventh espresso in twenty-four hours, not that I'd been counting. Frustration broke through. "Too much caffeine causes neuron activity, which triggers the adrenal glands into releasing stress hormones," I blurted out.

Raindrops splashed on the windshield. Mom hit the turn signal, then flashed the headlights before finding the wipers. Drowned bugs smeared across the glass.

"You know, Liv, you should put that photographic memory to better use than acting like a know-it-all. If you don't look at the heart of the matter, you'll miss the complexity of the . . . of the . . ." She floundered, searching for something that made sense. "Take the psychological impact of coffee, for example. It makes a lot of people insanely happy. I bet you won't find *that* in your *Scientific American*."

I nodded, tired of the tension that had plagued us through twelve states. I searched the GPS for a place that might be open. It wasn't working again, so I checked my phone. "I think there's a Starbucks off exit sixty-seven."

Mom swerved to the right as if it weren't four exits away. I nudged my thoughts in a better direction. With the three-hour time difference, school back home had officially started. I'd already missed forty-five minutes of my junior year. I pictured Sean moping through the hallways without me. I glanced at my phone for the hundredth time since we'd left and maxed the volume so that even the car three lanes over couldn't miss my incoming texts.

Mom found the exit. The lonesome Starbucks glowed like a spaceship on a desolate field. She parked the U-Haul between two compact spaces. "I'll take a double macchiato, please," she said, fishing coins from the ashtray.

I wanted to dump the money back into her lap, but Tom's warning echoed in my head. I climbed down from the truck and headed inside. As I waited for her order, I glanced at my reflection in the polished espresso machine. Without my flat iron, my blond hair had separated into tufts of frizz.

My heart lunged at the muffled chirp. Thoughts of my

mother flew from my head as my hand shot to my pocket. *Miss you so much!!!* I hoped the text would say. Sean wasn't an exclamation point kind of guy, but it was my fantasy, and I was sticking to it.

Oh, it was Audrey. *Hey Liv, was getting a muffin at Gourmet City. Saw there was a help-wanted sign for a manager. Weird. Thought your mom was laid off.*

My stomach tightened a notch. *I guess things are better now,* I texted back. Mom had been Employee of the Month three times at Gourmet City. Why would they lay her off only to hire someone else right away? I searched through my emojis, picking the toothy-grin face with heart eyes. *Wish I were with you guys,* I wrote. *Miss you a ton.*

The radio silence didn't stop me from checking six more times. I hoped she hadn't gotten caught texting in class.

Back in the truck, Mom blared Queen's "Fat Bottomed Girls" from the tinny speakers. As she reached for the espresso, the purple wrap bracelet that I'd given her for Mother's Day slid down her forearm. "One day at a time," it said. She never took it off, not even in the shower. A fact popped into my head: *90 percent of alcoholics who quit drinking have a relapse before achieving long-term sobriety.*

Mom "fell off the wagon" when I was eleven. Only once, and only for an hour.

"I'll never touch another drop," she'd promised the next day.

I'd believed her in Vermont. I could believe her in California, too.

. . .

11

"Livvy, wake up!"

A bag of peanut butter–filled pretzels landed in my lap. Breakfast, Mom-style.

My eyes stung, assaulted by sunlight. Before my vision cleared, my ears knew where we were. Honking cars, a truck beeping in reverse, sirens spilling through the streets. Our truck was sandwiched between two buildings that scraped the turquoise sky. San Francisco was loud, bold, and in my face. I put my sunglasses on.

A bicyclist, going twice as fast as us, shot around our U-Haul. Mom grumbled "messengers" before turning left. The next thing I knew, we were climbing the steepest hill I'd ever seen. All of our stuff slid down the truck bed and slammed into the rear door.

"This is California Street!" Mom announced. "Isn't it gorgeous? We're going a little out of our way, but I wanted you to see an authentic San Francisco street—one of the longest in the city." She slowed at the flashing red lights on a brief plateau before we went higher. We were on a roller coaster, cranking to the inevitable drop.

And then the ground rumbled. I grabbed the dashboard. An earthquake? No. The noise was coming from behind. In the passenger side mirror, I watched a real cable car motor up the silver tracks embedded in the road. It was gaining on us.

Finally Mom turned off the street. But now we were pointing down. The junk in the van changed directions, hitting the partition behind our heads. I squeezed my eyes shut.

When we finally leveled off, Mom said, "Thought you could use a wake-me-up." She pressed her lips together, holding back a laugh.

I tried to frown but couldn't pull it off. This felt better, like how it used to be. I relaxed into the vinyl seat.

As we cut through the city, she pointed to a row of Victorian houses. They looked glued together, one after another. "Where are the yards?" I asked, thinking about the hundred-year-old maple tree outside the window of my old room. It would change colors any day now. I loved spinning on the tire swing, my head cranked back to gaze at a canopy of red and orange.

"Probably in the back," she said.

A minute later, we reached the top of a busy street, flanked by people heading to work. Our van crawled down the hill, brakes whining. My head jerked from left to right. There were hip clothing stores and a café on every block and restaurants with outdoor tables. Even a place to get your eyebrows waxed.

Mom looked at me, full of expectation. "This is Fillmore Street. Our neighborhood. What do you think?"

I didn't know what I thought. A fun place for a vacation? It wasn't home. Couldn't be, not as long as Vermont was on the map.

That's when I noticed that the GPS was still on the blink. "Hey, how do you know your way around?" I asked her. Mom had told me she'd never been west of the Denver ski slopes.

Her head swept the street, searching for an elusive

parking space. She cursed at a motorcycle tucked between two cars, as if we could fit our clunky vehicle into the space. "Tom made sure I knew the directions before we left."

"He used to live here?"

"Yes, in college, I think."

Abruptly the street ran out of money. The stores looked shabbier; the sidewalks dirtier. At a red light, I stared at a homeless man crouched in front of a Mexican take-out restaurant with an *Out of Work* sign propped against his foot. I thought about my own jobless mother. What if her restaurant interview fell through? What if she dug in her heels and refused to leave San Francisco? The money we had left wasn't much of a safety net.

She pointed to a decrepit row of windows on the second floor above a food market. "There it is! That's our apartment!"

Mom pulled the U-Haul onto our concrete front yard. A dog had left us a housewarming gift.

Home sweet home.

CHAPTER

TWO

MY ARMS FELT WORKED OVER BY A TAFFY MACHINE.
I surveyed the moving boxes that littered the studio apartment. Thank God we didn't have to lug too much furniture
up the two flights of stairs.

We can't bring anything that won't fit into the U-Haul, Mom
had said. She'd invited her AA friends over for a farewell
party, insisting that everyone take at least five "party favors"
to remember her by, including our '50s chairs, the dining
room table, and the bedroom set that Dad had bought me
the summer he moved out.

I wished we'd had a garage sale. We could have made
some money.

Sweat snaked down Mom's neck. She opened her arms,
dropping a box to the floor. *FRAGILE* it read on the side.

"Got to rest," she announced, collapsing onto the couch.

"So, when's your interview on Monday?"

"Eight thirty."

"School's over at three. How about we celebrate your
new job?"

"Or we can celebrate your first day at school," she said,
adding, "There's one last box. Would you grab it? I'm beat."

15

I dragged myself downstairs. A policewoman stood behind our van, writing a ticket.

I pointed to the "U-Haul" emblazoned on the side. "We're new here."

"Parking on the sidewalk is illegal everywhere." She handed me the ticket. Eighty dollars! Where else were we supposed to unload our truck? There wasn't enough room in this city. Too many people, too many cars.

In my hometown, the city council had voted 6 to 1 against installing downtown parking meters. They wanted to welcome visitors, not scare them away. I clomped back up the stairs, a box of dish towels under one arm, and handed Mom the ticket without a word. She folded it into a paper airplane and aimed for a dust bunny.

Fifteen minutes later, we were on our way to a neighborhood called South of Market to return the U-Haul. Mom cursed at all the signs that didn't let us turn left. After we dropped the van off, we took an expensive cab ride back to our new neighborhood.

In the apartment, I made our inaugural meal: spaghetti topped with Paul Newman's marinara sauce, purchased from the market under our living room. Cost: $7.28.

Monday seemed a long way away.

· · ·

We spent the weekend in San Francisco doing touristy things. First stop, Fisherman's Wharf, where Mom and I shared an enormous bread bowl filled with clam chowder. After that, she insisted on buying me a T-shirt that claimed, *I love Frisco!*

"It's $3.99," she said. "We can't ignore a deal like that."

As soon as she found a place to fuel her caffeine dependency, I returned the shirt but kept the bag so she wouldn't know.

When we reached Pier 33, Mom pulled a pair of tickets out of her purse. I glanced at a ferry with "Alcatraz Cruises" splayed across the front. "I got them on the website," she said. "You should be happy. Buying them in advance saved us, like, six dollars."

The chowder threatened to come up when I saw the ticket price. Thirty-three dollars each! Almost as much as that stupid parking ticket.

"You can't give them back if you order online," Mom said, looking smug.

I forced a smile. "You got me."

On Sunday we went to Haight-Ashbury, where the hippie culture still had a pulse.

"Look, Liv!" Mom pointed to a thrift shop. "It's just like that store that you and Candace always went to."

Actually, with the cropped vests and peasant blouses, it was an upgrade. I wasn't going to admit it, though. I wanted to go inside, but I couldn't. And not because of Mom. A homeless woman sat on a step beside the entrance. She cradled a baby, bundled in a blanket. A sign, tucked between her bare feet, read, *God bless those that help.*

She caught my eye. "Do you have money for me and my newborn?"

Mom acted like she hadn't heard. She kept on talking as if the woman didn't exist. Then she ran ahead to find a bathroom, leaving me alone on the sidewalk.

"I'm sorry," I began. "I mean, I can't give you . . . but . . ."
I thrust my bagel at her. I was hungry, but probably not as
hungry as them.

As the woman tried to grab it, the blanket fell to the
side. My gaze pulled to the unblinking infant. Torn between
empathy and disgust, I stared at the painted face of the one-
armed plastic doll. I dropped the bagel in the woman's lap
and took off, my eyes on my shoes, until I caught up with
Mom.

Back at the apartment, I said I wanted to go to bed early,
tomorrow being the first day of school and all. Mom seemed
to buy my noble reasoning. Truth was, I was wiped. The
city was loud and bright and colorful and overwhelming.
My senses were amped up from urban assault. What I really
wanted was to be swaddled in the green cocoon of my
Vermont backyard, but that wasn't going to happen.

The living room was now Mom's bedroom. I had to sleep
in the walk-in closet opposite the front door. Quarters were
tight, but right then, there was something oddly comforting
in being able to touch the walls on either side of my blow-up
mattress. It reminded me of the old refrigerator boxes that
Candace, Audrey, and I used to drag down the street from
the appliance store the summer before sixth grade. We spent
all our time in there, sharing nothing and everything at the
same time—before boys and parties and homecoming dances
became more important than spending time together.

I put the flashlight on the shelf and turned on my ancient
laptop, waiting for the display to limp to life. Mom's resume,
which I'd transferred to my hard drive the day we'd left, was
riddled with errors and inconsistent formatting. Two hours

later, I saved the new and improved version, documenting her journey from banana walnut muffins at a supermarket to napoleons at Gourmet City. It wasn't *that* much of a leap to see her as a head pastry chef at a hot, new restaurant. Anyone could tell she was a hard worker—at least when it came to baking.

I loved the new resume. It was perfect. I sent it to the printer. Stretching out my hands, I brushed my fingertips along the walls and smiled in the dark.

. . .

Early the next morning, as I shuffled into the kitchen for a glass of water, something stuck to my heel. I peeled off a Post-it. *2846 Fillmore Street*, it said, circled twice. Mom's interview address, probably. I put it on the coffeemaker so she wouldn't miss it.

My thoughts switched to the first day of school. Grant High was huge—four times as many students as at my old school. At least I'd found a map on the website to mark my classrooms. What should I wear? And how many layers? Mom told me that each neighborhood had its own climate. Apparently Noe Valley was the hot spot, but right now it was cold enough for gloves. I sighed. My weather app was useless here.

I unplugged my phone from the charger, hoping to find a string of texts. Despite the three-hour time difference, there was nothing. I didn't get it. Sean, Candace, and Audrey *knew* it was my first day. I'd even posted yesterday to remind them.

Using the tiny mirror next to the door, I put on my makeup and straightened my hair, while telling myself that it didn't matter what I looked like because I wouldn't be at

19

Grant High for long. Even so, I was too well trained to leave the house without looking my best. Too bad it was for no one but myself.

With time to waste, I poured myself a glass of milk and shuffled to the window to look outside. White smoke streamed past Tomas's Taqueria. Wait, smoke? On the street?

"Oh my God!" I yelled. "Fire!"

"What?" Mom mumbled from under a pile of blankets on the couch.

I listened for sirens. Nothing. "Under us! In the store . . . no, down the street. Call 9-1-1!"

Mom sat up. A moment later, she snickered. I spun around to glare at her.

"Oh, Livvy," she said.

My eyes darted back outside. Smoke zipped by like clouds on a windy day. Mom cupped a hand over her mouth to hide a smile. Wait, what? That wasn't smoke? Blood rushed to my cheeks.

San Francisco.

Fog.

The two went together like clam chowder and bread bowls. Like cable cars and roller-coaster hills. How many photos had I seen of the wispy stuff weaving its way through the cables of the Golden Gate Bridge? I groaned, knocking my forehead against the glass. Mom giggled.

I pictured fire trucks screaming up the hill, cranking their city-sized ladders to our second-story apartment. All because a girl from Vermont had witnessed fast-moving fog.

It *was* kind of funny. Before I knew it, we were both laughing.

Mom went to take a shower, and I started breakfast. Cooking was a total challenge in the L-shaped kitchen. With the stove and dishwasher at perpendicular angles, I couldn't fry eggs and put away dishes at the same time. The single wedge of counter space to the left of the burners was barely enough room for the coffeemaker.

When she emerged from the bathroom, she was wearing a cotton shirt with a big red poppy on the front and a pair of gray wool pants. I squinted, spatula in hand. She didn't look the part of an executive pastry chef in one of the best restaurant capitals in the world. I slid the eggs onto plates and watched as she ate.

"I think I have something amazing for you to wear to your interview," I said.

She looked down. "That bad, huh?"

"You should dress how you want to be viewed. A lot of people can't see past the wrapping paper."

She rolled her eyes, my words falling on deaf ears.

"How long until you have to catch your bus?" she asked.

Because we'd transferred at the last second, the high school three blocks over was fully enrolled. Grant High was the next best choice—except it was a half-hour ride away. I'd almost fallen off the couch when Mom explained there weren't school buses to take me there. I'd have to take a city one like every other urban teen.

I glanced at the time on my phone. "It comes in fifty-seven minutes."

She laughed. "My girl. Always so organized."

"I still don't have a clue what to wear."

I reminded myself to keep things light before her interview. Too much was riding on this. I wished Mom could pick out a professional outfit. After some speed searching, I found my favorite silk top in the box that Mom used as a pedestal for her cactus plants. The careful packing paid off; it wasn't too wrinkled. The blouse was casual, yet tailored. Conservative, but creative. And the autumn colors—well, autumn back home, anyway—would bring out Mom's eyes.

"Now you'll look like a real professional," I said, draping the clothes across her lap.

She glanced down at her Birkenstocks. "My tiramisu speaks for itself."

I handed her my low-heeled wedge sandals. "They aren't interviewing your tiramisu, Mom."

I couldn't wait to show her what I'd been working on last night. I passed her the yellow folder with three freshly printed resumes, ready to go. I would have printed more, but I didn't want her to think I had doubts about this interview.

She mulled them over in silence.

"So, what do you think?" I asked. The folder in her hand looked cheerful, full of hope.

She ran a finger down a page, printed on heavy-duty ivory stock. "How thoughtful," she said, her voice tight. My eyes skipped from her to the folder and back again. Was she nervous about the interview? That would make sense, since we didn't have a lot of savings left.

"You'll do great." I squeezed her hand. "The San Francisco food snobs are lucky to have you."

"You're right," she said.

"I'm always right," I joked.

"You're always right." Her voice sounded robotic. The eggs I'd downed hardened like a rock in my stomach.

"Well, I'd better get ready," I said after a moment.

"I'm assuming you're going to catch the bus on Sutter, since that's closer, but it's near the projects. Better go three blocks up and then left at Webster. There's a stop kitty-corner to Donovan's Deli."

How did she know about Donovan's Deli? Or where the bus stop was? I'd mapped it out last night on my phone, but it wasn't like her to plan ahead. To plan at all, really.

She took in my expression. "I checked with Tom. He told me which streets to avoid."

Well, at least she was in touch with him. That was a good thing. I eyed the coffee table. The list of local AA meetings was where I'd left it.

Mom picked up her briefcase and flew out the door. From the window, I watched the fog wrap around her like a puffy comforter. I waved, but she couldn't see me through the haze. She pulled the folder out of her briefcase and tucked it under her arm, then jaywalked across Fillmore. When she reached the other side, she stopped. I watched as she lifted the resumes I'd made and, with no hesitation, dumped them into the trash can.

THREE

MOM STROLLED UP THE STREET LIKE A PERSON with nothing better to do than window-shop on a brisk summer day.

I swiped some money off the table and ran out the door, taking the stairs three at a time. At the corner, I waited for the light to turn. *Come on!* When it changed, I darted across the street to the trash can and reached in. The folder was drenched in soda. I dropped it and wiped my sticky hands down my shirt.

I didn't understand why Mom would throw the resumes away. Didn't she want a job? I considered all of our tourist ventures this weekend. Sure, it had been fun, but fun was expensive. Was I the only one who cared about our dwindling bank account?

I looked around but couldn't find her. With only eighteen minutes left to catch the bus to school, I jogged up Fillmore to search the cafés. My face began to sweat, and then freeze, in the cold morning air.

A bus hissed to a stop in front of me. If I rode it to the top of the hill, I could cover Fillmore faster. She couldn't have gone far. As soon as I found her, I'd make her explain—even if it was risky to push her, like Tom had warned. I took a deep breath, trying to still my jumbled thoughts. Maybe this was a misunderstanding. I didn't even know her side of the story. Whatever. I wanted answers. And after the time I'd wasted on those resumes, I deserved them. So I climbed on board.

Looking for bus fare, I reached into the pockets of my . . . *Oh, crap—pajama bottoms.* Worse, my *South Park* ones. The bus driver scowled at me as I pulled out the wrinkled five-dollar bill from home.

"Do you have change?" I asked.

He waved me back, grumbling incoherently. Didn't he want me to pay? I stuffed the money back into my pocket. Two girls with matching ponytails looked at me and giggled. My face flared brighter than the Day-Glo plastic seats. The bus jerked forward, careening me into the pole. I grabbed hold of it and spun around to land in the last available seat.

Maybe Mom had a decent reason for tossing the resumes—like there was an error that needed fixing. A mistake I'd missed that she'd caught? Unlikely. But what other reason could there be? Maybe she'd moved us out here because of a guy. Nah. Mom couldn't keep a secret—not when she was excited about something. Anyway, she knew I'd be thrilled if she met someone. Grateful, because then I wouldn't have to take care of her by myself.

As the bus lumbered up the hill, I scanned both sides of the street. A woman hobbled onto the bus, a protective boot on her left foot. I stood up, sliding between two burly men with briefcases. She smiled gratefully and lowered herself into my seat. I ducked down to peer out the window. There weren't any stores near the top of Fillmore, just houses.

Where *was* she? My time was almost up. I didn't want to wait the rest of the day to confront her, but I couldn't be late for school. I was always on time. *Always.*

I closed my eyes as the bus rolled past D & M Wine and Liquors. Checking might be bad luck. With that thought, my stomach clenched, my palms grew damp, and my heart began to pound in my ears.

The woman who took my seat asked, "You okay, honey?"

"Uh-huh." I dropped my chin to hide my face. Her toes, each nail painted a different color, peeked out from her bulky boot. Rainbow toes, dotted with smiley faces.

A man tugged a wire that ran above the window. Immediately the number 22 slowed. I had to get off, too, so I did the same.

"Heard it the first time," the driver said, frowning in the rearview mirror. The doors swung open and I ran off, shivering on the sidewalk as the bus squealed down the other side of the hill.

From up here, I could see all of Fillmore. Everything, and everyone, except my mother.

CHAPTER

FOUR

ON THE BUS RIDE ACROSS TOWN, I'D NEVER FELT MORE alone. Who knew where my mother was. Who knew where I was going, either. To school, apparently. *A* school. Not my school. And not with my friends.

As we crossed Market Street, I checked the time. Because of my mother, I'd missed the bus that gave me a fifteen-minute buffer to find my first class.

I stared out the window, thinking of my friends, already a few days into junior year. That's when I realized the date. I'd missed the Third Extreme Party in Audrey's backyard on Saturday.

I looked at the people on Castro Street, donning sweaters in August. In Vermont you could have a pool party long after the sun had gone down.

Last year's Extreme had been the best. For me, anyway. Though Sean and I didn't make it official until later in the year, it was the first time he spoke to me.

As the bus stopped to let a passenger off, I pressed my nose against the window and smiled, thinking about the "Dress Down to School Challenge"—a fancy name for skinny-dipping in Audrey's infinity pool.

"Livvy, what the hell?" Candace had yelled from the pool, her breasts skimming the top of the water. "Get in here!"

"I'm eating," I'd called back, clutching an enormous, purposefully timed bowl of potato chips. My two best friends embraced fun with no excuses. Me? Not so much.

Candace, as always, had her bullshit monitor perfectly calibrated. "Put that food down and strip!"

And then I'd heard the voice. Smooth. Melodic. Achingly familiar. "Leave her alone, Candace. She'll go in if she wants. We're talking, okay?"

Sean Holmes. Crush since month one of freshman year. Varsity baseball player. Sexy smirk. He was single for a few minutes each year, until some new girl snapped him up like a parking spot on Fillmore.

"Um, thanks," I'd told him, grateful that the dark hid the firestorm in my cheeks.

I couldn't tell if we had talked for five minutes or twenty. All I knew was that by the time he walked away, the temperature had dropped, Audrey was demanding someone fetch her a sweater, and people were running from the pool to the house under shared towels.

The bus jerked to a stop, arriving in reality. Everyone unloaded. I followed them up the street, both wanting and not wanting to find the way to my new school.

. . .

Instead of three buildings sprawled across generous acreage, like my school back home, Grant High was a cement rectangle five stories high. Stairs led up from each of the corners, with one elevator marked, *Handicapped Use Only!* and the other, *Out of Order.* I stared at the maze, trying to figure out which staircase would bring me closest to Algebra 2 on the third floor. Finally I picked the smartest-looking student and trailed behind. As I emerged from the stairwell, some girls were standing next to the water fountain, babbling about party hookups, summer boredom, and the endless amount of vacation homework that a lit teacher had assigned.

God, I missed my friends.

By the time I found Room 24, there was only one seat left. The boy sitting next to me swiveled my way. "Ready or not, here I am," he said, offering his hand. "Franklin D. Schiller." He emphasized the middle initial.

Franklin D. was as large as a lineman on a football team, but he looked more like the anti-jock type. The mass of brown curls on his head added inches to his height. I took in his black T-shirt, which read, $C_8H_{10}N_4O_2$.

"That stands for caffeine," he said, catching me looking. "The elixir of the gods."

Candace's voice popped into my head: *For a kid like that, "popular" is nothing more than a sixty-one-point Scrabble word.* It was one of her favorite lines.

"Where's our teacher?" I asked.

"Harrison's notoriously tardy," he said. "Hypocrisy, day one. It's what makes high school great."

I wasn't sure if I was supposed to laugh or not, so I checked my schedule for the fifteenth time.

"And you are?" he prodded.

"Livvy Newman," I said, my mind on Mom again. She couldn't have had time to print out more resumes. I wondered if the interview had been canceled and she'd been too embarrassed to admit it.

Franklin D. asked some questions about my past. I kept my answers brief, in part to avoid tripping over general cluelessness about why we'd moved here.

Mr. Harrison scurried into the room. He dropped the slab of a textbook onto his desk to wake us up. As he introduced himself, I rehearsed what I planned on saying to Mom when I saw her. In my head, the conversation would end with, "You're right, Liv. Let's go back to Vermont."

I hid my phone in my binder to check my social media. Sean, Candace, and Audrey had updated in the past hour. Standard complaints. Nothing about me. It was like I'd bungee-jumped off the face of the planet.

When Mr. Harrison wasn't looking, I added a post: *Some nice people showed me around my new school. Love my classes!* Of course, it was only first period, but I suspected my East Coast friends wouldn't connect the dots. I hit Send, convincing myself it was better to be a liar than a loser.

C-Lunch didn't start until the ridiculously late hour of one thirty. To avoid the cafeteria scene, I left campus. I trailed behind a small crowd to 24th Street and parked myself on a bench, where I picked at the walnuts I'd grabbed while rushing out of the apartment this morning. Through the window of Joe's Diner, I watched a waitress deliver sweet potato fries wrapped in a newspaper cone. My mouth watered.

Maybe I was worrying too much about money. If Mom got a job, we'd have money soon enough. Without giving myself time to think, I jumped to my feet and strode into the coffee shop next door. It turned out that a medium mocha cost a dollar more than a mega-cup size at Gourmet City. One sip later, I felt an overwhelming urge to return

30

it. California coffee tasted different. Like money dwindling away. Like eviction. Like sleeping under an overpass, covered with a blanket of fog.

Stop being so dramatic, Livvy. I took a large gulp and burned the roof of my mouth. I spit the drink back into the cup, which was so gross that I had to trash it.

I hoped Mom had enough sense to make her lemon éclairs for the interviewer.

. . .

The last class of the day was International Debate. I'd already taken it freshman year, but there wasn't much in the way of electives for last-minute transfers. I'd done okay in the class, mostly because of my research skills. Performance wasn't my thing. The secret to a decent grade was an extroverted partner.

I finally found the portable classroom, stationed across the parking lot, next to the dumpsters. No surprise, my new school had capacity issues. As I walked through the door, Franklin D.'s head whipped around. "Livvy No-Middle-Initial Newman! The most beautiful transfer student in the world." He patted the seat beside him. I plunked down and pulled out my phone to do some research. Who knew that there were more than three hundred thousand portables in the United States, with a useful life of only ten years?

Franklin D. planted his elbows on my desk. "Tell me, perchance, where you hail from?"

Perchance? Okaaay. "Vermont."

"Aha! The only state with a capital that doesn't have a McDonald's."

"Really?" I asked, drawn in by the unexpected fact.

"I detest all things McDonald's," he went on, "from Happy Meal Beanie Babies to the Big Mac. Personally, I think the gluttonous chunk of heart-clogging meat should be called the Gain-Some-Pounders so consumers are fully informed."

"'Two all-beef patties, special sauce, lettuce, cheese, pickles, onions on a sesame seed bun'?" I rattled off, then quickly added, "Um, that's a jingle from the seventies. Anyway, I think there's twenty-eight grams of fat in one of those things."

Wait, what was I doing? I didn't want to encourage the notion that I was friend material. My social life was 3,017 miles away.

Franklin D. nodded, clearly impressed. "You're absolutely right. That's more than half the recommended daily fat intake in an incredibly unfulfilling sandwich."

I snuck a sideways glance at his barrel chest and beefy arms. If he lifted weights, he'd have some impressive arm muscles. This made me think of Sean, who practically rented a room at the gym.

At my sigh, Franklin D. flicked a finger in the air. "I know what you're thinking, but don't judge this book by its cover. My father's side comes from Viking stock. My body fat's an acceptable twenty percent, midrange for males aged thirteen to seventeen."

"I wasn't thinking that," I lied.

The teacher had scrawled "Ms. Leslie Thurmond" across the board in hot pink chalk, underlining the "Ms." part twice.

"You will all be responsible for two debates this semester," she began. "I thought we'd start by looking at some possible subjects for the first one. I put a list on your desk to jump-start the process, but I really want to hear your ideas."

The class seemed more interested in working on their ability to sleep with their eyes open. They looked like they suffered from PLOD—Post-Lunch Operational Disorder. Ms. Thurmond waited, but no one said anything. She had *freshly credentialed* written all over her. As much as I longed to blend in with plastic walls, I couldn't watch a newbie crash and burn on her first day. My hand crept up to my chin.

"Yes, you in the black sweater," she called out.

"Um, whether schools should have an open or closed campus during lunch?" This reminded me of the sweet potato fries at Joe's Diner. My stomach rumbled, the walnuts not cutting it.

"That's a hot topic," Thurmond agreed. "What do you know about it?"

I could pull up three relevant facts right there, but I shrugged.

"That's why research is an important part of the debate process," she told the class. "Facts are the best way to prove a point. Anyone else have thoughts on the subject?"

An emo girl with tar-black hair said, "Some kids at Jackson High smoked pot at lunch and smashed their car into the side of a bank. If the school had a closed policy, it would have extended their moronic lives three whole hours." She swiped her chin-length bangs out of her eyes, revealing Sharpie tattoos up her arms. Skeletons, maybe. No, clowns. Zombie clowns, it looked like.

"They killed a cat!" a girl with a braid down her back cried. "A harmless animal. Someone's pet."

"Um, they killed themselves, too," Franklin D. pointed out.

33

"They were a bunch of rich kids who bought overpriced drugs from a disreputable dealer," said Emo Girl. "They get the Darwin Award."

"This subject seems to inspire passionate opinions," Thurmond said. "Anyone else have a potential debate topic they want to share?"

Franklin D. tapped the list on his desk, then spoke up. Loudly. "Number four here says, 'Does history repeat itself?' I was reading an article in the Sunday paper about all the revisionist pages popping up on the Internet."

"Revisionist?" Thurmond asked.

"Those morons who try to convince everyone that the Holocaust never happened," Franklin D. clarified.

Ms. Thurmond crossed her arms under her sizable chest. A guy behind me grunted in appreciation. "I'm not sure that a minimally held position that fails to honor the slaughter of six million Jews is a strong debate topic," she said.

"That's like neo-Nazi shit, right?" Emo Girl asked.

My eyes skipped to the teacher. She didn't wince at the French. Oh, right, urban school.

Franklin D. raised his hand. He didn't wait to be called on. "With all due respect, Ms. Thurmond, debating is a way of deconstructing the validity of their beliefs. *Ignoring* them is the worst thing we can do. With witnesses getting older and dying, white supremacists will continue to spread their lies to a new generation. It's up to each and every one of us to challenge their assertions."

Thurmond stared at him like she'd discovered that one of her students had two heads. She glanced down at the class list on her desk.

"Schiller," he offered. "Franklin D. Schiller."

"As I was saying, Frank, some topics are—"

"Franklin *D.*" He folded his hands in front of him. "Please."

"Heil Schiller!" someone called out, followed by a chorus of "heils" from the back row.

A fact danced on my tongue, begging to be let loose. I bet none of them knew that Hitler's own father was believed to be the illegitimate child of a Jewish man named Frankenberger and how DNA findings suggested that the Nazi leader had a chromosome linked to the Ashkenazi population. Of course, I didn't say all that. Franklin D. had to fight his own battles.

Thurmond's face turned the shade of a ripe eggplant. "Who said that? I won't have that kind of talk in my classroom."

"Schiller is a Jewish name," Franklin D. said, unruffled. "It's not our original surname, though. My great-grandfather, Hymie Lipschitz, changed it when he arrived at Ellis Island from Czechoslovakia. Can you blame him?"

More scoffing from the back. I twisted around in my seat, but the kids were smiling. And not in a mean way. Huh.

"Where's Czechoslovakia?" the girl with the braid asked me.

I almost pointed out that it had been called the Czech Republic since 1993. "Next to Austria," I said.

She nodded, thinking. Then, "Where's Austria?"

This school, and its culture of nonconformity, sent my head spinning. I turned around again, but this time, to take a closer look at my classmates. In the row in front of me, there were two Hispanic kids, a white boy whose makeup skills rivaled my own, and a Chinese girl who sat on hip-length, rainbow-dyed hair. The boy on my right—Ashaz, according to the name on the notebook in front of him—had a "Mom" tattoo on his forearm, underlined with birth and death dates. My old school had been as diverse as vanilla ice cream.

I cleared my throat. "I think Franklin D. has a point about the revisionists. If these . . ." I tried to come up with a word other than the indecent one in my head, ". . . *people* go unchecked, they'll only grow stronger."

Franklin D. slammed his palm on the desk. "I knew there was a reason I liked that girl!"

"Because she's hot," said a boy two rows over. I looked down at my lap, letting my hair hide my smile.

"Quiet down now. Let's stay focused." Thurmond's eyes skipped to the clock over the door. "Your homework for tomorrow is to choose three subjects from the paper on your desk and tell me why you believe they'd make an interesting debate."

"So much for listening to our brilliant ideas," Franklin D. mumbled under his breath.

"I want depth, people. Less than one paragraph and you fail the assignment," she added.

"How many paragraphs to get an A?" asked Braid Girl.

The bell rang. Kids jumped from their seats, ready to flee.

Franklin D. waited for me at the end of the row. "Think I made an awesome first impression, don't you?"

I did a double take, relieved to see that he was kidding. "Yes, definitely. The A's in the bag."

I edged past him, picking up speed toward the door.

Ms. Thurmond was making tight circles with the eraser, slowly eating away at her hot-pink name.

MAY 1945

When she opened her eyes, the first thing she saw was a male nurse, erasing a name off the portable blackboard. Her eyes wandered to the rows of cots lined up like matches in a box. Oh goodness, a cloth diaper between her legs? How utterly mortifying that someone, perhaps that male nurse himself, had changed her and might do so again. She tugged the blue paper gown as far down as it would go.

Another nurse ran to her side with a cup of ice chips and an assortment of pills displayed on a pink palm. "The war is over, dear," were the first words she heard. Words with a British accent. "You're at the Bergen-Belsen Displaced Persons Camp until you get your strength back."

She squinted at the calendar taped to the window. The words and dates danced across the page. "Who won the war?"

The nurse—she couldn't read the spinning name tag—laughed brightly. "Why the Allies, of course!" Her expression shifted, strained with sympathy. "You have a bad case of typhus. We had to shave your head, but those locks of yours will grow back more beautiful than ever. You'll see!"

She raised her hand to her bristly head and fainted.

. . .

When she woke next, that same nurse—Matilda, her name was—struggled to open the swollen window beside the cot.

"How long have I been sleeping?" she asked.

"Two weeks, more or less. You've been in and out." With a stage whisper, the nurse added, "The doctors

37

weren't sure you'd make it, but you've proven to be a strong young woman indeed."

Two weeks!

"Do you have any family left?" Matilda pressed gently.

She thought of her parents, her sibling, her home. She couldn't go back now, not ever. She wasn't even safe here, in this refuge for the ill. "No," she answered. "They're dead."

There was something else, but she couldn't remember. A person? No, an object. She ran her fingers over the scratchy sheet, searching for it.

"Are you looking for that letter? It must have been important to you, the way you clung to it. I'm sure it's here somewhere . . ." The nurse found it beneath a glass of water on the side table.

She wanted to say thank you, but the words lay swollen in her mouth. When she woke again hours later, the envelope was beside her pillow.

Matilda was back. "Where is home for you, dear?"

Home? There was no home anymore. She needed somewhere new, far away.

The nurse glanced down at the clipboard in her hand. "Someone might be looking for you. What's your name?"

She shook her head as if the answer eluded her. The nurse gave a sad smile and crossed the narrow aisle to the cots on the opposite side.

Three days later, she told them. And though Adelle— *the name of a classmate from primary school—rolled heavily off her tongue, it was something she could live with. Like the name of a newborn, it allowed her a fresh start.*

CHAPTER

FIVE

A FEW BLOCKS PAST MY USUAL STOP, THE BUS TOOK a nose dive. The decline was so steep that there were steps instead of sidewalks. Fillmore Street stretched out like an oil painting of jewel-colored homes, ending at the water. Sailboats flecked the bay. In the distance were more hills, studded with homes.

Like a fact, the address on the Post-it had engraved itself into my memory. Google Maps showed that Mom's interview was somewhere near here, but I didn't see any businesses. Only homes. Still, I tugged the cord and got off at the next stop.

I checked the text she'd sent an hour ago: *Be back soon. Final interview at four with higher-ups. Good sign!*

"Excuse me," a buff guy grunted, jogging around me.

I stepped to the side. "Sorry."

A girl and her black poodle danced up the incline. Farther down, a man in a wheelchair muscled his way up the hill. I headed down the steps, pressed to the side to avoid the fitness fanatics.

2846 Fillmore was on the opposite side of the street. It was a yellow Victorian duplex—a residence, like all the others.

Where was the restaurant? I'd planned on asking Mom about the resumes, but now there were more questions. I looked at the drawn lace curtains as if they might offer a clue.

As a garbage truck rumbled past, the right side door of the duplex swung open. I ducked behind a tree and peered through its branches. My mother, in her gray sweats and the *You Are Here* T-shirt she'd had since the '80s, tromped down the steps of the Victorian. She stopped halfway, then returned to the house. Thirty seconds later, she came out with her briefcase.

Where was the interview outfit I'd picked out for her? I pictured my blouse crumpled up in the briefcase. Was her portfolio of photographed desserts even in there? Maybe she'd already scored the job, but these clothes were unprofessional for a first day.

I was about to cross the street to intercept her when Mom put her phone to her ear. "You have no idea, Tom," I heard her say. Relief rolled through me. At least she was talking to the one person who could help her with her problems, whatever they were. My eyes skipped back to the house. 2846 Fillmore. A home, not a restaurant. But *whose* home? And why was my mother wiping tears from her eyes?

I waited until she was a block away before darting across the street and up the steps to the alcove porch. Twin mailboxes hung on the stucco wall. One was slightly open. I slid my hand inside and found an ad for a credit card, addressed to *Resident*. Not helpful.

"Mailboxes are federal property. You will be punished for stealing mail!"

The letter slipped through my fingers and dropped on

the doormat. An old woman, peering through a half-opened door, glared at me. She wore a calf-length corduroy skirt and a cream-colored blouse with lacy frills that curled up the front. Her eyes were like a Siamese cat's, almond-shaped and watery brown. Black eyeliner jagged around her lids.

"I wasn't trying to steal anything," I stammered. "I was just . . ." *Just what?* "Leaving. I was just leaving."

"Don't you dare go anywhere!"

I thought about running, but the authority in her voice stopped me.

"Why were you snooping?" she demanded.

I scrambled for an excuse.

I thought this was where a friend lived.

I was bringing her mail in.

I found this ad on the sidewalk and was going to put it back in the mailbox.

It dawned on me that if this was Mom's new boss, the three of us might meet again one day. I didn't want to make up a lie that I'd have to take back later.

My arms dropped to my sides under the lady's withering stare. "I . . . I saw my mom leave your house, and . . ." What could I say that wouldn't send the message that I didn't trust my own mother?

"And?" the lady echoed.

"My mom said she had an interview here this morning. I was supposed to meet her when she was done. I thought I had the address wrong, so I checked the mailbox to—"

Her lips puckered. "I suppose you look like Lee Newman."

My dad? How did she know *him?*

"Gretchen was the one who left, you know," she added.

41

I stared at her, bewildered. If anyone had run away, it was my father. He'd gone to Australia, leaving me with a mom fresh out of rehab. The words tripped out of my mouth. "Did she tell you about him?"

"She shouldn't have married that man. Now she's all alone with a child to raise."

When I was twelve, Mom had dragged me to an AA meeting, where she spilled her entire life story in fifteen minutes to a room full of strangers. She wasn't stupid enough to do the same thing with a new boss, was she?

The old woman shuffled closer. Her hand trembled near my face, finger crooked as if beckoning me closer. I stepped back. No way was she touching me.

"You look nothing like Gretchen," she said.

Well that part was true. My eyes were blue, and my hair, almost as white as marshmallows, was a nod to Dad's Swedish side. I didn't escape Mom's curls, but it was nothing that my flat iron couldn't handle.

"I am Adelle Pfeiffer," she said, pausing between words as if announcing the Queen of England.

I smiled politely. "Nice to meet you. I'm Olivia Newman."

Her nod seemed to say, *I know*. Oh, God, what had Mom said about me?

"You look cold, dear," she said. "I remember how to make tea." I watched her limp down a dark hallway that sliced the house into narrow halves. One of her heels clicked against the parquet floor, the other dragged behind it.

I hesitated, glancing over my shoulder at the street. I could leave. Nothing was stopping me. I could use the perennial homework excuse, which never failed with adults. But the thing was, she'd met with my mother. If I could deal with the woman's dizzying tangents, maybe I could get some answers.

"I want to talk about Gretchen," the woman called out, her back to me.

At least we had *that* in common.

Swallowing my nerves, I followed the woman down the hall. When we reached the kitchen at the other end of the apartment, she turned around. "Someone has taken my teapot."

I cleared my throat and pointed to the silver kettle peeking out of the papery leaves of a dehydrated ficus tree. This was getting weirder by the second. "I have to go in a few minutes," I told Mrs. Pfeiffer. "You said you wanted to talk about my mom?"

She extracted the pot, sending a flurry of leaves to the floor. After she put it on the stove, we sat at a round table by a bay window that overlooked a blocky patch of yellowish grass caged in by a wood fence. She glanced at the pudgy dog in the backyard, nose twitching in a hydrangea bush. A wrinkle caved between the old woman's eyebrows. She pounded a fist on the single-paned window, which shook against the assault.

"*Scheisshund!*"

The dog's head jerked up. He tucked his tail between his legs and scampered off.

"Is that his name?" I asked.

"Yes. It most certainly is."

The teapot gave a breathy whistle.

The basset hound waddled back into the yard. He thrust his snout into a flower bed again. "Is he your dog?" I asked, hoping for the animal's sake that the answer was no.

"Ha! That menace belongs to my neighbor. Those type of dogs are vicious, trained to kill, you know."

A laugh of shock bubbled out of me.

She slid a plate of cookies onto the table. They smelled like Christmas—cloves, nutmeg, and cinnamon. I hadn't eaten anything since my walnut lunch. I nibbled on one as Adelle Pfeiffer brought out a pair of china cups, dotted with pink and lavender roses, and a silver bowl filled with sugar cubes—the kind you see in fancy restaurants. With trembling hands, she poured the hot water into teacups.

"What's my mom going to do for you?" I asked.

"Who's your mother?"

I stared at her. Was she kidding? "Gretchen? Gretchen Newman?"

"Of course," she said. "I hired Gretchen to do odds and ends for me. I . . . I don't do as much as I used to."

Odds and ends? "You mean, like helping you with your restaurant?" Though at this point, it was pretty clear that Mrs. Pfeiffer didn't own a five-star bistro requiring a top-notch pastry chef for overpriced desserts.

She looked at me blankly. "Do I have a restaurant? I'd remember if I had a restaurant . . . Yes, I would. I would definitely remember something like that." Her face swelled with uncertainty. "Wouldn't I?"

"I'm sure you don't have a restaurant," I said. "Guess I

heard wrong." Fact: My mother was a big fat liar. I dunked my third cookie into the tea.

"You look like my *oma*. Chiseled cheekbones, and eyes like the deepest part of the ocean. She had another name . . . her name was . . ." She dropped her chin into her hand and stared out the window. "I don't know."

She wasn't making sense. Time to get to the point. "What exactly is my mom going to do for you? Cook?"

"I'm fabulous in the kitchen; better than her, better than that Vickie person the agency sent."

I had a sinking feeling that Mom had abandoned her goal of finding a pastry job. But caregiving? I couldn't see her doing that.

"Thanks for everything." I stood up, catching most of the cookie crumbs on my lap in my hands. "I have to read three chapters of Faulkner for my Honors English class."

"Ah, the gentleman who said, 'Facts and truth really don't have much to do with each other.'"

"He said that?" It was the dumbest quote I'd ever heard. Facts were the only thing you could count on. Without them, there were only the imprecise perceptions of witnesses.

"Don't go, Livvy," she muttered from behind her teacup.

Livvy? I'd introduced myself as Olivia. "How do you know my nickname?"

She cocked her head to the side. "Do you know who I am?"

"Um, Mrs. Pfeiffer? The person who interviewed my mom?"

"Gretchen's my daughter," the old woman said. "I pay her to protect me."

I stared at her, the words in my brain trying to sort themselves out. "My grandmother's dead. She died a long time ago."

Mrs. Pfeiffer shut her eyes. "So that's how the story goes."

Story?

"It's a fact," she said, "that I am not yet pushing up daisies."

This woman's driveway didn't meet the street. She had to be making this up, or hallucinating, or lying for some reason. I edged toward the door.

"There are people who know the truth," she said, wagging her crooked finger.

I rushed down the hallway, not even slowing. Mrs. Pfeiffer shouted my name. It sounded ugly, the way she cut O-LI-VI-A into four sharp syllables.

I slammed the door shut behind me.

CHAPTER

SIX

I NEVER MET MY GRANDPARENTS. THEY GOT MARRIED
after World War II. My grandfather died of a heart attack
right before Mom went to college. My grandmother passed
away in her sixties from the flu, or maybe it was pneumonia.
Mom hadn't said much about them, but one thing I knew, she
wouldn't tell a lie this big.

I tried to collect my thoughts on the way home. When I
got to the apartment, it was empty. I looked out the window.
Couples huddled together at café tables on the sidewalk across
the street, heat lamps glowing above them. The downtown
bus pulled up to unload the business crowd. A man's tie lifted
in the wind, swatting him in the face.

I texted Mom. *Need to talk.*

She wrote back. *What's the emergency?*

Just come home.

She called a minute later. I let it go to voice mail. I had
to talk to her in person, see her face. But while I waited, I
needed to do something to take my mind off the old lady.
The apartment was filled with boxes, the same as the day
we'd moved in. I hadn't wanted to unload them and repack
later. But right now, the chaos closed in on me like the sides

47

of a trash compactor. I pushed all the boxes against the walls to clear space in the middle. There, that was better.

I hired Gretchen to do odds and ends for me, the old lady had said. Mom could pipe frosting on cakes like no one else, but if the task involved grunt work, she became an expert delegator. She wouldn't last two weeks at a job like that.

Anyway, Adelle Pfeiffer was a fruitcake with extra nuts in the mix. She said Mom was her daughter, but daughters didn't work for their mothers. Not for pay. They helped out because that's what families did.

Not to mention, my grandma was stone-cold dead.

I was draping tablecloths over cardboard boxes at either side of the couch to make end tables when Mom stormed into the house. "Jesus, Liv, are you okay?" Her splotchy cheeks shone with sweat.

I stared at her "job hunting" outfit. Wrinkled pants, and my blouse, last button undone. Gone were the casual clothes I'd seen an hour ago. I pointed to her briefcase. "What's in there?"

Mom's gaze flicked around the room, landing nowhere. "Just the usual crap I need for interviews. Paper, pens, the photo album of desserts . . ."

"What about the resumes?"

"Yeah, sure," she said, heading to the couch.

"I found a Post-it with an address on it, so I went there after school. I saw you leave that house, Mom."

"What?" she asked blankly.

I waited, hoping beyond reason that she could explain this in a way that made sense. Instead she murmured, "I didn't realize you felt the need to spy on me, Livvy."

As if I had nothing better to do than stalk my own mother. "I *saw* you throw away those resumes, Mom. I know you didn't wear the clothes I picked out for you. What's going on?"

Mom painted a smile on her face. "I didn't want to tell you that you'd wasted your time. It's not the way business operates in my industry. Proof of my skills depends on how I bake, not what I say on a piece of paper or what I wear." She tucked an errant curl behind her ear, but it sprang back.

"That address was a house, not a restaurant," I said.

I could barely make out Mom's features in the darkening apartment, but her sigh was clear. "Liv, not now, please. I'm so tired, I could . . ."

So tired she could what? Drink? *Don't go there, Liv.* "Who is Mrs. Pfeiffer?" I demanded.

She looked at me as if I was speaking another language.

"She said she's my *grandmother*." The only sound in the room was a distant siren, growing closer, before fading away.

"Adelle's a confused woman," Mom finally said. "She gets mixed up a lot."

I recalled the woman's words: *Gretchen's my daughter. I pay her to protect me.* Who was wrong? The demented old woman, or the one person I thought would always be truthful with me? "Come on, Mom. What's this about?"

"Listen, I know I haven't been completely honest . . ."

"*Completely* honest?" I repeated. "A person's either telling the truth one hundred percent or she's a liar. There's nothing in between."

"Everything's so black and white with you," she snapped. "Your grandmother was dead. At least to me."

49

Wait, *what?* Her words were like raindrops, bouncing off my skin. It took a few seconds to absorb the meaning.

"I didn't plan on seeing her again," she went on. "It was easier to bury her six feet under, metaphorically speaking."

The lady wasn't wacked after all; Mom was the insane one. Adelle Pfeiffer was my *grandmother.* Mom had buried her, all right—alive. White-hot anger fueled my words. "You don't like your mother, so you tell me she's dead? That's sick, Mom!"

She seemed to shrink before my eyes. "Try explaining to your kid that you hate your mother when she thinks her own mommy's an angel."

Oh my God, I have a grandmother. "Believe me, I never thought that," I snapped.

She clamped her lips together, tears welling in her eyes. My body tensed, a stony exterior meant to keep out her drama. That left me feeling as empty as the hollow guts of a ghost.

"I didn't want my mother to ruin you the way she ruined me," Mom said through tears. "Saying she was dead put an end to that possibility."

"What gave you the right to decide that for me?" I thought about my father, who lived across the ocean with his new family. I had no one left but my mother—not a single relative. That's what she'd told me. That's what I'd believed.

"If you'd grown up with my mother, you'd understand."

"We had tea and cookies, Mom. She's a harmless old lady."

"I know you like everything to be precise and factual, easy to explain, but my relationship with my mother isn't that simple," she spat out.

My cheeks burned as if I'd been slapped. "Why are we living in the same zip code if she's that horrible?"

Mom opened her mouth but answered with a shrug. I pushed past her, out the door.

"Where do you think you're going? Get back here!" she called.

I was on the street, heading in the opposite direction from the one I'd taken this morning. Minutes later, I ran into a cluster of run-down buildings. I knew from Mom's warnings that this was San Francisco's version of the projects. People milled about—some talking to neighbors, some to themselves. I felt self-conscious in my cashmere sweater— like I was pretending to be somebody I wasn't. Truth was, at this point Mom and I probably had less money than some of the people who lived here.

I headed for the empty playground across the street and scuttled up the slide, parking myself at the top. Mom tore around the corner. I drew my knees to my mouth to muffle a sob. When she spotted me, she kicked off her shoes and attempted to climb the slide, but her stocking feet kept sliding out from under her. She strung together some major league curse words before tiptoeing across the sand to the stairs at the back of the structure.

When she dropped down beside me, I scooted back until the safety bars dug into my side.

"Adelle was a lousy mother," she began. "She'd be a lousy grandmother, too."

"Then why'd you move us here?" I persisted.

"My mother was diagnosed with Alzheimer's three years ago. I guess that's why she didn't tell you her married name, Adelle Friedman."

I pictured the teapot, nestled in the branches of the ficus plant. Pfeiffer must be my grandmother's maiden name.

"She makes stuff up all the time," Mom said. "Last month a policeman found her wandering around Crissy Field. She got lost, even though she's lived here for twenty-five years. She told him she was Cleopatra. Luckily, there was an expired driver's license in her purse."

"When was the last time you saw her?"

She glanced at her hands. I saw that her nails were ragged, bitten to the quick. A fleck of silver polish remained on her thumb. "Adelle moved here after my father died," Mom said. "The last time I saw her was the summer before my junior year in college. Visiting her was like shelling out money for a root canal."

She searched my face for a smile. I wouldn't give her one. "So that's why you knew all the streets around here. You never asked Tom for directions. He didn't even live here." I swept my fingers across the grate. Dirt sifted through the holes to the ground. "What could she have possibly done to make you hate her so much?"

Mom shrugged. "Which story do you want to hear?"

"Any."

"My mother was . . . is . . . an impatient person. Raising a kid was too messy, too slow for her. Barking orders got immediate results, or at least that's what she thought."

I remembered the way Adelle had spit out my name when I'd tried to leave.

"One time, when I was seven, we went to a friend's pool party," Mom said. "I was content to hang my feet over the edge, but Adelle insisted that I get in the water. I couldn't swim, but she promised to hold on to me. We waded out to the middle, me in her arms, and all of a sudden . . ." Mom spread her arms like eagle wings. "The third time I bobbed to the surface, I saw her in the shallow end of the pool, watching me. Some man I didn't know jumped in, clothes and all. My mother berated the poor guy for a half hour. She told him I would never learn to swim if people interfered. Pretty much everyone thought my mother was a nut job. I never got invited to another party." She hardly inhaled before switching stories. "When I was twelve, I wanted a CB radio for my birthday. No surprise, I didn't get it. It cost about a hundred and fifty dollars, I think, which was a fortune back then. Still is. Anyway, I saved up all my paper route money, and a year later, I bought it myself. My mother had a fit, said it was a waste. She threw it against the wall and broke it into a heap of plastic. 'One hundred and fifty dollars worth of garbage, that's what you bought yourself,' she told me."

The examples weren't nice, it's true. No one would want a mother like that. But they didn't really seem bad enough to sever ties with her forever.

"She shouldn't have had a kid in the first place," Mom finished.

"You and I wouldn't be talking right now if she hadn't," I pointed out.

"So I should put up with her cruelty because she gave birth to me? God, Liv, grow up. Being a parent means more than carrying a baby for nine months."

Like you'd know, I thought. *You drank through the first eleven years of my life.* I shook my head, trying to dislodge the thought. My mother was a good person who'd behaved badly.

"At the end of my last trip to see her, I left on a train headed to the East Coast and I didn't come back. I haven't regretted my decision," she said.

I couldn't hide my shock. "You mean you didn't even talk on the phone?"

"Not until last month when I got a call from her lawyer. He said she needed full-time care, which meant he had to hire two caregivers to share the day. The first thing I did was look for a decent care facility. My mother could afford the Ritz-Carlton of retirement homes. She was a poet who never earned much, but luckily, Dad's life insurance invested well."

A poet? This didn't jibe with the portrait my mom painted of a tyrannical mother.

"Of course she refused to go into a home, even though she's probably close to ninety," Mom added.

"You don't know how old she is?" I asked, surprised.

"Her records were lost before she came to the U.S. She took advantage of it, I can tell you that. She was thirty for at least a decade."

"This doesn't explain why *you* have to be her caregiver."

Just then two boys around my age walked by, jeans slung halfway down their hips. They wore oversized sneakers that flopped on their feet. They saw us on the slide and nudged each other with their elbows.

"Shit," the tall one said. "Looks like some doves flew into the wrong jungle."

Mom tensed beside me. I knew what she was thinking: guns, knives, drug dealers. But there was something about those boys. They didn't sound angry. In fact they reminded me of some kids in my classes. I considered the mixed-up rules of life at Grant High, and something inside me shifted. I bent my arms and cooed like a bird, grinning so they knew I was playing along. We traded smiles as they turned the corner.

"What the hell do you think you're doing?" Mom hissed. "This isn't maple sugar Vermont."

"They're people, Mom. Like you and me, trying to get by on too little."

She nodded. "That's why we moved here, Liv. For our future. Adelle's lawyer told me that if I didn't help take care of her, my mother might write me out of the will. I didn't even think I was still in there." She covered my hand with her own. I flinched and pulled it back. "I have more than myself to think about now. So I quit my job."

Audrey's text about how Gourmet City was hiring popped into my head. *Thought your mom was laid off.* Yeah, that's what I'd thought, too. The lies were piling up faster than farm manure.

"I got a good deal, Liv. I work from eight to four every day, and then the other caregiver takes over until morning."

Gourmet City had paid Mom a good wage. And I'd covered most of my own expenses with babysitting money. Besides, selling out to collect an inheritance seemed greedy.

"Her attorney will pay our living expenses and a stipend. We get the first check next week. It should be enough to survive on until . . ." She stopped, leaving me to fill in the rest.

Until my grandmother dies.

Mom looked over my shoulder, lost in thought. I wondered how much of the inheritance she'd already spent in her mind.

"How long does she have?" The question felt dirty as soon as it left my mouth.

A car ripped by, the thud of bass shaking its sleek silver frame. Mom waited for it to zoom past. "Adelle isn't far enough gone to demand a memory-care facility."

Far enough gone. I shuddered. For the first time, I truly considered who Adelle Friedman was. It added up to more than a sick old lady. And then I remembered how she'd quoted Faulkner. "Are you sure she has Alzheimer's?" I asked.

"Absolutely. Vickie—that's the other caregiver who helps me out—says my mother has good days and bad days. Seems to me it's more like good minutes and bad minutes. She can't even remember what a rotten mother she was." Mom stood up. She brushed the tanbark off her pants. "One thing, Liv. I want you to promise me something."

"What?"

"Keep your distance. You don't need her in your life."

I didn't know what to say. *One day, this will all be over,* I thought. *We'll go back to Vermont. We'll stay with Tom and his wife until Mom finds a job making panna cotta at some upscale Italian restaurant, and then we'll rent a new home, or maybe buy one of our own, because we'll have money—a whole lot of it.*

"I promised to take care of her until she gets too difficult to handle," Mom said. "Could be months . . ."

Months? That was no time at all, really. I could be home in time for prom.

". . . or it could be years. The disease doesn't work the same for everyone."

"Are you saying I could end up *graduating* from Grant High?" I blurted out.

"I don't think it will be that long. She's already confused, forgetting things, losing stuff. But it'll be worth it one day, Liv, you'll see."

What I was thinking was almost as awful as Mom's reason for moving us: *Imagine not having to take out college loans one day.* The thought soured within me. We were discussing my grandmother's death like it was an event to be put on the calendar.

Last year in Honors English, we'd learned a German legend. A man named Faust had traded his soul to the devil in exchange for worldly pleasures.

This didn't feel a whole lot different.

SEVEN

As I was about to walk into math on Tuesday morning, my phone buzzed. I freed it from my jeans. It was Candace. *Think someone should tell you . . . Sean's hanging out with Kendall Perry. SORRY. Thought you should know. I'd want to know.*

I read it again, trying not to overreact. I reminded myself that I wasn't the jealous type. No point starting now.

Probably just a friend, I texted back. My eyes began to sting.

A minute later: *Probably.*

I deleted the text, wishing that Candace could ignore her "altruistic" urge to share bad news.

A blur of movement snatched my phone from my hand. Franklin D. shoved it under his sweatshirt.

"Excuse me!" a voice bellowed. Mr. Karnofsky, our extremely short, extremely stout, very loud chemistry teacher, glared at me. "Was that a cell phone I saw? Might I remind you of the school policy: no cell phone usage during class time?"

Franklin D. rolled his eyes to the caged clock in the hallway. "With all due respect, Mr. K., the bell has yet to ring. I believe we have another—"

The bell rang. Franklin D. finished his thought. "We *had* another twenty seconds. So technically, Ms. Newman has adhered to all the policies, guidelines, and rules of our institution."

"Mr. Schiller, would you like *your* cell phone taken away?"

"No, sir."

The teacher served a pudgy palm to me, flesh side up. "You may be a new student, but you received the handbook like everyone else."

"I don't have it." I pulled out my pockets to show him, arching my eyebrows like I wasn't sure what he'd seen, but it hadn't been *me* breaking the rule after only one week in school.

"If I see it again, it's gone." He walked away.

Franklin D. passed me the phone, which I buried in the folds of my jacket. "I'd hate to see your main connection to the world get stowed in a desk drawer for forty-eight hours," he said.

We walked into math and made our way to our desks. Mr. Harrison wasn't there. Late again.

"What's so important that you'd risk the wrath of Karnofsky, anyway?" Franklin D. asked.

This brought back the text, with all its flaming agony. My eyes filled up.

"Now that's what I call gratitude," Franklin D. said. "I bring the lady to tears."

I looked up, having already forgotten he was there.

"You okay?" he whispered, leaning in.

I pulled back. "Yeah, thanks. It's, um, personal."

"No problem. Would you like me to reserve a seat for

you at my lunch table?" He glanced at an invisible watch on his wrist. "At, say, one thirty, sharp?"

"I have a meeting at lunch," I said, thinking fast. "Prom committee."

Franklin D. nodded. I'd meant to say homecoming, but he didn't seem to know the difference. Though the no-cell-phone-usage-where-you-might-be-caught policy had officially commenced, I checked my screen one last time before putting it away.

"Another time then," he said. He ripped off a corner of notepaper, scratched out a phone number, and placed it on my binder. "You can text me if you have questions about the school, or meaningless policies, or whatever."

I raised a hand in acknowledgment and pulled out my homework.

. . .

The next day, Mom stormed into the apartment. She headed to the living room and fell onto the couch.

I was sitting on the floor, algebra homework spread in front of me while *Jeopardy!* played on the TV. Math was my favorite subject. As long as I was careful to get two questions wrong on every test, I wouldn't screw with the grading curve. I'd learned this the hard way, back in sixth grade.

Stupid spelling test, Candace once said to me. *It's totally unfair that you get an A and you don't even have to study.*

"It's like she gets to have an open book with every test," Audrey had chimed in.

"Maybe she's cheating," Candace had said.

I denied it, but that was all. I wanted to tell them about

60

my memory, but they'd be jealous. It would be easier to hide my ability behind a few mistakes.

On the TV, Alex Trebek announced the Daily Double: "After the 1906 earthquake, prisoners were transferred to this island until local jails could be rebuilt."

"What is Alcatraz Island?" I shouted. I tapped Mom on the leg. "Ha! Beat you to it."

We always competed for the answers. Granted, I won most of the time. My memory gave me an unfair advantage. That didn't stop me from gloating, though. It was tradition.

When Mom didn't roll off her usual retort, I studied her more closely. Her face was pale, and her eyes ringed with dark circles.

"We were just there. Alcatraz? Overpriced, nonrefundable tickets?"

She nodded.

"How was your day?" I probed.

"Fine."

I picked up her coffee mug from the morning and took it into the kitchen. I turned the tap on and raised my voice, hoping my question would sound casual above the blast of water. "How are things working out with Adelle?"

"I spent an hour searching for her damn purse," Mom grumbled.

It was good to hear her complain. Better than silence.

"I found it in the pantry, between a can of kidney beans and an empty cereal box," she said.

According to the Alzheimer's website, misplacing stuff happens to everyone, but putting items in weird places? Not so much. I threw out a question that had been marinating in my head all day. "So, are there other relatives I should know about?"

"Not that I'm aware of."

"What made you stop visiting your mother when you were in college? I mean, was it something specific?"

"Livvy, please, can't you see I'm exhausted? Another time, okay?"

I sighed, not sure if there'd ever be enough time for my questions.

. . .

The following Monday, I sat on the steps across the street from the yellow Victorian and waited. Mom wanted me to forget about my grandmother. I'd tried. Really. For a week, I told myself that I was too busy with school to visit Adelle. If Mom's stories were true, then who needed the drama, right? But with each passing day, the guilt tugged harder. Mom had issues with Adelle—that was obvious—but I didn't. Maybe I could get to know my grandmother on my own terms, not my mother's.

At exactly four, Mom sprinted from the house with freedom on her mind. I ducked behind a car and watched her hike up the hill with determined steps.

My heart beat double time as I crossed the street. On the porch, I raised my fist to the door, but didn't knock. An ornamental box with Hebrew lettering, nailed to the doorframe, stopped me short.

At a friend's bar mitzvah in the seventh grade, I'd asked Mom about our nonexistent religious life. *We're human beings above everything else*, she'd said. Typically, when Mom used the word *God*, it was attached to something profane. As for me, I didn't know what I believed in, and so far, I'd been okay with not knowing.

I pulled out my phone to Google *Jewish* and *door*. The search engine brought up the word I was looking for: *mezuzah*. I skimmed the Wikipedia entry about the variety of decorative cases designed to hold parchment with verses from the Torah.

Adelle Friedman, my grandmother, had a mezuzah. I didn't get it. Why hadn't Mom told me we were Jewish? Or maybe it was my grandfather. But then why would Adelle hang one up when she'd moved to San Francisco *after* her husband had died?

I wedged my phone into my back pocket and leaned against the wall, wondering why I'd come here. What was the point? It was already too late to know my grandmother. The disease had shrunk her brain. After hearing some of Mom's stories, I didn't think I'd care for the wholly intact version, anyway. Maybe Mom was right. Maybe I was better off staying away. It wasn't too late to turn around and . . .

I jumped from the wall as the buzzer sounded in the apartment. Great, I'd butt-rung the doorbell. My eyes skipped back to the mezuzah. I couldn't help but wonder if God was sending me a message: *Your grandmother is family.*

No, I couldn't run away like a scared kid. I had to find out for myself if Adelle Friedman was the monster Mom made her out to be. It wasn't that I thought Mom was lying, but she was definitely capable of exaggeration.

I smoothed my hair and stepped onto the doormat. "Hi," I whispered when Adelle finally got the door open. There was a hint of a smile on her face. I matched it, then raised her a grin of my own. "It's me. Olivia. I mean, Livvy."

Adelle backed into the foyer, gesturing with her bent finger for me to follow.

"Cookies?" she asked.

"Oh, um, no thanks. I just ate."

In the kitchen, she brushed past me to the oven door. She bent down stiffly to peer through the glass window. "Do you know how to get them out of the heat?"

The mitt on the counter was scarred with black burns, but when I opened the oven, it was cold. The cookies inside were burned disks. I set them down on top of an unwashed pot from another night's dinner. Adelle didn't take her eyes off me. Not wanting to appear rude, I plucked the least overdone cookie off the tray.

"I've been trying to make them all day," she said, putting the teapot on the back burner. She turned on all four gas flames.

Oh, God. "These are really great, thanks," I said.

"I used to be a cook. The neighbors would stroll past the open window to get a whiff of roast goose with apples and salt and . . ." Her eyebrows drew together in confusion. "*Gottverdammt!*" she shouted, marching over to the trash can to peer inside. "Gottverdammt, gottverdammt, gottverdammt!"

That sounded like German—and not very nice German, either. Come to think of it, so was the name she'd called the neighbor's dog: *Scheisshund.* Mom had never really said where Adelle had grown up.

I followed my grandmother's gaze to the trash can, topped with what looked like discarded chunks of coal, burned beyond recognition. Several batches of cookies had been thrown out. "Doesn't my mother help you?" I asked gently.

"Gretchen was ill today. *I* took care of *her*."

I imagined Mom spread out on the couch with a "headache." My grandmother could have burned the house down on my mother's watch.

The teapot howled like a coyote calling its pack. Adelle transferred it to the counter but left the burners on. She shuffled back to the trash can, retrieved a cookie, and tossed the rock to me.

"Thanks," I mumbled. When she turned around, I leaped across the room to turn the burners off and slid back into my chair.

"Where's Gretchen?" Adelle asked.

"She went home."

Her face seemed to crumple in on itself. She must've thought I meant forever.

"She'll be back tomorrow," I said, quickly adding, "It must be nice having my mom around to help, right?"

"She'll do."

Not exactly a ringing endorsement.

"But she steals things," Adelle said, wrinkling her nose.

I almost dropped my cookie on the floor.

"First she took my gloves, and then my keys. She wants me to think I'm going crazy so she can send me to an insane asylum." She ground her fists into her eye sockets. "Herbert wouldn't care for her plan. He wouldn't care for it at all."

Herbert. My grandfather.

Adelle's voice was an urgent hiss. "That woman is out to get me, you know."

Paranoia. Mid-stage Alzheimer's symptom. Still, I didn't like that she thought this about Mom—even if it wasn't worlds away from the truth.

"My mother's taking care of you so you can stay at home," I explained. *Though you might need to go to an assisted-care facility one day.* "She's happy to have this time with you." When she looked away, I stuffed the charred cookie into my pocket.

"She wants to stop me from doing everything I love, like baking for Herbert when he comes to call."

Panic roped around my chest, squeezing the breath from me. What if Mom had lied about my grandfather, too? Could he still be alive? I had no idea how old he'd be.

"Where's Herbert?" I whispered.

"I'm friends with the dearly departed," she said.

I exhaled, relieved. My grandfather survived only in the snarled nest of Adelle's brain.

"What's your name, dear?" she asked.

I swallowed. "Livvy."

"Yes, Oh-livia, Livvy! That was my mother's name."

Something else I hadn't known. Thanks, Mom.

Adelle looked around the kitchen as if there might be spies lurking behind the refrigerator. "Those people at the cuckoo farm want to steal my cookie recipe." She tapped the side of her head. "They'll have to torture me to get it. Unleash their ravenous mutts and whip me until I can no longer stand, and even then I will not tell."

Ravenous mutts? Whips? "There's no one here but me," I told her.

She set a cup down on the table and poured the hot

water into it, forgetting the tea bag. The water overflowed and dripped off the edge. I dropped a stack of napkins on the floor, sopping up the puddle with my foot.

"Victoria says I have to sleep every day, but I don't remember when, Oh-livia," she said. "Is it time for my nap?"

Victoria? Oh, right, Vickie—the other caregiver. Where was she, anyway? She was supposed to start her shift when Mom's ended. I stood up. "I'm pretty sure it's nap time now, Adelle."

"Don't call me that!"

"Sorry . . . uh, Grandma." It felt weird saying it out loud, as if I was making it up.

"Oma. Call me Oma. That's what the Dutch children do."

"Was your . . . oma . . . from Holland?"

She paused, the wrinkles on her forehead bunching together as if she was solving a complicated math problem. "All the great writers lived in the capital, you know." She took off, limping down the hallway. She stopped at the front door and stood at attention like a porter at a fancy hotel. "You must come again."

"Sure. I'd like that." I opened the door and escaped down the steps to the sidewalk. But then I stopped and turned around. I didn't want to leave her alone like this.

Right on cue, the other duplex door opened. A woman in her twenties stepped onto the porch. She was tall and thin, with short brown hair that clung to her scalp like a cap. "Where do you think you're going?" she asked Adelle.

My grandmother looked at me. The woman tracked her gaze, spotting me.

"May I help you?" she asked.

"This is my granddaughter," Adelle said proudly. "Her name is . . ."

"Hello, Livvy! Your mother's told me all about you. I'm Vickie."

Damn. Now this Vickie person would tell Mom about my visit. "Nice to meet you," I said, climbing back up the steps.

She shook my hand vigorously and turned to Adelle. "I thought you were trying to escape, you silly girl."

"It's impossible to escape," Adelle said. "No one makes it out alive."

"I can tell you're in a hurry to go," Vickie told me. "Has school already started for you?"

I nodded, and she smiled. "I'm sorry to hear that." She laid a hand on my grandmother's shoulder and nudged her forward. "Go on, give your granddaughter some love."

We hugged awkwardly. Adelle rested her cheek on my shoulder, arms hanging at her sides as if she didn't have a clue what to do with them.

"Promise me you'll visit again, Gretchen," Adelle said in my ear. "Please, dear, please. Promise?"

My eyes stung at the sudden realization that I wouldn't be coming back. Adelle couldn't even remember my name. Whatever chance I'd had for a real grandmother didn't exist anymore. "Um, okay," I said.

Her mouth curved into one of those near-miss smiles.

For the first time, I was glad that Adelle's memory was a sieve, and that this moment, like so many others, would sift right through.

MAY 1945

Herbert was a Buchenwald liberator who volunteered at the Displaced Persons Camp. Adelle thought it funny that he referred to the patients as "guests"—a fancy name for the sick and dying refugees housed in the former quarters of the German army. Everyone used pretty words to scrub away the scum of war.

She implored him to return on three separate occasions. Each time he did, she asked who he was. On the fourth visit, she fixed those brown eyes on him and said, "Hello, Mr. Friedman."

He smiled, telling her, "My name has never sounded better."

. . .

The American soldier was older than her—somewhere in his twenties—and she knew he found her attractive, although he kept his thoughts to himself. "You aren't as thin as the others," Herbert commented one day.

It took her a moment to compose a response. In broken English, she said, "I was in the camp hospital. A nurse gave extra rations sometimes."

"A Nazi gave you food?" Herbert said incredulously. "I can't believe it."

"Perhaps she didn't want me to die on her watch." These soldiers were so simpleminded, Adelle thought, viewing everyone as either good or evil when the world was much more complex. There's a decent heart in most of us, *she wanted to say,* if you'd only open your eyes.

Herbert's jaw had tightened. He didn't agree, she knew

69

that. He'd seen the damage firsthand, the destroyed lives, the rotting corpses. He was incapable of finding humanity in the soul of a beast. And yet, he didn't try to change her mind. He didn't argue. He kept his feelings to himself, tucked away where they belonged.

In time, she felt a spark in her chest, as if her heart had cracked open the tiniest bit.

. . .

One afternoon, Herbert brought her a gift.

She pulled the Star of David necklace from a bed of cotton. The single overhead bulb caught the tiny diamonds, casting a shiver of light across her hand. She thanked him and politely returned it to the box. Later she discovered that people wouldn't ask difficult questions as long as she wore the necklace. No one dared resurrect the trauma.

From then on, she never took it off.

CHAPTER

EIGHT

A COOL MIST SETTLED ON MY FACE AS I TREKKED over the Fillmore Street hill. I ran my hands down my hair in a lame attempt to keep it straight. The sun had vanished behind a bank of fog. God, I missed the late-night warmth of an East Coast summer. I used to escape to the roof outside my window and stargaze in a tank top and shorts. What I missed most, though, was the tree outside my bedroom. I could track the changing seasons by the color of its leaves. In a few days, summer in San Francisco would turn to fall, and I needed a calendar to know it.

"Mom, you here?" My voice echoed through our sparsely furnished apartment. The blinds were drawn, blotting out the last rays of daylight. I flipped on the light switch.

"Turn it off," Mom said, her voice hoarse.

I did as she asked. She lay on the couch, sneakers on the armrest.

"Are you okay?" I asked.

"I have a headache."

"You want me to get you an ibuprofen?"

She waved me off. "I need to rest."

I sat down at the opposite end of the couch, careful not to disturb her. Mom used to get migraines back when she was fighting with Dad.

"What happened today?" I asked.

"Adelle's a bitch."

Even though that word was tossed around a thousand times a day at school, it sounded worse when applied to a little old lady. And not any old lady—my grandmother.

"She's always criticizing me: 'Gretchen, where did you hide my necklace?' 'Did you steal my diamond ring?' 'Gretchen, you didn't put enough sugar in my coffee . . . It tastes like seawater!' " Mom's imitation was close, but she exaggerated the almost undetectable European accent.

"I read that volatile moods can be a sign she's getting worse," I said, hope and sadness warring inside me.

"My mother's always had a crappy disposition."

"She likes having you take care of her." I figured that Adelle had to be grateful on some level, even if she didn't always show it.

Mom rolled onto her back. Shadows spread across her face, sinking into the hollows of her cheeks. Had she been eating these past weeks?

It'll be okay, I'd told Tom. *I'll keep an eye on her.*

I wasn't doing a very good job of it. Mom's face was flushed, eyes glazed with exhaustion. Was she getting sick? I ran my palms down my jeans. It didn't seem like the best time to tell her, but I knew if I didn't say something, Vickie would do it for me. "Mom, I met the other caregiver."

Her head snapped to the side. "You visited my mother when I specifically asked you not to?"

72

Her tone floored me. It sounded so . . . Adelle-like. "I stopped by after school."

"Why?"

"How can I live a few blocks away and not see her? She's my grandma."

"Save yourself the trouble."

"But Adelle seems nice." The innocent adjective was a weapon, I knew that, but I didn't care. "She made me cookies again."

"She always was a good cook. I can say that for her."

I searched for a hint of sympathy in her rigid features. Finding none, I said, "She has a disease, Mom. She doesn't have much longer."

She rolled toward the back cushion, tucking her face into a crevice. "One can only hope." I was about to accuse her of being immature when something sweet and sour hit my nose. Oh, God, Chanel No. 5. I hadn't run across that particular scent in a long time. When I was a kid, I called it the Cover-up Smell.

"Jesus," I said, bringing my fist to my nose. "Mom, you didn't. You couldn't. Not after all this time."

"I'm tired, Liv. Just wanna sleep."

"No!" I climbed over her, inserted my hand between the couch and her shoulder, and flipped her onto her back. "Five years, Mom, five years! You wouldn't throw it all away, would you?"

Her pupils flared. "It was a little bit, Liv. To take the edge off. I needed something to help me relax."

I started to cry. As much as I resented my own tears, I couldn't help it.

"Don't do that," she pleaded. "Don't look at me like that. Not until you've lived my life."

"Mom—"

"Yesterday was my parents' anniversary."

I wiped my tears away so I could see her more clearly. "What?"

"I thought maybe it wasn't too late to connect with my mother. It might be easier than before because at least now she was incapable of pulling up a laundry list of resentments."

"I don't understand . . ."

"I threw us a party, Liv. Just her and me. To remember my dad."

Oh, God. Please let it have gone well, I thought to myself. But I knew it hadn't. A person didn't abandon five years of sobriety because she'd finally connected with a difficult parent.

"So I pulled out my photos of my father," she continued. "He looked so handsome in his military uniform. I even found one of them on their honeymoon. They were learning to surf in the Bahamas. My dad was on a surfboard with her, and he had both his arms wrapped around her middle to keep her from falling off. She looked so safe, so secure. It was an amazing picture, because, you know, I can't remember ever seeing my mom like that. I guess I thought that if she saw the photo, it would resurrect a feeling of being cared for." Mom stared up at the ceiling. Then her voice dropped. "I brought her a heart-shaped balloon. Oh, and I made her a cake. An anniversary special, with peach fondant roses, and icing like lace, and . . ." She stopped. Tears spilled over, running down her cheeks, leaving splotches on the pillow where her head rested. "The balloon popped. It popped, and she fell to the floor, and she covered her head, and she screamed. She screamed that I wanted to shoot her. That I had already stolen from her, and now I wanted her dead."

The softness in her eyes melted away, like a snowball with a rock packed inside. My own anger hadn't subsided yet, but I knew that she needed a hug. All I could manage was a touch on her wrist. "I'm sorry," I said, dragging the words out.

"The party lasted ten minutes. Ten minutes, Liv, until I was so upset that I tossed the cake in the trash. And then you know what I realized?"

I shook my head, even though Mom was looking at the ceiling and not at me.

"I realized that my mother can't be fixed. Even this disease won't wipe away who she is, deep inside."

"But Mom, Alzheimer's makes her do—"

She talked over me, lost in her own world. "When Vickie came in for her shift and asked how her day was, you know what Adelle said?" She turned to me then, as if I had the answer. When I didn't guess, she went on. "My mother said, 'Gretchen spilled my food!' She didn't remember the party. She didn't remember the cake that took me four hours to make. The photo montage. None of it. All she could pull out of that brain was a complaint. Just like it's always been."

I felt a familiar swell of emotions. Pity. Sympathy. Sorrow. Emotions that tamped down anger. But I wasn't going to let them do that this time. "Where's the bottle, Mom?"

She finally turned her head and fixed her eyes, brimming with hurt, on mine. "What do you want to do, make things worse?"

What did I want to do? Yell and scream and break

75

everything in sight, for starters. But I had a better idea and grabbed my phone off the table.

"Who are you calling?"

"Tom."

"No, don't!" She swung at my phone. I pulled it out of reach.

"I'm calling him if you don't tell me where the booze is!"

"Don't call him. Please." She inserted a hand behind the cushion. Out came a bottle of Scotch, two-thirds empty.

"Just a little bit," I said, "to take the edge off."

"It's my first slip, Liv. I swear it'll be my last."

I wanted to believe her. I really did. The thing was, hope, as a cure for heartache, had worn thin. "I think we should call Tom," I said. "You guys need to talk."

"I'll call him after we both get a good night's sleep."

"Okay," I conceded, but only because it was three hours later on the East Coast. I'd call him tomorrow morning, whether Mom wanted me to or not.

Her meek smile had all the right ingredients—shame, apology, gratitude—but her eyes scared me. They were dark as snuffed-out candles.

.   .   .

Five years ago in March, Mom almost ran over an eight-year-old boy riding his bike to the park. This was what recovering addicts called rock bottom—the moment when you need to make a choice: recover or lose everything. When Mom rehashed the story at her AA meetings, she always ended with, "I could have killed someone's child."

Within a week of the accident, she admitted herself to Evergreen Center, a rehab facility with shuffleboard and a swimming pool and group therapy sessions under the fringe of a willow tree. I loved visiting her there. Tom was her counselor. Mom said that he had a heart the size of Manhattan and a ten-year sobriety button pinned over it. After she finished the program—and discovered that Dad was on his way to Australia with the "other woman"—she trekked thirty miles each way to go to the same AA meetings as Tom. Not long after, she asked if he'd be her sponsor, and he said yes.

She fell off the wagon three months later. Not because Tom was a bad sponsor. Or because a calamity overwhelmed her, like going bankrupt, totaling her car, or having our house burn down. No, the reason was way less impressive than the catalyst for sobriety.

My mother drank again because we ran ten minutes late to my sixth grade performance in *Sleeping Beauty*. She got caught behind too many red lights.

I remember being on stage that night. I played Olivia Oak in Maleficent's forest. Standing on stage, I had lots of time to scan the audience for my mother. Twenty minutes in, I saw her sit down. Third row, chin to her chest, mouth open wide enough to swallow a bee. As soon as the curtains fell for intermission, I darted down the steps, wove my fingers through hers, and led her out of the gymnasium. God knows how we made it home in one piece, but when you're eleven, the threat of embarrassment trumps safety.

You know what else? Our director didn't even notice I was gone.

NINE

MY BRAIN, CRAMMED WITH WORRIES, LEFT LITTLE ROOM for the trifling details of high school. During Spanish, I tuned out irregular past-tense verbs and considered if it was possible for Mom to drink one day and stop the next like a normal person. Maybe she *had* downed the booze for no other reason than it helped her relax, and not because the monster that lay dormant inside her all those years had stirred.

And maybe I really was the queen of Liechtenstein.

After class, Franklin D. appeared beside me, pinpricks of sweat on his forehead. "Ready or not, here I am," he said, spreading his arms wide.

"Hello to you, too," I said.

"You're a fast walker, Livvy Newman. Have you considered joining track? I like a girl who can reinvent herself. Prom planner one day, mega-jock the next. You always keep me on my toes."

"Prom?" Oh, right, my excuse for not sitting with him during lunch that first time.

"Girls sure like to plan ahead," he said pleasantly. "Prom's, what, seven months away?"

Guess he wasn't as clueless as I'd thought. "I'd rather be

by myself at lunch. I'm not feeling very social these days."

"You really miss your old school. Creston High, right?"

I stopped suddenly, which caused Franklin D. to slam on the brakes. The guy behind us swerved to avoid a collision. We moved to the wall so we wouldn't cause a traffic jam.

"I asked Hilda in the office. That was all I could get out of her," he admitted.

My groan was swallowed up by hallway noise.

"What you need are good friends, and since I'm stuck here eight hours a day, I have nothing but time to charm you," he said. "I'm failing epically, aren't I?"

I laughed, wanting to deny it, but caught myself. "Listen, it's not your fault. I'm not in the best space for friends right now. It's—"

Franklin D. pulled an imaginary sword from a holster and thrust it through his heart. "Argh, a variation on the 'It's not you, it's me' speech! I thought those days were over in middle school."

I laughed again, acknowledging my own epic failure to build a fortress.

Franklin D. cleared his throat. "'Friendship sought is good, but given unsought is better.' *Twelfth Night*, Act three, Scene one."

"Shakespeare?" I rolled my eyes. Secretly I was impressed with his ability to pull a quote on demand.

"The Bard of Avon has something to say for every occasion." Franklin D. shrugged. "Well, if we're going to get all technical, the way it goes is, 'Love sought is good, but given unsought, is better.' I didn't want to freak you out by saying the 'L' word or anything."

79

His thoughts flowed from brain to mouth like water through a colander. Oddly I found his unfiltered honesty refreshing. I didn't have to weigh the truth of his words, like with Mom, or decode subtext, the way I had to do with Candace and Audrey.

He walked me to chem lab and took off. Fifty minutes later, he was back. "I was wondering if you'd changed your mind about having lunch with us?"

"Us?"

"Me and my friends."

I had to admit, I was curious. Kids back home would've chopped this guy up and used him for kitty litter. I shrugged, noncommittal. "I don't like cafeteria food."

He patted his backpack, designed like a TARDIS from the *Doctor Who* series. "I'll share my sandwich with you. Today we have the PB&J special. The *J* refers to my mother's tantalizing homemade plum jam."

I pushed the double doors open and shielded my eyes from the blinding sunlight. "I appreciate it, but I have money for lunch."

He followed me toward Alvarado Street. As we walked, he shed his green parka, revealing a sweatshirt with the message "Counting in binary is as easy as 01 10 11." Then he stopped under a tree. "This seems like a nice spot for lunch, don't you think?" He snapped his jacket out and spread it on the ground like a picnic blanket.

I gestured to his backpack. "Peanut butter and jelly, huh?"

He took a sandwich out of a lunch bag and tore it in half, giving me the bigger share. My last PB&J had been somewhere around fifth grade. The plum jam tasted sweet and tangy. The peanut butter was smooth, the way I liked it.

He put his finger to his knee and coaxed an ant to crawl on, then delivered it to a fallen leaf. "This is an excellent first step, Livvy. Tomorrow, we'll try the cafeteria. I've trained my friends not to bite—unless you attack first."

I folded my arms across my chest.

"Is that body language for, 'Sure, I'd love to?'"

"I don't know . . . maybe."

"I'll take 'maybe.'"

I think I might have nodded, but I didn't say anything that would imply a verbal contract.

. . .

The next day, figuring it would take Franklin D. thirty seconds to get from his class to mine before lunch, I tore out of school and sped across the parking lot like there was a tsunami coming. I found a bench two blocks away and sat down to write him a text. It took me three tries before I came up with *Sorry to miss lunch. Had to go for a walk to clear my head.*

I checked e-mail. Only a message from Dad.

> *Dear Liv,*
> *How are you? Your mom told me about the move.*
> *I don't know what to say, except I hope you're okay.*
> *San Francisco is an exciting town. Life here is good. The*
> *boys start preschool this year, and they joined a Peewee*
> *T-ball . . .*

I skimmed through the details about the boys' first game, their new pet wallaby named Bob, who hopped around the backyard and had the life-span of a small dog, and Maggie's booming business making jewelry from recycled wine corks. I cut to the end.

> *How about an Australian getaway over winter break? You'll like summer in December.*

As if it all came down to sunshine.

I was about to close the e-mail when I saw that he'd brought up my address by hitting reply to an old one I'd written him years ago.

> *Hi Dad,*
> *Did you know that over 75% of people who marry their affair partners end up divorced? That's a fact.*

> *Dear Livvy,*
> *All the statistics in the world can't touch true love. So, when do you want to visit?*

This particular e-mail had come three weeks before Dad threatened to sue for partial custody if Mom didn't put me on a plane to Perth. I spent my summer—their winter— avoiding my father and stepmother by playing Twister with my half-siblings.

> *Dear Dad,* I wrote now, *I'm thinking of auditioning for the school play. That means rehearsals in December and January. Mom's bugging me to do chores. Later—*

Lunch was almost over, but there was still something

I had to do. I punched in Mom's cell number, holding my breath as it rang.

"Did you call Tom yet?" I blurted out when she answered. I'd called him myself yesterday morning, but I hadn't told her. He suggested I give her a few days to phone him on her own. *It's better if she takes initiative*, he'd said. *No one can make her stay sober.*

I hoped he was wrong. I was going to try, anyway.

"Yes, I did," Mom said, her voice a half octave too high. "It helped, thanks."

So she hadn't called him. I said good-bye and went back to school.

· · ·

In debate class, Franklin D. dropped a note on my desk.

> *I'm sure you are unaware of the fine dining opportunity you missed this afternoon. All our seats are booked months in advance. Please know that we have a twelve-hour cancellation policy. However, we are willing to extend the offer one more time (for now): tomorrow, at 1:30. Please nod your head once to confirm acceptance of this most auspicious invitation.*
> *—Franklin D. Schiller*

I fought back a smile, knowing his eyes were on me, and tucked the letter inside my school planner.

After class I sensed him nearby. I turned around, and he walked right into me. "That was exciting," he said, taking my elbow to steady us.

"Listen," I began. "I can tell you're a nice person, but I

have to be honest with you. I'm happy on my own. I have a lot of friends in Vermont, and I'm really not lonely."

He tilted his head. "You call that being honest?"

Blissfully my cell phone chirped, saving me from an answer. I whipped it out like a druggie looking for a fix. Sean! I *knew* he was going to say that it was me, always had been. Well, for the seven weeks we'd been together, anyway.

> *Livvy sorry I haven't answered your texts. Christ this is too damn hard. Maybe we should see other people . . . think about it. It's only fair. Hope you are having fun in SF*

What?! I felt my insides curdle up like milk left out overnight.

"Bad news?" Franklin D. asked.

"My boyfriend," I whispered. "He just . . . he just . . . he just said he loved me."

"Oh." He took a second to recover. "It's good to be loved."

I hadn't meant to lie, but I didn't feel like sharing a humiliating breakup-by-bytes.

The rejection barely slowed him down. "With all due respect, I think you need friends on *this* coast. Therefore, the offer to join our illustrious lunch table still stands. Tomorrow?"

I shoved the phone in my pocket, my thoughts consumed with Sean. "I don't think you get it," I said, arriving at my locker. "My boyfriend won't like it if I'm hanging out with another guy." I focused on my combination, unable to face his reaction.

"Livvy," he said, cheerful as ever. "I feel the whole male-female thing has gotten in our way. You see, I truly am interested in getting to know you. But not as a boyfriend. It pains me to tell you that you're not my type." He gave me an appraising look. "You *do* think that men and women can be friends, don't you?"

I took in his placid smile. "Of course," I said. "We can get bumper stickers made: 'Friends always stalk friends.'"

He laughed. "Oh, yeah, my bad. I have social OCD."

I wanted to go home, to mope in the blissful darkness of my walk-in closet. It wasn't like I was delusional or anything. Sean hadn't stayed in touch since I'd left, but I'd told myself that he'd never been into social media.

I once read in *Psychology Today* that it was impossible to swallow and cry at the same time, so I made a beeline for the water fountain.

"You're a very interesting woman, Olivia Newman," Franklin D. said as we headed outside. I was surprised to see that the trees lining the parking lot had softened to a seashell pink. They weren't the brilliant hues of the ones back home, but at least they looked different. Franklin D. kept talking. "I feel like you have more important things on your mind than the usual high school drama. Like real life, to be exact."

Sadly that was true. Real life did get in the way of fun.

"I wasn't lying when I said I wanted to be your friend. I do. I get that you have a boyfriend, and that you're madly in love with him and blah, blah, blah, so, like, that's cool as a cucumber, okay?"

My heart gave an unexpected thump at the vulnerable look on his face. "Well, now that I know you won't turn into some kind of lovesick stalker type, it does take the pressure off," I allowed.

Franklin D.'s shoulders slumped with a dramatic exhale.

"Okay, I'll eat lunch at your table tomorrow." Crap, that sounded alarmingly like a commitment.

His grin dwindled as he glanced down at the pocket watch in his hand, chain and all. "Holy Christ and Batmobile, my archery lesson starts in twenty." He rode the handrail to the street.

When he was gone, I shook my head and smiled. Franklin D. was growing on me. Kind of like a wart, but whatever.

TEN

I SAT AT FRANKLIN D.'S LUNCH TABLE ALL WEEK, surrounded by his eclectic friends. The first person I met was Elizabeth. She spent her extracurricular hours making fundraising calls for Greenpeace. She moved through the cafeteria like a bride at a reception, chatting up people, gathering trash from the tables, and sorting it into the proper receptacles.

"You know what's strange about this place?" I asked Franklin D. while watching Elizabeth collect a Coke bottle from a cheerleader, offer a perky thank-you, and glide to the next table.

"What?"

"This place lacks cliques. Where are the jocks, the geeks, the drama freaks, the brains, the slackers?" I still wasn't used to the kids at Grant High and how they seemed to march to their own drummers in a dissonant marching band.

He shrugged. "They're here, if you feel compelled to categorize."

"But they blend," I went on. "They talk to each other like it doesn't matter."

"Everyone is who they are. We accept each other as is. Like one big bargain-basement clearance sale."

I arched an eyebrow. "That doesn't seem natural."

Franklin D. scratched his head, thinking. He leaned forward, placing both palms on the table. "Picture a pot on the stove, filled with meat, beans, vegetables, tomato sauce, whatever. When you take a bite, you don't taste every single ingredient, right? They meld together, creating a mouthwatering, delectable chili."

Just then, this guy slunk by, greasy hair, orange Converse boots—yes, orange—with black laces and a plaid shirt. Franklin D. and I watched him approach a table of girls and snag a French fry off one of their trays.

"Not all ingredients are as fresh as others," Franklin D. commented.

"Evidently." I turned back to him. "Let's take you, for example. It seems you take pride in your . . . unusual personality."

"Don't you?"

I started to laugh but realized he was serious. "It's hard to connect with people when you're different," I said.

"We're all different. We can't help it. Why deny the one thing we have in common with everyone else . . . our uniqueness?"

I crossed my eyes. "Huh?"

My friends back home would have summed Franklin D. up with one word: *weird*—a default adjective used to describe anyone they didn't understand. I remembered how our English teacher never let us use the word in our papers because it was too vague.

Alex, another one of Franklin D.'s lunch buddies, walked up to the table, his tray loaded with an extra apple and a package of Twinkies. He was as short as a middle schooler, with rust-colored hair that he tried to hide with a buzz cut. I watched as he scanned the cafeteria, lingering on every female who strolled by.

"What if I told them they were the hottest girls on the planet?" he asked Franklin D. out of the blue.

"Hmmm, Jenna Cortez, Sydney Gellini, and possibly Cheryl Vanderhoff, on the right day," Franklin D. responded.

"What if we were all drunk?"

I winced at the casual reference.

"Robin Smith, Liz Barney, and Rebecca Reilly. That was easy," Franklin D. rolled off.

"I don't get it," I whispered, though Alex could hear me fine.

"He wants to know which girls would sleep with him under specific and varying circumstances," Franklin D. explained. "I try to be as generous as possible with my answers."

"How about you, Livvy?" Alex asked me. "'Cause I think *you're* the hottest girl on the entire planet."

"Livvy's mine," Franklin D. said. I gave him a look, which he ignored. He smiled kindly at Alex. "If she weren't pining after me, she'd be all over you, dude."

The bell rang and we stood up. A tall blond in a girls' wrestling team shirt strutted over to our table. "Hey, Liz, you know where the Mathletes meeting is today?"

Elizabeth told her and the girl left.

"See? That's a perfect example," I whispered to Franklin D. "A jock in Mathletes. My God, what's this world coming to?"

He patted my hand. We inched with the crowd toward

the stairwell. "Since we're now buds and all, will you be my partner in debate?" he asked.

I hesitated. I'd be giving up an easy A if I joined forces with him. Ms. Thurmond failed to see Franklin D.'s passion for exploration. She rarely called on him in class, even though his hand whipped in the air like a flag in a tropical storm. He didn't seem to notice. The next day, it would creep up the flagpole again.

"What's your GPA?" I asked as we took our seats. I figured teacher payback would manifest itself in substandard grades.

"3.87, unweighted. No one's perfect." He smiled, holding my gaze for a moment. "My test scores are nothing short of impeccable. Harvard's sending me swag already."

"I'm surprised they'd bother mailing anything, since their acceptance rate was only 5.4 percent this year."

He gave me an approving look. "Has anyone ever told you that you're a walking trivia master? Twenty-seven grams of fat in a Big Mac . . . 5.4 percent admission rate for Harvard."

"Twenty-eight," I corrected. "Twenty-eight grams of fat in a Big Mac."

He raised an eyebrow.

"I like to research things," I said. God, what was I doing? I didn't want to reveal my obsession. "Forget it."

"'Fess up," he said.

"No, it's weird."

"Livvy, a little weirdness will only add to my esteemed perception of you."

I shook my head.

"I'll tell you something about me that's bizarre," he said. "You know what my favorite snack food is?"

"Jalapeño pretzels?"

"Silken Berry Tofu shakes. Bayside Café makes decent ones—however, I've deconstructed the recipe and have vastly improved on it."

Yeah, that was pretty strange. "Okay, fine, so I like to look up statistics and stuff. It's, like, a hobby." I didn't tell him how facts imprinted themselves on my brain. How they didn't fade away over time the way they did for other people.

"Statistics and stuff, huh? That's sexy . . . If you were my kind, which you're not." He stopped outside the debate room. "Throw one my way, and make it good."

Over by the lockers, a girl buried her nose in a yellow bouquet that probably came from the guy sneaking a peek down her shirt. My mind wandered to last year, when Sean asked me to help him out with his math homework. He said it would free up time for us to be together. I'd been skeptical, because I wasn't born yesterday, but he kept his promise, and we talked for an extra hour on the phone after baseball practice every day. Each time he got an A, he brought me a rose from his mom's garden. It was sweet, really.

Then again, maybe it wasn't.

"Did you know that the average person spent over a hundred dollars on Valentine's Day last year, according to the National Retail Federation?" I said. It was $133.91, to be exact, but I decided to keep the amount to myself.

Franklin D. followed me into the classroom, nodding his head as we took our seats. "Impressive. You even knew the source."

"But do you know the change in divorce lawyer requests right after Valentine's Day?"

91

"I assume it drops, due to the chocolate-flavored truffles and chemically preserved floral arrangements."

"Wrong! It goes up." I held back the exact number: 40 percent.

He cranked an eyebrow. "Aha! From all the suckers who forgot to buy chocolate-flavored truffles and chemically preserved floral arrangements."

"Exactly." We slapped each other five, which was a totally dorky thing to do. I looked around, relieved no one had noticed.

Ms. Thurmond reviewed the rubric for the first debate, explaining how our classmates' assessments would be worth 50 percent of our grade. I wondered if maybe I *could* be Franklin D.'s partner without risking complete failure.

After class we stopped at his locker. I waited as he loaded up his backpack. A minute later, we made our escape into the Real World. It was a gorgeous day. I was sweating beneath my blue pullover, which I'd worn because of the bone-chilling temperature this morning.

Franklin D. ran his fingernails down the railing. "You never told me if you'd be my debate partner."

Oh, what the heck? "Sure. Why not?"

He tipped his invisible top hat at me. I curtsied before dropping onto the bench to wait for the city bus.

. . .

When Mom opened Adelle's door, I leaned in to kiss her, inhaling the scent of her skin. She smelled sober. "How was your day?" I asked.

She reached for her purse, which hung on the coatrack next to the door. "It's after four now, so it's about to get a whole lot better."

"Who's there?" Adelle called out.

"Just me," I said, stepping out of Mom's shadow. "Livvy."

I'd been doing a lot of research on Alzheimer's. The disease was a ticking time bomb. Who knew how long my grandmother had left? It felt wrong to turn my back on her, at a time when she needed me the most.

When I told Mom how I felt, she'd muttered under her breath, "Your funeral."

"Livvy's going to stay with you while I make a clean getaway," Mom said now to Adelle.

"Where's Vickie?" I asked. "Isn't it time for her shift?"

"Right here!" came a cheerful voice. Vickie waltzed by, drew Adelle to her, and planted a kiss on her nose. "How's my old girl?" She turned to Mom. "Oh, Gretchen, you won't believe what I found last night. In a Kleenex box, of all places." She pulled a gold bracelet out of her pocket.

"I was wondering where that went," Mom said. "One moment she was wearing it, the next it was gone."

"They stole it!" Adelle cried, making us all jump.

"No one stole anything, dear." Vickie slipped the bracelet on Adelle's wrist. She didn't even need to unclasp it. "It's right here, you see? You need to stop hiding your jewelry."

"Has she lost weight?" I asked. "Maybe it slipped off."

Vickie shrugged. "I wouldn't know. I started working here the same time as your mother." She turned to Adelle. "Guess we'll have to fatten you up, won't we?"

Mom grimaced. "Oh, darn, I forgot her three o'clock snack."

"I've got it covered," Vickie assured her. "Though I'm

not as good a cook as you, Gretchen."

Mom thanked her. To me, she said, "Happy bonding," and left.

"I'd like to make your grandmother a shake, but we're out of milk," Vickie announced. "Would you mind watching her for a minute while I go to the corner store?"

"Sure," I said.

When we were alone, Adelle limped down the hallway to the kitchen. *Judge Judy* was on the tiny TV that Vickie had brought over from her apartment.

"What kind of tea do you want?" I asked.

"The hot kind," she said.

I moved her to a chair in front of the TV, wondering if it had been on all day. Did she get any exercise? I turned it off, relieved when she didn't object.

"Do you know how to do a jumping jack?" I demonstrated, and then helped Adelle to her feet.

She couldn't move her arms with any kind of synchronicity. Her body wasn't functioning much better than her mind. I watered down the routine to standing jacks, waving my hands overhead like I was hailing a cab. Adelle tried, then hunched over her knees, panting. I turned the TV back on and waited for her to recover.

When Judge Judy asked about a photograph, I had an idea. Family albums. They had to be somewhere, right? Adelle was happily humming commercial jingles, so I snuck off. I started in the library—looking on bookshelves, in desk drawers, in the sitting room across the hallway, and the formal living room . . . but I couldn't find any. Not one.

When I returned to the kitchen, Judge Judy was declaring

her verdict. I filled the teapot and put it on the stove.

"Where do you keep your pictures? You know, of Mom when she was little, of you and Grandpa Herbert?" I asked.

She whipped her head from side to side like a horse shaking off a fly. "No pictures!" She brought a finger to her mouth. "Shh, I'm a secret! No one can know I'm here. They'll kill me if they find me alive."

I sighed. Why did I even bother? Adelle couldn't remember what she had for lunch, much less where she kept her albums.

I heard the front door shut and glanced at the clock. Thirty minutes was a leisurely jaunt to the corner store.

"I want my ginger tea!" shouted Adelle.

"Someone's being bossy," Vickie sang from down the hall. She meandered into the kitchen, slow as a city bus in afternoon traffic. "What's the word, dear?"

Surprisingly, Adelle found it. "Please?"

I cringed when Vickie clapped.

"How was the store?" I asked as I poured lukewarm water into a china cup. I didn't want Adelle to burn her mouth.

"They were out of organic milk. I'll go back tomorrow."

Vickie sat down beside my grandmother and checked her e-mail on a laptop, her lips curving in a distant smile.

"Have you always been a caregiver?" I asked.

"I was in finance at one of the largest accounting firms until the economy took a nose dive."

"Do you like working with the elderly?"

"I've been doing it since I was laid off from my real job."

I bit my lip. *Real* job?

"But I adore your grandmother," she added, catching

Adelle's eyes. Grandma tried to smile, but her mouth sagged into a frown.

I studied Vickie more closely. She could be patronizing at times, but at least she was organized, which helped balance Mom's scattered nature.

She shut the laptop case. That's when I realized that it was the same blue Dell that Mom had used to order a refill of Adelle's prescription.

"Isn't that my grandmother's computer?"

"Your mom and I are sharing it. It's in the contract. We agreed that it stays in the house at all times. That means you can't take it out, either, Livvy."

I stared at her, surprised. I had my own laptop at home. It was five years old—officially defined as "vintage" by the Apple store. I could fold an entire load of laundry while it booted up, but it wouldn't have occurred to me to sneak Adelle's computer out of her house.

Vickie patted my grandma's hand. "It's not like you use it anymore, right, hon?"

Next to the computer, I spotted a stack of envelopes. Adelle's water bill was on top. "Doesn't my mom pay the bills?" I asked.

"She has enough on her mind. I told her I'd help out." She winked. "At least they'll get sent in on time." She considered the pile. "Most of these are mine, sadly."

I softened. Vickie had to be making less as a caregiver than she had at her accounting firm. "Do you want some tea?" I asked.

She nodded, her smile returning. "Ooh, we can have our

jasmine in the living room, like fancy ladies," she said to my grandmother.

"Do you want to have tea with Vickie and me, Adelle?" I asked, silently hoping she'd say, *No! Just Livvy!*

"That's not my name," she said instead.

"Sorry." What was I supposed to call her again?

"You're my granddaughter, Livvy?"

I smiled. "Yes, I am."

"Then I'm your oma!"

Vickie and I led her down the hallway to the living room, where Adelle—I mean, Oma—stared at the room as if she'd never seen it before. "Isn't this a pretty place, Livvy-my-granddaughter?"

I placed the teacups on the coffee table, beside a gaudy gold vase shaped like a heart. The room was a museum from the Edwardian era. On the bureau, a stained-glass lamp with beaded fringe gave off almost no light. By the fireplace, a white porcelain cat crouched, its cold marble eyes trained on me.

When Oma and I sat on the high-backed couch, dust rose into the air. Vickie coughed.

"Maybe we should get a housekeeper," I suggested. Neither Vickie nor my mom seemed to be doing much in that department.

"We must save our money. I could never afford that, not in the Great Depression!" Oma cried.

"Great Depression?" Vickie rolled her eyes. "You have enough money to hire all the maids in Buckingham Palace if you want, darlin'."

I detected a subtle twang that I hadn't picked up before. "Where'd you grow up?"

"Why?"

"I thought I heard an accent."

Vickie snapped her fingers and pointed at me as if I'd won a point. "Guilty as charged. I tried to shake it, but it's not easy taking a South Carolina drawl out of a girl."

"Did someone from Buckingham Palace beat you with a whip?" Oma asked.

Vickie sat down on one of the matching rose-print armchairs on either side of a jade-tiled fireplace. I slid behind the ruby-colored settee to part the brocade curtains and roped them back with the tassel tiebacks. A swath of light cut through the lace panel, striping the parquet floor.

"I don't want to go to Buckingham Palace," Adelle said with undeniable urgency. "The British are coming! The British are coming!"

She searched the room for something unseen. Making sense of her hallucinations was like trying to see a picture in a dot-to-dot after skipping from 1 to 29, and back to 16.

"Oh, is Paul Revere stopping by for a spot of tea?" Vickie said, nodding at me as if we shared a private joke. I didn't react.

I jumped when a warm liquid ran down my leg. Adelle's teacup was upended at my feet. "Uh oh," she said, her hands tightening into fists as a flush spread across her cheeks. She looked like an injured toddler, revving up for a blood-curdling yell.

Vickie bent down and swooped it up. "Everything's fine! I can glue that handle back on so it's as good as new."

Adelle relaxed, her eyebrows settling back in place. Vickie's quick response had stopped my grandmother from a tantrum. *Whew.* I let out the breath I'd been holding.

After Vickie went to get another cup of tea, Adelle whispered in my ear. "My sister calls me Lazy Lillian. All she cares about is homework and report cards. Not me. I have more important concerns."

Lazy Lillian? The Alzheimer's website said that recent memories were the first to disappear, but patients could sometimes remember precise details from long ago. I guess older memories were ingrained from years of recall—at least until the disease progressed, and everything collapsed into a sinkhole. If Adelle was forgetting her name, the situation was worse than I'd imagined.

"I'm a little like your sister," I said, trying to silence my depressing thoughts. "I can't even sleep until my homework's done and in my backpack."

"I don't have a sister," Adelle said, her lip trembling.

I sighed.

"I like to write," she went on, "about boys and sunshine and flowers. I like journals, too. I have so many of them." She leaned in close. "You can find them for me."

"I don't know where they are, do you?"

The question seemed to float past her and dissipate into the air. "I need them now!"

"Okay, okay, I'll check. Be back in a sec. Wait here and whatever you do, please don't yell."

In the library, the half-moon stained-glass window cast a lavender light across my Vans. I walked to the bookcase and scanned the shelves. The books were as old as the room

99

itself—row after row of titles from the 1800s. Maybe that's why the anachronism stood out, despite being sandwiched on the bottom row between *Uncle Tom's Cabin* and *The War of the Worlds*. I opened the thick poetry anthology to the author index and skipped to a familiar name. I smiled. Mom had told me the truth about Adelle's writing after all.

Her poem had a weird foreign title: "Anne Frank Kastanjeboom." I typed *Kastanjeboom* into my phone and saw it was Dutch for "chestnut tree." I dug deeper, searching for more information. Apparently the famous teenager who'd died in the Holocaust had mentioned it a few times in her attic diary.

I skipped to an article describing a fungal infection that had plagued the chestnut tree outside Anne's window. A few years ago, a foundation tried to save it by attaching it to an iron structure, but it toppled over in a storm anyway.

I flipped to page twenty-three in the anthology, relieved that the poem was published in English. The last few lines described the fallen tree, so I knew the poem couldn't be that old.

I returned the book to the shelf and searched Oma's desk, looking for the journals she'd mentioned. No surprise, they didn't seem to exist.

I went back to the living room and said, "I didn't find any journals in the library."

Adelle's nose flared. Her cheeks brightened like beets. Crap, why hadn't I changed the subject? She couldn't hold on to a thought for more than thirty seconds, anyway.

"No journals! No journals!" A tear took a circuitous route down the contour of her cheek.

"I'm sure they'll turn up, Adelle."

Her hands fluttered in her lap like a captured butterfly. "Don't call me that!"

"Oh, right. Sorry, Oma." I repeated it in my head, making it stick: *Oma, Oma, Oma.*

"I am not Adelle!" Her left foot dug into the carpet, leaving indents in the wool piling.

Vickie swung the door open. "Inside voice!"

Oma went still.

"I'm sorry, Livvy. She's too tired for a visit today." Vickie picked up Oma's hand. "It's nap time, isn't it, doll?"

She led my grandmother out of the room.

CHAPTER
ELEVEN

I WALKED INTO THE APARTMENT TO FIND MOM IN the kitchen, the counter crammed with ingredients. She was making spaghetti casserole, which was one of my favorites. Half the meal seemed to be spread on the front of her shirt.

"A little dash of this. A dash of that." She shook two spices into the saucepan at the same time, swinging her hips, hula style.

I hadn't seen Mom this happy in a while. I dipped a spoon into the sauce to taste it. "Someone had a good day," I said.

"Hardly," she said. "I've been trying to show Adelle how to put her dirty clothes in a hamper instead of dropping them wherever she takes them off. Jesus, you'd think I was trying to teach her to . . . I don't know, to balance a checking account or something."

I bit back a comment. Mom didn't even know the password to the bank website. It fell under my domain, had been that way since she bounced the payment for my eighth grade Girl Scout camp. "Speaking of money, is Vickie in charge of Oma's bills now?"

"*Oma*, huh?" she said, voice dripping with sarcasm.

"That's what she asked me to call her."

"Well, you know how bad I am about sending bills in on time, but I do most of the grocery shopping to make up for it."

"So you like her? Vickie, I mean?" I added a teaspoon of basil and a few shakes of salt to the sauce, then put the spices back on the rack, turning the labels out so they could be read.

"What's there not to like? She loves responsibility, and I don't."

I shrugged. "She seems nice, but a little *too* nice, you know?"

"Oh, right, I can see where that might be offensive."

I sighed. "She acts like a preschool teacher. Like Oma's a helpless child."

Mom raised an eyebrow.

"Come on," I said. "You know what I mean."

She shook her head. "Vickie's a godsend. I couldn't do this by myself. I'd go crazy. Sometimes I think your grandmother uses the Alzheimer's thing as an excuse. It's like she doesn't *want* to remember."

"Alzheimer's thing? Oma's sick, Mom, really sick."

She plucked a strand of spaghetti from the pot and flung it against the wall to see if it stuck. The al dente test. I'd have to wash the wall later.

"Listen, Liv, I have to keep reminding her that my father's been dead for a few decades." We watched in silence as the spaghetti curled in on itself and flopped to the floor.

"She still remembers things from when she was young," I said. "How she loves to write, and about her sister—"

Mom gave a strangled laugh. "My mother never had a sister. Only a brother named Hans, but don't ask her about him, or she'll start screaming about how he bit the head off her doll."

"She told me her grandmother lived in Holland," I said, wondering how much Mom knew, how much she'd tell me.

"For Pete's sake, Adelle's family was not from Holland. I think she was from somewhere in Germany." Mom reached absentmindedly for the pot of simmering sauce. "Damn it!" She yanked her hand back, flicking off the pain.

"Could we be Jewish, Mom?"

"No."

"What about that silver box on Oma's door?"

"My mother's delusional, Liv. Maybe she *wants* to be Jewish."

I passed her an ice cube from the freezer. She closed her fist around it. "Isn't Friedman a Jewish name, though?" I asked.

"It's also Swiss. My father's parents immigrated from Lucerne to Pennsylvania, where he was born. No one's Jewish."

"Is it possible Oma converted later on?" I pressed.

Mom laughed as if the idea was ludicrous.

"You think she's making this all up?"

"Listen, Liv, there's no point pushing her on the details. She's obviously a hostage to her warped imagination."

"Maybe there are things you don't know about her." I made my voice sound mysterious. "You know, secrets she's never told you."

Mom plucked the whittled ice cube from her hand and pitched it into the sink. "She's not altogether right up there. Never was. My mother was a liar before the disease. Difference is, when she does it now, no one blames her."

· · ·

At lunch on Thursday, Alex, Franklin D., Elizabeth, and I went to Grant High's first-ever Chess Lunch Club. Alex, a nationally ranked chess player, was president. I'd never played before. Elizabeth taught me Scholar's Mate, a way to win a game in only four moves. Inexperienced people don't see it coming, she told me. As I played Franklin D., Candace's voice rose from the recesses of my brain: *Are you out of your mind? Chess is for nerds.*

If chess was for nerds, what would Candace have thought of my memory? I'd never told her or Audrey the truth. Having a talent for recall and a love of facts would probably move me into the same category as my new friends.

Shut up, Candace, I thought, banishing her from my head once and for all.

After school I stopped by the apartment to drop off my backpack, then hiked over the hill to Oma's. The other day, I'd told Mom that Oma needed exercise. I couldn't believe it when she agreed.

"Why don't you come directly from school and take her around the neighborhood?" she said. I figured she liked the idea of knocking a half hour off her shift.

No one answered my knock on Oma's door, so I rang the doorbell. Where was Mom? I remembered her saying something about an extra key in a plant on the porch. A fake-looking palm sat in the corner. I ran my fingers through its plastic leaves until I found the key, hammocked on a leaf and covered in a coat of rust. It had probably sat outside for the last twenty years. It took a minute of finagling before I could turn the lock.

I stepped into the foyer. "Hello?"

No answer. Only a distant squeak like a train moving away. Had Mom forgotten to mention a doctor's appointment?

Wait, I recognized that sound. The teapot! The whistle stuttered as it ran out of steam. Someone must've left the stove on. My palms went clammy at a horrible thought: *Please, God, don't let me find my grandmother dead.*

"Oma? Are you here?" I called, not very loud. I flicked on the hallway light. A yellow gauze spilled across the floor. I walked toward the kitchen, the heel of my boot striking the floor with each step. The door was closed. I rested my hand on the cold metal knob, took a breath, and turned it.

My grandmother glared at me, wide-eyed and alive, a frying pan raised above her head.

I flattened myself against the wall. "It's me, Oma!"

"You missed roll call."

I gingerly pried the pan from her fingers. "Well, I'm here now, okay?"

The teapot gave a final hiss.

"Please don't take me back to camp."

"What's wrong with camp?" I said, desperate to keep things lighthearted. "There's swimming. And canoeing. Sleeping under the stars . . ."

Mom was right—in the past few weeks, she'd gone downhill. I turned off the burner, then spotted the note on the fridge.

Liv,
Need a cup of coffee. Go ahead and walk Adelle. Vickie should be here when you get back. See you at home.
Hugs,
Mom

Walk Adelle? She made my grandma sound like a dog.

Getting Oma's sneakers on was no simple task. She curled her toes, giggling like a child. "It's a warm day, Oma. How about we take off that blouse and get you into a T-shirt?"

She clasped her hands behind her back. "No! No! No!"

Vickie and Mom had warned me about Oma's need for privacy. She never let anyone help her get dressed, even though it took her a half hour to do. Lately we had to help her eat so all the food wouldn't end up in her lap. Still, I couldn't blame my grandma for clinging to the last bit of independence. "I'll get you a shirt," I said. "You can put it on by yourself."

"So cold." Oma drew her elbows together.

I threw my hands on my hips, frustrated. "Fine." Maybe if she got good and hot, she'd be more cooperative the next time. If she remembered.

Ten minutes later, I knitted my fingers through hers, and we started up Fillmore toward the bakery on Sacramento Street. Oma had a sweet tooth. I knew she'd love the almond bear claws. At the intersection, I waited as she leaned against a traffic sign, fanning herself with a hand.

"Hey, remember when you told me about your sister? That she was obsessed with getting good grades?" The conversation I'd had with Mom had been bugging me all day. How could Oma have forgotten the gender of her sibling?

Oma looked at me blankly.

I inched forward with my questions like a soldier through a minefield. "When did you move to the United States? Did you meet my grandfather here?"

"Herbert's a soldier. He comes to visit me when I'm sick, and he stays a very long time." She frowned. "Belsen wasn't such a nice place, after all."

Belsen? "Why not?" I persevered.

"Potato peels!" She pounded her fists on the signpost, laughing at a joke that made sense to no one but her. "Potato peels and turnips!"

Her hands would get bruised if she didn't stop, but if I grabbed them, she'd freak out. I tried to keep my voice calm. "Oma, if you're hungry, we can . . ."

"The sister, Margaret, wants bread, lots of it. Not me. I prefer bean soup. It's cheap and good to eat. But Herbert says we have plenty of money now. We can eat whatever we want."

The disjointed babble blurred in my head. "It's okay, Oma. I'm here. It's all good."

She lowered her fist from the sign. "Did you have a nice day, Gretchen?"

I laughed, not because she was confused, but because her shifting moods threw me off balance. "I'm fine."

"Where did you go?"

"To school."

"That's good. I went all the way to the eighth grade. Are you in the eighth grade?"

"Eleventh."

"Oh, aren't you a smarty!"

"Would you tell me about your sister?" I prodded gently. "Her name was Margaret?"

"The war made her disappear. Do you think she left on

the last train out? Perhaps she escaped. Perhaps they both did. Perhaps I did, too."

Maybe Oma had kept her sister a secret from Mom, but I couldn't figure out why she would do that. I considered how Mom had lied to me about my grandmother in the first place, and an uncomfortable thought came to mind: Was keeping secrets a family trait?

"*Who* escaped?" I demanded.

"Oh, no, the train's leaving, heading away from hell. Hurry, get on it now!"

The word *train* shook a memory loose. Hadn't Mom mentioned leaving that way to the East Coast, the last summer she'd visited her mother? Maybe Oma remembered, on some level, that the woman who took care of her now was the college student who left her all those years ago.

"Gretchen's come back to take care of you," I said, watching for a reaction.

"Oh, are you Gretchen?"

I sighed. "No, I'm Livvy. Your granddaughter."

A woman walked by with her dog. He sniffed the signpost. I cringed, afraid Oma would start shouting *Scheisshund!* Instead, she leaned back as if she was afraid that the poodle was going to bite her. Her teeth began to chatter. She gripped her chin, leaving an angry mark with her fingernails. I gently pulled her hand down, blurting out the first thing that came to mind. "I met a new friend named Franklin D., Oma. He gets in trouble sometimes because he blurts out whatever's on his mind."

The good thing about Alzheimer's—if there was anything

good—was that Oma's fear vanished once I got her mind off the dog. I kept talking as the woman walked the poodle up the hill. "Our teacher doesn't like Franklin D. much, but what he says keeps the rest of us from slipping into a school-induced coma."

A furrow lodged between her eyebrows. "Tell that friend of yours not to say too much."

"I meant that he asks questions that most people don't have the brainpower to answer," I clarified.

A tiny smile cracked her hard exterior. She rarely smiled, but when she did, it changed the entire landscape of her face. She looked like somebody's sweet grandmother. *My* grandmother.

"What's his name?" she asked.

"Franklin D. Schiller," I repeated.

"Jewish?"

I thought about when Franklin D. had defended himself in debate class, telling everyone about his great-grandfather, Hymie Lipschitz. "Yeah, I think so."

"God bless his soul," she said somberly.

As we headed up the hill again, I couldn't stop myself. "You're Jewish, too, Oma, right? Just like . . ."

"Shh," she whispered, her head whipping around. "They might hear you. Hide your jewelry! They like gold and diamonds. In the middle of the night, they come and steal it."

"Who? Who steals it?"

She wrapped her arms around a parking meter. "I don't know! I don't know! I don't know!"

I tried to unknot my shoulders, hoping to look calm

and in control. "Anyway, it doesn't matter—your religion, I mean."

"What's going on here?" Vickie, a grocery bag on her hip, glared at me. Where had *she* come from?

"Oma and I are taking a walk."

"I can see that."

"I've lost everything," Oma murmured. "Everything. Everything. Everything."

I rubbed the headache pressing against my temples. Vickie pried my grandmother's arms from the parking meter. "You shouldn't talk about the past. It upsets her, Livvy."

Oma slipped her hand into Vickie's like a compliant child. I watched helplessly as they continued up the hill. A bewildering sense of guilt spread through me.

"I'm sorry, Oma," I whispered to myself.

SUMMER 1945

For weeks Herbert held washcloths to her forehead, dabbing at the stubborn fever that wouldn't let go. She didn't say much, so he talked, and she listened, smiling at his dreams for the future and frowning when he ventured to the past.

"I've lost everything," was all she would say. "I can't talk about it."

He soon stopped asking.

It was eight weeks later, under a blue moon, that he placed his calloused hand on hers. "I must know. Do you think you will ever be capable of loving again?"

Could she? The hatred mixed black as coal inside her blood. She wasn't even sure what or whom she hated anymore. "If you can accept me as I am right now, you will never be disappointed," she told him. Had it been so long since she'd believed that everything was rosy with the world?

He pondered her response. She saw the flash of hesitation, an uncertainty. Silence pressed down on her lungs, leaving little room for air. "I'll take my chances," he said at last. "Hope is all we have to rely on, anyway."

It was that same hope that carried Adelle from her birth country to Brooklyn, New York. Her new husband, always a gentleman, averted his eyes from the abyss of the past, and in doing so, permitted them a future.

CHAPTER

TWELVE

I CALLED MOM FIVE TIMES. HER PHONE RANG UNTIL
it went to voice mail. Darkness seeped through the apartment, deepening my sense of dread. To take my mind off my
worries, I began researching an assignment, but ended up
looking up terms other than Arthur Miller and *The Crucible*.

Belsen, I typed into my laptop.

Bergen-Belsen concentration camp was the first to pull up.
A link took me to a black-and-white photograph, where a
room full of sad female prisoners gazed into the camera lens.
A barrack block at Belsen, the caption read.

My grandmother had been in a concentration camp. Oh,
God, how could I have been so stupid? I thought about what
I'd said to her about camping. *Swimming. Canoeing. Stars.*
Then I remembered Oma standing in the kitchen, frying pan
in the air. *You missed roll call!*

A metallic taste climbed up my throat. I clicked and read,
then read some more, before ending up at the United States
Memorial Holocaust Museum website.

*During its existence, approximately 50,000 persons died in the
Bergen-Belsen concentration camp complex including Anne Frank
and her sister Margot . . .*

I'd read *The Diary of Anne Frank* in the eighth grade. After the Frank family and the other residents in hiding had been discovered by the Nazis, Anne ultimately ended up at Bergen-Belsen. The website said that she and her sister had died only weeks before British soldiers liberated the camp. How horrible that she hid for two years in an attic, only to die right before the end of the war.

I navigated to an old newsreel on YouTube that showed the British liberation of the camp. The images turned my stomach: Bodies strewn across the ground like branches after a storm; Jews with sunken eyes peering into the camera lens; impassive Nazis forced at Allied gunpoint to haul human remains. I watched in disbelief as a female Nazi officer and a guard lifted a dead body by its hands and feet and swung it like a jump rope, tossing it into a mass grave.

It.

It was a human being. A him. A her. A murdered Jew.

I closed my laptop, not wanting to think about Bergen-Belsen anymore. I connected my iPod to the stereo and cranked the volume, hoping the music would chase away the images that threatened to burn into my memory.

The music cut out, then thudded back. I crawled around the red-and-white striped armchair we'd bought at a garage sale last weekend to push the loose stereo plug into the outlet.

And there it was. An empty vodka bottle. Correction, *almost* empty. A few drops of liquid remained, too valuable for its owner to throw out. I crawled back out and collapsed against the chair, propping the bottle between my knees. *Damn it.*

Mom's keys jangled in the door. I tightened my grip

on the bottle neck in case she tried to snatch it away. One slipup I could justify. She was stressed, worried about money, exhausted from the move, with a sponsor who lived in another state. But drinking twice was a different story—one I didn't want to hear.

"Hello!" she called out. "Hey, what are you doing over there? Why's it so dark in here?" She switched on the lights. They were way too bright.

Her eyes landed on the bottle. She exhaled a groan. "I'm sorry, Liv. I tried not to let it happen again. It's just . . . life's so hard right now. And my mother's so . . . but excuses don't change anything, do they?"

It was nice to know she'd learned something at her AA meetings.

"Speak to me, Liv."

"What do you want me to say? You made a promise and you didn't keep it." At the word *promise*, tears I hadn't even known existed tumbled down my cheeks.

"Alcoholism is a disease I have to fight every second, every hour, every—"

"Don't," I said, borrowing Oma's *Do it now!* tone. I couldn't bear to hear the cliché. Drinking wasn't like other illnesses. A disease caused deterioration, but alcoholism could be stopped.

Mom's mouth was open, but she couldn't retrieve the words. She slumped to the ground and cried instead.

I knew there'd been a moment when Mom had considered how this would affect us, what drinking might do to our lives, and yet, inexplicably, she'd brought the bottle to her lips. Her tears couldn't soften my heart. I wouldn't let them.

"I only have two more years until college," I said, my voice whittled to a sharp point. "Couldn't you have waited until I was out of the house before self-destructing?"

"I know I can stop. I've done it before—"

"No! I won't listen to promises you're going to break tomorrow. I'm moving out, Mom. I'll get legally emancipated if I have to." I had no idea what I was talking about. Realistically, no court would set me loose without a way to support myself, but that was my story, and I was committed.

Mom took a ragged breath and wiped away her tears. "You don't know how hard my life's been lately," she said. "I used the last of our savings to rent this hellhole, to try and support you, to—"

"You won't have to pay for me anymore. That should free up some money for a Costco liquor run." I swept my foot back, knocking the bottle over. It spun across the floor, clinking against the couch leg.

Mom turned her face to the wall. "I need to get out of here. I can't take this right now."

"Are you going to a seedy bar somewhere?"

She opened her mouth to deny it, but a plaintive sigh escaped. "I don't know."

No, I wouldn't feel sorry for her. I wouldn't. I couldn't.

I jumped up and ran into the bathroom, where I spun the shower faucet to the hottest setting.

"To Adelle's, okay?" she called through the door. "I'm going to sleep at my mother's. I need time to think."

I dropped down onto the toilet. The steam swirled to the ceiling, where it clung to the ventilation fan before dropping tears on my head. I stayed like that until the mirror fogged over. I felt totally drained. All I wanted to do was curl up into a ball and go to sleep. *No!* I told myself. *That was the old Liv. This one has to fight back. For myself. For Mom.*

For Mom. Despite the hardened shell I'd built around me, my center was soft. I loved her, flaws and all. It hurt like hell to see her like this.

I turned off the shower and opened the bathroom door. A blast of steam rolled into the living room.

Mom was gone. I picked up the list of Bay Area AA meetings, the grid-like wrinkles giving away the number of times she'd opened it, then folded it back up. The sight of her cell phone made my stomach inch up into my throat. *Oh God, what have I done?* There'd be no talking her down from a drinking binge now. I looked closer, hoping to find her wallet under the pile of receipts, but she hadn't forgotten that. I scooped up my keys and ran out of the apartment. Jogging down the hill, I headed toward the part of Fillmore where liquor stores were more common than restaurants. Three within a four-block area. Mom wasn't in any of them.

At the foot of Fillmore, I called out, "Mom!" Then, "Gretchen!"

"Shut up!" someone yelled back.

Maybe she *had* gone to Oma's. I needed to bring her home—and then call Tom to beg for help. He'd know what to do.

I was gasping for air when I reached Oma's house. I ran my hands through the fake palm and unlocked the door with the key. From somewhere inside, I heard Oma snoring. The door to the sitting room was open. I peered inside, expecting to find Vickie conked out on the futon couch, but she wasn't

117

there. I'd tell Mom this, I decided, before remembering that I had bigger problems than Vickie sneaking off during her shift.

I crept down the hallway. A new sign, in my mother's cramped handwriting, was taped to a door—*Adelle's Bedroom*. Two of the saddest words I'd seen. My grandmother needed a map to her own home.

I peeked inside. Oma was curled on her side, hands braided under her chin. Sleep smoothed out her skin, making her seem younger. She'd kicked off her blanket, so I tiptoed in to cover her up. Then I went to the kitchen to look for Mom. She wasn't there. Not in the living room, either. The library was also empty.

I texted Tom, because it was too late to call. *Mom had a relapse, need help.* I read it again, adding, *We're both okay.* That would be his first question.

A vibration under my feet broke the stillness. I froze in place, listening. Outside, the garage door groaned open. I ran to the sitting room window, which faced the street. The headlights of a car cut through the curtains, blinding me. I swept the sheer material to the side. Oma's old Mustang reversed into the street with a jerk as if the driver didn't know the difference between an accelerator and a brake. As the car idled, Mom lowered the bottle from her lips. Our eyes locked. I darted from the room to the porch and then leaped to the sidewalk, my knees buckling when I hit cement.

I managed to open the back door before she came to life. The car lurched, and I dove inside, landing a full belly flop onto the cool white leather. I grabbed the front bucket seat to steady myself while shutting the door with my free hand.

Mom tore past the stop sign. She spun the wheel to the left, flinging me against the side of the car. She made two more turns, then gunned it up the steep hill.

"Mom, stop! You're going to kill us!"

She slowed down long enough for me to yank the old-fashioned seat belt across my lap. Gurgling sobs rose from her as she swerved around a trash can, nicking it with her back tire. It tipped over and skidded down the hill a few feet.

"Mom, please," I begged. An unwelcome fact popped into my head: *Every fifty-three minutes an American dies in an alcohol-related crash.*

"I've screwed up everything!" she said. "I couldn't even take care of a helpless old woman or my own kid. I trashed five years of sobriety. Couldn't pull it off. Just a drunk at heart. A damn drunk!"

She wrenched the wheel around. We spun in the opposite direction, heading downhill in a zigzag pattern, even though the road was as straight as a balance beam. Red-and-blue lights flickered in the rearview mirror.

Thank God, I thought, a moment before coming to my senses. *Shit, we're in a world of trouble.*

Mom steered with one hand while burrowing through her purse with the other.

"Keep your hands on the wheel!" I shouted.

The police turned on the siren. Mom pulled out a pack of Listerine breath strips, freed one, and slapped it on her tongue. We heard a warning blast from the cop's horn. Thankfully Mom slowed. The patrol car inched behind us for three blocks, until she turned into a church parking lot.

As the officer walked up to our car, Mom snapped on her

seat belt. "Keep your mouth shut, Livvy. I'll do the talking."
Whatever. I was too stunned to speak.

He tapped on the window. Mom rolled it down and gave him a cheesy smile. "Yes, officer?"

"May I see your driver's license, registration, and proof of insurance?"

Her hand trembled as she reached for Oma's glove compartment, found the cards, and handed them to the officer. She took her wallet out of her purse.

"My license is here somewhere," she mumbled, rifling through a wad of balled-up cash, mixed with an assortment of credit cards. "Whew, here it is."

"Ma'am, that's a Macy's card. I asked for your driver's license."

She took it back and handed him another one.

"Is this your car, ma'am?"

"It's my mother's. Her name's Adelle Friedman. I was picking up groceries for her."

"Do you know why I pulled you over?"

"No, sir," Mom said, sweet as corn syrup. "I don't suppose you're here to ask me out?"

"Did you see the stop sign at the street back there?"

"Oh, gosh, officer, I'm sorry. My daughter dropped her cell phone and it startled me."

I dug my nails into my hand.

"Is that your daughter?" he asked, peering around her. Why was he looking at me that way? Oh. My stomach contracted like a fist. He wasn't looking at me; he was sniffing Mom's breath.

The officer excused himself and returned to his patrol

car. An eternity passed before he came back to her window. Meanwhile a second police car pulled up. The other officer looked like a recruit, only a few years older than me. He stopped a few feet back and observed as the first officer fired questions at Mom: Was she diabetic? (Nope.) Was she sick or injured? (Nope.) Finally he came to the one I'd been dreading. "Have you had anything to drink tonight?"

"No, sir," Mom answered. "Not with my daughter in the car."

My mouth dropped open at that one, but I snapped it shut before anyone saw.

When he described field-sobriety tests, I thought I might throw up all over Oma's vintage car. "I'll need your consent, ma'am, or you can take a blood test at the station," he said.

Shit. Shit. Shit.

"Absolutely," Mom said. "But could you stop with all that ma'aming business and call me Shirley?"

I winced, knowing where this was going.

"Would you please step out of the car?" he asked.

"Shirley you're not serious, officer!"

When he didn't return her grin, Mom flicked her fingernails at him. "Just trying to inject some humor into the sit-chew-ation." She swung the door open and almost knocked him into a patch of ice plants.

I climbed out of the car, watching in disbelief as Mom tried to follow the horizontal movement of his pen with her eyes. Next he asked her to take nine steps along the crack in the sidewalk and nine steps back. She did okay, but I think she turned around on the seventh step. Then she stood on one leg while flexing her other about six inches off the ground.

That lasted three seconds before she had to grab his uniform for balance.

"Would you recite the alphabet, ma'am—straight through, without singing?"

Mom took an exasperated breath, the letters coming out in groups of four. *A-B-C-D*. Pause. *E-F-G-H*. Pause. *I-J-K-L* . . . She launched into song, skipping over the *N*. I couldn't watch anymore, so I turned my back. The lights went on in the house across the street. A family watched us from their living room window. When I looked back, Mom's hands were behind her back, and the policeman was walking her to the patrol car. I glanced at the backup cop. He shifted in place like there were sharp pebbles in his black shoes.

"Do you drive?" he asked me.

My head felt like a balloon with too much air. "No, I can't." Realizing I might be misunderstood, I added, "I don't mean I've been drinking. I just got my learner's permit, and I can't drive by myself."

Officer McDougall, according to the name tag on his uniform, told me to wait right there. Not that I was going anywhere. He went to Mom, took her keys, and climbed into the Mustang. He parked Oma's car in a legal spot that had miraculously opened up at the end of the block. When he came back, he offered me a ride home. I couldn't deal with our empty apartment, so I gave him Oma's address. I climbed into the passenger seat of the patrol car. No way was I riding in the back.

"Your mother can pick up the car tomorrow," he said.

"Tomorrow?" I repeated.

"She's going to county jail. Most likely, they'll release her when she sobers up."

"What happens then?"

"Well we took away her license, but she'll get a temporary one that lets her drive for the next thirty days."

"No, I meant what happens to *her*."

"It's almost the weekend. Nothing will get done until early next week. The D.A. will file charges, and she'll have to make a plea, guilty or not guilty."

He didn't say anything else, and I didn't have the guts to ask more. We drove to Oma's house in silence. When he pulled up in front, he said, "Is there anyone I should talk to about this?"

"No, it's fine. We live with my grandma," I lied. "Trust me, you don't want to wake her up. Besides she'll find out soon enough."

He looked relieved. "All right then. Good night."

I got out of the car and walked up the steps to the porch. He waited for me to unlock the door. I turned around and gave him a lame wave.

Officer McDougall nodded once, backed out of the driveway, and drove away.

THIRTEEN

I woke up on Oma's sitting room futon, numb from the previous night. I didn't know if Mom had been released yet. She wasn't answering her texts. That was fine with me. She was better off in jail, nursing a whopper of a headache.

I couldn't believe I had to be in class in an hour. I thought about calling in sick. It wasn't a lie. I *felt* like throwing up. But then I remembered the test in chemistry and the quiz in math. *Crap.* And Vickie was still missing, having never shown up for her night shift.

Mom was supposed to go on duty soon, and I couldn't leave Oma by herself. I had no idea what to do, so I padded down the hallway to check on her. She was still asleep.

In the bathroom, I studied the clothes I'd worn to bed. I considered Oma's closet for about a second and a half, then decided I could deal with wrinkles for one day. I rinsed my mouth out and pulled my fingers through my hair. Oma didn't have a flat iron or a blow-dryer. I studied my reflection in the mirror. My hair lifted in soft waves that rippled across my shoulders. It really wasn't bad this way. I couldn't even remember why I'd made such a big deal about straightening it in Vermont.

"You'll survive," I told the girl in the mirror. She didn't look like she believed me.

Outside, the fog slapped me in the face like a wet washcloth. I zipped up my hoodie and raised my fist to Vickie's glass door. She slid the curtain open, tightened her robe around her bony body, and opened the door.

"Livvy, what are you doing here?"

"I stayed overnight."

Vickie rearranged her features into something resembling concern. Instead of asking me what was wrong, she launched into an excuse for missing her shift. "I came home last night because I had to get something. The next thing I knew, it was morning. Must've passed out cold. Well it's a good thing Adelle sleeps like a log at night. Probably didn't even know I wasn't there. Anyway, it worked out well with you staying over, huh?"

Vickie's eyes stayed on me as she spoke.

"Yeah, sure," I said. "Listen, last night, my mom had too much to drink, and a cop pulled her over. He took her to the station. She gets out this morning, he said, but I have to go to school now, because I have this test and a quiz and—"

Vickie brought her hand to her mouth. Through her fingers, she said, "I can take care of Adelle. Go on, get to school. When your mom comes back, we'll figure out what to do."

"Please don't tell anyone."

"I won't say a word, but I can't promise your mother's behavior won't speak for itself," she said.

I mumbled good-bye and darted down the porch steps.

. . .

"Earth to Livvy. Hello? Come on, partner, we only have three minutes left to pick our subject. What, you daydreaming about me again?"

Franklin D.'s voice snapped me back to where I was—in debate class. It was like any other Friday, except for the fact that my mother had spent the night in jail.

"Because, you know, it's pretty much useless to fantasize about me, Liv. I've made the decision to join the priesthood."

I hoped Mom was home where she belonged. "No worries," I said, only half-listening. "I'm not interested."

Franklin D.'s lower lip poked out. He blinked and looked away. I didn't have the energy to banter. What was going to happen to Mom and me? Did she still have a job, or had Vickie complained to Oma's lawyer the minute I'd left? She probably knew her overnight absence would pale next to my mother's offense.

Franklin D. glanced at the sheet in his hand. "Choice number one: Lowering the minimum legal drinking age to eighteen."

I'd fact-surfed at lunch, pretending to do homework so I wouldn't have to talk to anyone. What I'd found had been depressing. *At .08 blood alcohol level, even experienced drivers may show serious impairment.* Mom had definitely drunk more than that, which meant that I had the cops to thank for our lives.

Franklin D. looked at me with concern. "I know I can be a flippant bastard at times, but did I say something inexcusably rude to you?"

"Huh?" I focused back on him.

He reached into his backpack for a tattered package of

Kleenex. I took one, not bothering to make up an excuse for my watery eyes.

"Two minutes left, people," Ms. Thurmond announced.

"You can pick our topic," I told Franklin D. "I don't care."

"Don't you have an opinion?"

I didn't answer. He glanced at the list. "Could these subjects be any less stimulating? Number seven: 'Teenagers should be allowed to have televisions in their bedrooms.' How old is this thing, anyway, from the eighties?"

"Franklin D., do you have something to share with the rest of us?" Ms. Thurmond's voice sounded kind, but it was a front. She'd emphasized the *D* in his name.

"Sure. Livvy and I were contemplating the relevance of some of these questions. For example, who needs a TV anymore? The other day I watched a documentary on the history of lobotomy on my phone while getting my teeth cleaned."

"Your geek is showing," I said under my breath.

I looked behind me, expecting whispers and laughter— at Franklin D.'s expense. What I found were smiling faces. Franklin D. slid a fist behind his chair. The boy one seat back bumped it.

Once again, my rule book from home didn't hold up in the City by the Bay.

Franklin D. spun his one-piece chair and table unit my way. "Well it's a good thing I met someone as cool as you, Livvy, to keep me on the straight and narrow."

I couldn't tell if he was serious or sarcastic.

"I'm sorry, I didn't catch that last part?" Thurmond said.

Franklin D. folded his hands on top of his desk. "With

127

all due respect, Ms. Thurmond, some of these topics are as overdone as slutty on prom night."

I grabbed the paper from his hand, brought a finger down, and read number twenty-one out loud. "'Euthanasia should be legalized on a national level.'" I slid my foot across the aisle, nudging Franklin D.'s leg.

"That could be decent, I suppose," he said, sounding unsure.

Problem solved. A hundred more to go.

"Remember, everyone, partners need to pick sides," Mrs. Thurmond said.

Franklin D. began to talk, growing more animated with each word. "You know, maybe I could wrap my brain around that subject. As a society, we put pets to sleep, no problem. And what does the vet say? 'It's humane.' So the pooch gets to take a nap, drifting off to doggie heaven. Meanwhile it's a completely different story for people."

My thoughts landed in dangerous territory. Oma could be in the final stages of Alzheimer's. I couldn't believe I'd ever wished for that. It wasn't the kind of disease where a person went to sleep one night and died peacefully. Pneumonia was usually the cause of death—air sacs that filled up with fluid, forcing the lungs to shut down. I prayed it wouldn't be the case for my grandma. She'd suffered enough for one lifetime.

"Humans are expected to lie in a hospital bed, wasting away in agony," Franklin D. continued, "while we dwindle to nothing, comatose, only to die a horrible, drawn-out death. But wait, if we're lucky, the medical establishment might follow a living will and withhold food and water until we shrivel up like a dried sponge because God knows *that's an easy way to die.* Well give me that shot they gave my retriever anytime. If I'm in a wheelchair, using Depends, drool running out of my mouth, being spooned applesauce by some resentful employee at a smelly nursing home, kill me off already, okay?"

Ms. Thurmond's mouth fell open.

"I guess I'll take *con*," I said.

. . .

On the weekend, Mom stuck to me like Velcro, apologizing in all the wrong ways.

"Adelle's brought out my bad side," she said over takeout pad Thai.

I stabbed a fork into a crispy spring roll. "So you're blaming her for your adventure behind the wheel?"

"I didn't mean it that way, Liv."

I scraped my chair back and carried my dish to the sink. She could bring her own.

"It's not easy taking care of her, that's all," Mom went on. "She's always screaming about stuff she's misplaced. Yesterday, it was a silver ring with three rubies in it. Probably fell down the sink. Nothing's ever lost, it's always 'stolen.' And half the time, she doesn't even remember who I am. There's never a thank-you, never."

"Did you ever thank her for raising you?"

She half-laughed, half-snorted. What I pictured was her face through Oma's windshield, eyes red and bulging, cheeks inflamed from booze.

"Kids don't thank their parents very often," she said, giving me a pointed look.

Yeah, well, I wasn't about to start now. I turned my back

to load the dishwasher. Ten minutes later, I strode to my closet and shut the door.

. . .

Monday was a teacher workday. I woke at six but stayed in bed an extra hour, waiting for Mom to leave for Oma's. When the house was quiet, I ventured out. But she was still there, gazing out the window, her coffee on the ledge beside her. I drew in a sharp breath. Tom was next to her, sitting on a box with his sneakers resting on his army-green duffel bag.

"I really screwed up this time," Mom was saying. She hadn't noticed me yet. "Do you think they'll make me give my sobriety pin back?"

This was my mother's lame attempt at humor. I kicked the closet door shut behind me. Their heads whipped around in unison. Tom smiled, big and warm. "I flew in an hour ago," he began. "I thought I'd—"

I leaped over a box and threw myself into his arms. He folded them around me, where I stayed. When we pulled apart, I didn't miss the flash of hurt in Mom's eyes. Did she really think I was going to hug her?

"How are you doing, Liv?" Tom asked.

I couldn't answer, not without collapsing like a tower of cards.

Mom couldn't take the silence. "Vickie's helping me out with Oma today. She's been so helpful! I'm meeting with a DUI attorney at ten, and in the afternoon I have an appointment at Adelle's with her personal lawyer." She was looking at Tom, but I knew her words were directed at me.

"Since when do lawyers make house calls?" I asked. I turned to Tom. "Why are you here?" That didn't come out right, so I tried again. "I mean, I'm excited to see you. It's just . . . well, how long are you staying?" Forever, I hoped. I was doing a lousy job of holding my mother together.

"A few days. Your mom needs my help right now. I'm sure she's not the only one," he said.

"We're a family. We'll pull through this," Mom said.

"Whatever." I shrugged away her hollow sentiment. "I'm late for school. Gotta run."

I doubted Mom knew I had the day off, since I kept track of school holidays on my calendar app. I walked out the door, leaving my backpack on the dining room table to make a statement, though I didn't have a clue what I was trying to say.

. . .

When I showed up later that day at Oma's, Mom was meeting with her lawyer in the living room. His gravelly voice boomed through the house. I stood near the door, trying to hear her, but her voice was too soft.

Tom peered at me from the kitchen door, wearing rubber gloves that reached his elbows.

"I hope those pans didn't attack you," I said, meeting him halfway down the hall. "Maybe you should wear a hazmat suit."

"Your mom's been in meetings all day. Thought I'd get something done. How was school?"

"What school? It was a staff workday. I took *Grapes of Wrath* to a café and downed four mochas." I lowered my voice. "So what did the DUI attorney say?"

"His name's Mr. Bortel. He's the best in the Bay Area, Liv. Your mom's in good hands."

The *best* of anything couldn't come cheap.

Tom guessed at what I was thinking. "I've got it covered."

131

"You know she can't afford to pay you back."

"I'm not worried about it. I want to do this. Not just for her—for you, too."

I blinked the tears back. "Is she going back to jail?"

"Mr. Bortel thinks he can get her sentence waived if she completes a rehab program. There'll be fines, though. Big ones. Years of probation, too. But he says since it's only her second offense in ten years and no one got hurt, it's classified as a misdemeanor."

Only her second offense? I guess these people had seen worse.

"Why is she like this?" I asked.

"She keeps a lot bottled up inside."

"So to speak." I rolled my eyes, which made Tom laugh, but then his face grew serious.

"Livvy, I came here for a reason. I want to take her back to Evergreen. They have an excellent twenty-eight-day program . . . Well maybe I should let your mom tell you about it."

"What? No, you tell me. I have to know. She and I aren't talking much."

He studied me for a moment. "We have to go in three days. Our flight leaves Thursday night at seven."

"Thursday?" I repeated dumbly. That was so soon.

"I don't work at Evergreen anymore, but I'm still her sponsor. I'll be able to check in on her and make sure everything's okay."

"What am I supposed to do while she's gone?" I said, panicking as his words sank in.

In all the time I'd known Tom, he'd never once raised

his voice. He was the world's most patient person, prepared to sit out any storm. This time was no different. "There's a ticket for you, too, Liv. You can come stay with me while your mom's in the program."

"What's Lynn think about this?"

Tom shifted uneasily, his eyes jumping to the living room door. "Lynn left me."

That shocked me into silence. They'd been married for twelve years.

"She met someone else. A guy who throws caution to the wind and, I'm pretty sure, an alcoholic. I think she missed having an enabler around."

"I'm really sorry. That sucks." I thought about what bad news did to my mother. My body tensed, preparing for the worst. "Did you drink again?"

Tom's "rock bottom" story involved popping peppermint patties and drinking gin until he weighed eighty pounds more than he did now. It wasn't until he collapsed from a heart attack in Walmart that he paid attention to his doctor's dire warning. Tom once said that if he'd taken one more drink, he would've become a permanent resident of Bennington Cemetery.

He shook his head. "No, it made me want to go to the gym every day and lift a hundred pounds."

He *did* look better. "So that's why you have muscles now."

"The silver lining." The hurt behind his eyes dampened the small stab at humor. "If you want, when we get to Vermont, you can call your friends. Maybe they'll invite you over for an extended sleepover. If not, I'll take the couch. We'll make it work."

I felt an unexpected twist in my gut. "What am I supposed to tell them?"

"Don't worry. We'll make up a reason. No one has to know the details. By the way, your mom notified your school this morning. They can prepare an independent study program for you to do while you're away."

My heart thwacked in my chest. *Vermont*. Maybe when Mom came out of rehab, she'd see how happy I was to be back home. Maybe she'd let me stay with my friends for the rest of the year.

Strangely the thought felt constrictive, like an outgrown pair of jeans.

A laugh erupted from the sitting room. My mother was laying on the charm for Oma's lawyer.

"I've heard that all you've talked about is going back to Vermont," Tom said. "I'm sure you'll want to see your friends again."

Right. The same friends who'd barely contacted me since I'd left. And then there was Sean, who'd broken up with me in a text. I realized I hadn't thought of him in weeks.

My eyes filled up, spilling over the floodgates. Tom put his arm around me, and I cried into his shoulder, leaving a wet spot on his Grateful Dead T-shirt. It felt good to let loose, to feel someone else hold *me* up for a change.

"Can't I stay here by myself?" I dragged an arm across my eyes. "It's no secret that I take care of Mom, not the other way around."

"I don't know, Liv," Tom said. "That's a conversation for you and your mother."

Right on cue, Mom stepped into the hallway, followed by

a giant man with the broadest shoulders I'd ever seen. They looked at Tom and me, and we looked back. Finally Mom broke the silence. "Oh, Liv, hi," she said. "This is Adelle's personal lawyer and trustee, Mr. Laramie."

"Nice to meet you," I said. Mr. Laramie's grip cracked my knuckles.

"Everything's going to be fine," Mom assured me. "We'll hire a second caregiver to help Vickie until I get back."

Mr. Laramie was going to let Mom come back?

"Adelle says she wants me to keep helping her," she explained, lowering her chin so I couldn't see her eyes.

"Where's Oma?" I asked.

"In her room. She's watching TV."

"I want to say hello." I walked to Oma's door, resting my hand on the knob for a moment before turning back to Mr. Laramie. "If Vickie can switch shifts to the day, can I stay in San Francisco to help take care of Oma? I mean, Adelle . . . I mean, my grandmother . . . from the afternoons until I have to leave for school the next morning . . . until my mother gets back?"

I couldn't believe I'd said that.

Mr. Laramie cleared his throat. "Aren't you a little young for the responsibility?"

"I'm sixteen. And there's a caregiver living right next door." As soon as I said it, I realized I didn't want to leave Oma. What if she died while I was gone? Besides, my grandmother deserved someone who loved her. Vickie was okay, but I could take care of Oma better than anyone. "I've been alone with her many times, and I handled it fine. It's easier because Adelle likes me."

135

"Don't call me that!" Oma shouted from her room. Mom and I both laughed, but I stopped myself, not wanting to share a moment with her.

"We're packed in this tent like sardines in a can," Oma continued. "Livvy, tell them to stop this ruckus right now!"

I exhaled with relief, because today, at the right time, she'd remembered my name.

"I'm coming, Oma. I'll be right there," I said with textbook calmness.

She settled down, her sigh drifting out into the hall. It occurred to me that if I stayed at Oma's house, it would be easier to piece together her past, to really get to know her. Maybe I could find out what had happened to her. If I could do that, maybe I could figure out the root of the bitterness that made my mother drink. I had a feeling the two were connected.

I pulled my shoulders back in a show of confidence. "Why don't we ask Oma if she wants a new caregiver . . . or me?"

"I want that grandchild!" Oma hollered. Mr. Laramie smiled, which I took as a good sign. Mom's lips were pressed into a white line. Tom's eyes swung from Mr. Laramie to Mom to me.

"I'm not sure that my daughter is prepared to—," Mom started. Mr. Laramie cut her off with a raised hand.

"Please excuse me while I talk to my client." He passed by me into Oma's bedroom.

Through the door we heard her wail, "We have to leave this scary place. We have to climb the fence and run, run, run, run. They're chasing us!"

"Welcome to Casa Crazy," Mom said to Tom.

A minute later, Mr. Laramie sidled out of Oma's room.

"I'll think on this. We'll discuss it tomorrow, Gretchen." He shook everyone's hand again, crippling me for the second time.

I slipped into my grandmother's room and sat down on the edge of her mattress. Oma clutched her blanket to her chin like a child afraid of the dark. Her skin felt soft and warm as leather under my fingers. "It's okay, Oma. I'm here. They aren't chasing you anymore." I didn't know who "they" were, but the curve of Oma's mouth let me know that I'd said the right thing.

"You can't keep them away if you're a Jew," she whispered, tugging on a necklace chain under her sweater.

"But you're safe here."

She searched my face. "Do you think we're Jewish?" Her eyes shone behind a sheen of tears.

I didn't know what to say, so I grasped the only truth I knew. "It's okay to be Jewish, Oma. The war happened a long time ago."

"But it's not good to be German. They're the bad guys."

"Things are different now." I started to explain why but stopped myself. Her timeline was a knotted ball of yarn. She was living the same years over and over again.

Oma pulled the necklace out from under her shirt. She traced the tiny diamonds that edged a star. I counted the points—six of them: the Star of David. The silver was tarnished, almost black.

"Where did you get that?" I asked.

"God," she said.

"Would you like some ginger tea?"

She nodded. "Yes, Gretchen. Thank you very much."

CHAPTER

FOURTEEN

". . . AND I WANT DETAILED UPDATES EVERY WEEK when we talk, Liv, okay?" Mom said. "I have reservations about this, but if Mr. Laramie's willing to give it a try . . ."

"It will be fine," I said for the hundredth time.

"If Adelle hadn't been so adamant . . ."

"I'll be responsible," I said, thinking, *I'll do a better job than you did.*

"If your homework suffers, or there's any negative impact at all, the deal's over."

I nodded, careful not to roll my eyes. Mom switched the maternal gene on and off as it suited her.

"Don't forget to lock up the apartment when you move to Oma's. And Mr. Laramie will send you money—"

"I know."

"—for food, incidentals, and a stipend. Anything you need, really. And of course, Vickie's right next—"

"Mom, I have it!"

She was quiet for a moment, then, "Don't forget that Fridays are your days off, and you switch to a day shift on Saturdays only. On Sundays, you'll go back to the overnight evening schedule until Friday. But Mr. Laramie is paying

Vickie extra to be on call when you're working, so if you need anything, anything at all, feel free to knock on her door."

Mom's eyes went from frantic to wet in a blink. I had to look away. "I'm sorry, Liv . . . I let the alcohol do the thinking for me." There she went again, blaming the booze, not herself. I tensed, trying to fend off a tidal wave of emotion. *Don't say anything, Liv. Now's not the time.*

There was a honk. Tom in his rental car. Mom glanced at her twin suitcases, lined up at the door.

"He's probably circling the block," I said.

"I guess I'd better go. I think that's Tom." It was as if she hadn't heard me.

The question on my mind was a big one to throw out as she was leaving, but I didn't know when I'd get another chance. "Mom, was Oma a prisoner in a concentration camp?"

She looked down as if the answer was etched in the frayed rug. "My mother has Alzheimer's. If you try to piece together a puzzle with most of the pieces missing, you could come up with the wrong picture."

I wanted to ask more, but Tom's triple honk signaled his impatience. Mom looked relieved, as if she was glad to get away from me. I just hoped she was happy to be heading to rehab.

"Be safe and call if there are any issues," she said.

I fought an urge to hug her. Soon there would be thousands of miles separating us. Before I could figure out what to do, she picked up her suitcases and headed out the door.

I ran to the window, waiting for her to exit downstairs.

A minute later, she stood at the curb, the weight of the suitcases pulling her shoulders forward.

I raised my fists and banged on the windowpane until she looked up. Then I ran across the room, flung the door open, and almost tripped down the stairs.

Outside, her arms were open wide, waiting for me.

. . .

After school the next day, Franklin D. and I researched our debate topic in the library.

"I have to leave in half an hour," I reminded him.

"I know. You have somewhere to be. You've told me three times since school let out."

Oh, wait. "Sorry, I don't have to go. I got it wrong." It was Free Friday, my day off. I wasn't used to all the schedule changes.

"I know something's wrong, Livvy. You haven't turned a page in that book for the past ten minutes."

I started to deny it but shrugged instead.

"Come on, what gives?"

"My mom's away for a while," I told him.

Twenty-eight days, to be specific. Despite everything that Mom had done, I missed her. More than I had expected. Or maybe I missed the person she'd been before all this happened—my fun-loving, quirky, clueless, big-hearted mother.

"You mean you're staying by yourself?" Franklin D. asked. "For what, the weekend?"

When I didn't answer, he said, "Your mother left you *alone*?"

"Well, not really," I backtracked. "She'll be gone for a month. I moved in with my grandmother for now. I want

140

to help take care of her." At the surprised look on his face, I tried to clarify. "My grandma's got Alzheimer's. Every day, she gets worse. I want to know her for as long as I can."

"That's noble," he said, "but it sounds like a lot of work."

"There's another caregiver, too. Vickie lives in the apartment next door." I didn't tell him how awkward she made me feel. What kind of feeling was *awkward*, anyway?

I dropped my chin down on the stack of books on my desk. The top title, *The Righteous Death: Euthanasia Explored*, loomed large. Franklin D. paused, then said, "Well, then, you have a whole month of teen bliss! You can sleep till noon on the weekends, eat chocolate for breakfast, and take selfies at two in the morning."

I smiled. He was a goofball, but his attempt to raise my spirits was sweet.

"Or you can go in the opposite direction. You know, rely on your friends for support. For example, you're welcome to join my family for Shabbat dinner tonight."

Sha-*what?*

"It's nothing too outrageous," he continued. "A prayer or two, and then you get to eat bread and drink wine."

"I don't know any prayers," I said, about to add that I wasn't Jewish. But I wasn't so sure of that anymore.

"Just move your lips. That's all anyone does at synagogue, anyway. Oh, and at the end, say, 'Amen.'"

"Ahh, men," I said, wiggling my eyebrows.

Franklin D. turned pink. "Cute. Anyway, you have to promise not to make fun of my mom and dad. They're, um, interesting."

I wouldn't expect anything less from parents who'd

turned out a kid like Franklin D. "I'm sure mine take the prize," I said.

"It's just that they're so . . . so . . . frustratingly perfect."

I stared at him.

"I mean it. I have the ideal mother and father. My dad comes home at four to spend quality time with my brother and me, and my mom bakes cupcakes for our after-school snack."

I must've sighed, because he looked at my face and nodded. But I wasn't thinking about how weird his sitcom parents were; I was thinking, *Lucky guy*.

"Teenagers are supposed to pull away from their controlling, out-of-touch parents. It's a fundamental stage of independence so we can skip out the door to college. Well, not me. I'm going to actually" —he lowered his voice— "*miss* them."

I laughed. "Wow, so tragic."

"How about it? You want to join a Disney channel family for some Friday night fun?"

When was the last time I'd been around a real family with an intact parental unit, anyway? "Thank you," I told him. "I'd love to."

He looked shocked by my easy acceptance. He scrawled a time and address on the back of my hand. "In Sharpie," he said meaningfully, "so it won't wash off."

"I'll be there," I promised. To convince him, I added, "Five minutes early."

. . .

"Livvy, it's so good to hear from you!" Mom gushed.

"Yeah, well, I wanted to make sure you got to Evergreen

okay." I'd waited a whole day for Mom to get settled and call before giving in and calling her myself.

"Everyone's really supportive here," she said. "So how's it going at Casa Crazy? Is Adelle behaving? Things working out with Vickie?"

I looked around the sitting room, which was now my bedroom since it had a futon. All my chargers were in a plastic bag on the window ledge facing the front street, and my clothes were still in the suitcase, shoved in from yesterday's move. "It's fine, I guess. I mean, it's only been a day since you left."

I thought about telling her how Vickie, with her preschool ways, had actually given Oma a "time-out" yesterday, and how I'd missed turning in my math homework for the first time since forever because I ran out of time last night. But Mom needed to focus on her recovery. That was a thousand times more important than my list of grievances.

"I'm so glad Vickie's there to help, Liv," Mom said. "It gives me peace of mind."

My ear hurt from jamming the phone against the side of my head. I switched to the other side.

"It's been great hearing from you, Liv, but they don't want me to talk to people on the outside during my time here. They've asked for my cell so I won't be tempted. I'm giving it to them in an hour."

"Oh, okay."

"Of course, if there are any emergencies, any at all, you can call the Evergreen switchboard or, better yet, phone Tom."

"Got it." So now I couldn't even speak to my own mother.

143

"Good-bye," I said, hanging up before she could say anything that made me feel worse.

. . .

The tangy scent of yeast filled the foyer of the Schiller home. My lust for homemade bread must've shown, because Franklin D.'s mother said, "The challah's almost done, dear. My son tells me this is your first Shabbat."

"Yes. Thank you for inviting me."

"We're happy to have one of Frankie's friends join us."

Franklin D. grabbed a chunk of his curly hair and pretended to pull it out. "Mom!"

"Oh, I'm sorry." She covered a toothy grin. "Franklin D."

"It's hopeless," he said, turning to me. "Liv, if you ever call me Frankie in public, I'll—"

"Frankie, it's not polite to threaten a guest." Mrs. Schiller circled an arm around my shoulders and led me into the kitchen. She slipped on a pair of oven mitts that said *Happy Hanukkah!*

"Can I help you with anything?" I asked. Wow, the kitchen was really clean.

"Absolutely not," she said, pulling a braided loaf from the oven.

Mr. Schiller came in. He had a head full of salt-and-pepper curls and a solid gray beard. He winked at me in place of a greeting and began to open the wine. I liked Franklin D.'s parents right away. It was strange, but I felt as if I'd been coming to their home for years.

Mr. Schiller examined the cork. It seemed to have splintered in the bottle. "Holy crapola!" he said.

"Not Shabbat-sanctioned language, Dad," Franklin D.

called from the other room. I could hear the tease in his voice.

Mr. Schiller screwed his eyes shut. "Oops. Sorry, Livvy."

I laughed, wondering if Franklin D.'s father might actually be goofier than his son.

"I don't suppose you have experience getting broken cork out of a wine bottle?" He squinted into the neck of the bottle.

"She's our guest," Mrs. Schiller reminded him. "Her job is to relax."

"Actually I have a PhD in Cork Crudology," I said.

Mr. Schiller had the same wide grin as his son. He raised a thumb to Mrs. Schiller, giving his vote of approval.

I considered the problem and asked for a flour sifter. Holding it to the lip of the bottle, I poured the wine through. Chunks of cork tumbled into the mesh screen. I repeated the process a few more times until the liquid ran clear.

"Livvy saved Shabbat," Mr. Schiller announced. "You can't have Shabbat without blessings from the vine. It's a sin, you know."

Franklin D. popped his head into the kitchen. "Hey, everyone, time for the big show."

We moved into the dining room. There were five unlit candles on the mahogany table.

I thought about what I'd read last night about the lighting of Shabbat candles. "Aren't there supposed to be two?"

"In our house, we light a candle for each person in the family," explained Mrs. Schiller. "The first one's for our youngest, Toby. He's on an outdoor ed trip with his fifth grade class."

"That's why it's so peaceful around here," Mr. Schiller said.

"The other one's for you, Livvy," Franklin D. said in response to my unspoken question.

"You're a member of our family tonight," Mrs. Schiller explained.

Something like cork stuck in my throat.

"Where are the matches, Mom?" Franklin D. asked.

"Oh, Curtis! Did you forget to pick them up yesterday?"

"Did I forget to pick them up?" Mr. Schiller said. "I'm sure you could have paused *Oprah* long enough to run to the store."

"That talk show hasn't been on in, what, half a decade?" Mrs. Schiller laughed. "My poor husband is out of touch."

It took me a second to realize they weren't arguing. When Mr. Schiller thought I wasn't looking, he gave his wife a playful pat on the behind. Franklin D. blushed redder than the miniature roses on the buffet.

The thing was, I liked it. The roses. The house. His parents. Everything.

Franklin D. left and came back with a butane lighter. The flame shot out, melting beads of wax down the sides of the candles. Mrs. Schiller covered her eyes and raced through a Hebrew prayer. Because I was prepared, I had my "Ahh, men" ready.

After the fruit of the vine blessing, Mr. Schiller poured some wine into a misshapen ceramic cup that looked like a kid's second grade art project. He took a sip and passed it to me. I let the liquid play against my lips but didn't let it go further. For me, wine was the enemy. I hoped God wouldn't hold it against me.

There was one more prayer, and then we each ripped off

a chunk of warm challah with toasted sesame seeds on top. I bit down, my face melting into a puddle of ecstasy. Mrs. Schiller looked amused. "I'll get you the recipe. It's not hard to make."

Dinner was a bizarre mishmash of foods. According to Schiller family tradition, each person prepared a different part of the meal. Apparently no one knew what the others made until it was all laid out on the table.

"More fun that way," Mr. Schiller said, removing the tinfoil from a bowl of mashed potatoes. Mrs. Schiller heaped whole-wheat pasta with Alfredo sauce on my plate. Franklin D. yanked a cloth napkin off his offering: banana bread.

Once I got over the eclectic assortment, it was surprisingly delicious.

After we cleared the table and had moved into the living room, the question popped uninvited from my mouth. "Did you ever know anyone who was in a concentration camp?" I turned red, embarrassed by the intrusive question.

Mrs. Schiller looked unfazed. "Two cousins from my father's side were killed at Treblinka—an extermination camp in Poland."

"I'm so sorry," I said, wishing I could come up with something more original to say.

"I often think about how one murdered life affects an entire family line. Someone's child never had the opportunity to be born, or to create future generations," she said.

My breath hitched in my throat. Fifty thousand people had died at Bergen-Belsen. What if Oma had been one of them? Mom wouldn't be here right now. *I* wouldn't be here right now.

A timer went off in the kitchen. A rich smell of chocolate filled the room. Franklin D. sniffed appreciatively. When Mrs. Schiller returned, plate in tow, he tried to snag a chocolate meringue. She slapped his hand away. "Guests first."

We crowded onto the couch to watch a documentary called *Who Killed the Electric Car?*

An hour and a half later, as the credits rolled, I whispered to Franklin D., "Your mom and dad are awesome."

"They take after me," he said.

I thanked his parents, and then Franklin D. and his dad gave me a ride home. I was quiet, letting them fill the car with witty repartee. How was it possible to feel joy and longing at the same time? It felt like homesickness for something I'd never had.

His dad stayed in the car while Franklin D. walked me to the door. "Shabbat was great," I said. "I think I feel a Jewish stirring inside me."

A smile played on his lips. I took a wild stab at his thoughts and blushed. *No, Livvy, don't go there.*

When I said good night, we looked everywhere but at each other.

CHAPTER

FIFTEEN

THURSDAY AFTER SCHOOL, I POUNDED ON A PIANO in a practice room as Elizabeth belted out "My Favorite Things" from *The Sound of Music*—her song for play auditions next week. When she traipsed off to Environmental Club, I parked myself on the steps outside the history classroom and waited for Franklin D. to finish a make-up test. Today was our last chance to practice for the euthanasia debate. We were going to my house, but already, I was having doubts. We'd get there around five, the start of my shift with Oma. It might be hard to work, but a part of me wanted him to meet her. I'd met his family, after all.

As we got off the bus, I warned Franklin D., "My grandmother isn't always the easiest . . ." I bit back a yawn. The last few nights, I hadn't started my homework until after she was in bed and the day's mess had been cleaned up.

"So you told me. I like old people, Liv. Besides, we need to practice the con part."

He was right; we were going to be the final group up in the last class of the day at the end of a very long week, and I'd barely had time to review the note cards we'd made. On top of that, the words didn't fly from my mouth the way they did for him.

"Oh, I almost forgot," I said when I reached the bottom step of Oma's porch. "I ran across this article last night. Thought it might be helpful for your side." I pulled a printout from my binder that listed the ten most common diseases along with the odds that the average person would suffer from each by the age of eighty. Franklin D. looked touched, and I skipped up the steps to hide my blush.

His phone chirped. He checked the text. "Rats. My mom says we're going out to dinner in an hour to celebrate my brother's first soccer goal last weekend." His thumbs flew across the screen. "The restaurant's in the Marina. I can walk to it from here." He glanced at his phone again. "She asked if you want to join us."

I *did* want to go out with the Schillers. When I was with them, I could almost convince myself that they were my family. But they weren't. Mom was. And Oma.

Before I could say anything, Franklin D. remembered. "Oh, right, your shift. Never mind."

I inserted the key in the door, hoping that Oma wouldn't do anything embarrassing in front of Franklin D. Last week, I found her dancing in the hallway, wearing a knit sweater and panties. A German polka, she'd said. Actually it had been a lot of fun learning it, even though I was pretty sure she made most of it up.

Vickie was at the kitchen table, paying bills. She jumped when we walked in. "Oh, you scared me!"

What did I care if she did her business while Oma was

napping? I glanced down and saw Oma's bank account statement. Beside it was an open checkbook. Vickie followed my gaze.

"I'm paying the phone bill. I think we should cancel the home service since we all have cell phones. No point in throwing your grandmother's money away. What do you think?"

I was confused. "I took care of that bill already, remember? I told you a few days ago."

"Oh, right. I guess I'm just used to your mom trusting me to handle them. I forgot you offered to take some of them over."

There was an awkward pause before I said, "No, you can do it. I haven't sent it off yet, so no problem."

Vickie shut the laptop as if that put an end to the conversation, which I guess it did. I quickly introduced Franklin D. "I hope it's okay if he and I work on our—"

"I'm not your mother. You can do what you want," she said.

"We have a debate tomorrow." I wasn't sure why I was justifying myself to her. "He's just a friend."

Franklin D. hiked an eyebrow. "A very, *very* good friend."

I sent my elbow into his side.

"I gave Adelle a quesadilla and green beans for dinner," Vickie continued without reaction. "It took me ten minutes to find the stove handles."

"Oh, yeah, sorry. I took them off so Oma won't burn the house down. She keeps trying to make cookies."

"Well, she's napping now. See you tomorrow morning."

She stacked the bills on top of the laptop and stood up. When she reached for the baby monitor on the window ledge behind her, my chest tightened. Yesterday Vickie had explained the features of the deluxe model. I told her that we didn't need it. Oma was plenty loud when she needed help.

"Your grandmother could choke on something in her sleep or cry out," Vickie had said. "You might not be listening. You mentioned you slept through your alarm clock this morning. Imagine if you slept through an emergency."

I wanted to remind her that *she'd* slept through her entire shift the night Mom was arrested, but I didn't want to bring up Mom again. "I fell asleep because I had an essay on progressivism in Roosevelt's 'Square Deal' speech that I couldn't start until eleven at night," I told her.

"Unfortunately, justifications won't help in a life or death situation. If something goes wrong, I could lose my job."

God forbid a family tragedy would affect her paycheck. I glared at her, trying to think of a response but failing.

"Nice to meet you," she said now to Franklin D.

He nodded but didn't say anything. I got the feeling he didn't care for Vickie. I was glad. Vickie was bossy, demeaning, and controlling—especially toward my grandmother. But if you asked Mom, she was the Goddess of Caregiving.

One of the things we'd worked out with Mr. Laramie was that Vickie and I had to share Oma's laptop. It was a lot faster than my old dinosaur. If I needed it for school, I got priority. "I have an essay due in geography tomorrow," I said, glancing pointedly at the Dell.

"I'll leave the laptop on the mantel like we agreed," she said and left.

Franklin D. smiled. "You don't take geography, do you?"

I laughed. "I can't believe you told her that you're my 'very, *very* good friend'!"

"I didn't like how she was talking to you. I'm very loyal to my buddies, in case you haven't noticed."

"She's usually more friendly. Well, to Mom, at least." Vickie had changed a lot since Mom was out of the picture. She seemed to resent working with a sixteen-year-old.

I listened for the front door to shut. "Let's practice the affirmative and negative before my grandma wakes up."

We went to the living room. I tugged on the lamp's pull chain and was rewarded with a dim glow.

"I want to ask you something," Franklin D. said.

I curled up on the couch and kicked off my shoes, ready to begin debate practice.

"Where exactly is your mom, Liv?"

The question caught me off guard, but the words tumbled out as if they'd been sitting on the tip of my tongue, dying to be spoken. "In Vermont. She got a DUI, and she had to go back to a facility to dry out."

Why, why, *why* had I said that? I traced the herringbone pattern on the parquet floor with my big toe. When I raised my eyes, the warmth in his gaze startled me. "Life is messy sometimes," he said.

"I do my best to keep it neat whenever possible," I said softly.

"You can't control the whole world."

For some reason, I felt an overwhelming urge to share the story. Clinging to the facts out of comfort, I moved through my family history in logical order. How Mom had been so

153

involved with her AA meetings in Vermont; how she'd taken off stone drunk that night in the car; how rehab would be a substitution for prison time.

Franklin D. was a surprisingly good listener. I explained how I hadn't even known my grandmother existed until two months ago. I told him how Oma couldn't answer a direct question without going in a random direction. I even told him how my mom was so traumatized by her childhood that she didn't want me to know my own grandma was alive. I finished, shocked into silence by my monologue.

I felt ashamed when I saw the look of pity on his face.

"God, I sound like you," I said.

"In what way?"

"Have you ever tried to pour water out of a pitcher, and all of a sudden, the ice gives way and the water gushes out?" That came out harsher than I'd meant. I smiled to soften my words.

He frowned. "I lay it all on the line so everyone knows who I really am."

"I'm sorry. I have no idea why I said that. I guess I'm not used to talking so much about personal stuff."

"You should try it more often. It takes the guesswork out of communication." His face smoothed out into a smile.

Maybe he could handle the weird parts of me, after all. "My grandma talks about Bergen-Belsen, a concentration camp in Germany, but my mom says she wasn't there. She says Oma didn't grow up in Holland, either, even though Oma keeps mentioning it. And my grandma said she had a sister named Margaret, but Mom insists she only had a brother."

"Your grandmother has Alzheimer's," Franklin D. said.

"By definition, a lot of mixed-up things come out of her mouth."

"But my mom's honesty record is in the toilet right now."

"Do you think your grandmother didn't tell your mother the whole truth, because her memories were too painful?"

"My mom said that Oma was a closed book when she was growing up."

"But it doesn't sound like she's like that anymore."

Yes, I realized, he'd nailed the irony. Alzheimer's had torn down the walls, causing Oma's memories to spill out. If only I could figure out which were real.

"Do you know where your grandma might keep her personal records, like a passport or a birth certificate?" he asked. "Then you would know where she was born at least."

He was right. I took off without a word, him tagging behind. In the library, I searched through a squat file cabinet, obscured by a pile of tattered blankets haphazardly thrown on top. The metal rods inside sagged under the weight of paperwork. My grandmother had kept every utility bill from 1992 to 1999. Somewhere around 1996, I found a folder labeled "Records." But only plane tickets from vacations were inside: Jamaica, Grand Cayman, the Mexican Riviera . . .

No passports. Nothing.

Franklin D. gnawed on his lower lip as if he was biting back the urge to ask something. Predictably his impulse won out. "So if your grandma's remembering right, and she really was in a concentration camp, that would make you Jewish."

"There's a mezuzah on the door. I don't know why she'd put it up if she's not Jewish." I buried my face in my hands.

God, this was nuts. It was like I had a key to a whole new world, but I didn't know which door it unlocked.

He lifted a hand in the air. "High-five, baby. You've joined the club!"

I slapped his hand, laughing in spite of myself. What a dork.

"You can be an honorary member until you get confirmation." He shook his head, the curls flying in random directions. "This is a major mystery, worthy of being solved. You've got your mother saying one thing, and your grandmother saying something completely—"

"THAT'S NOT MY NAME!"

We jerked around. Oma was at the door, hands on her hips. I slammed the file cabinet shut. "She doesn't like to be called grandmother," I whispered. To her, I said, "This is my friend, Oma. Remember I told you about him?"

She blinked twice. No recognition.

"*Oma* means 'grandma' in Dutch," I told Franklin D. as we headed back to the living room, where we could all sit down.

"Dutch?" Franklin D. raised an eyebrow. "Or some other language?"

I saw where he was going with this. If Oma was from Germany, like Mom said, then wouldn't she want me to use the German word for "grandma"?

"Are you from Holland?" Oma asked Franklin D. "Nice people live there."

I thought about the poem I'd found in the anthology on Oma's bookshelf. She'd written about the demise of Anne Frank's chestnut tree, so she might've had some connection with the city of Amsterdam.

156

I pulled my phone out of my pocket, typed in the word, and sighed. "*Oma* means 'grandma' in *both* German and Dutch." A failed clue.

I walked over to the window and spread the curtains. The sunset cast an orange glow on Oma's face.

"Love your home," Franklin D. told her. "Edwardian, right? Awesomely antique."

Oma's head swung to him. "I most certainly am *not* an antique."

"I bet you weren't even born when this house was built," he said. "So that makes you a spring chicken."

Oma lowered her chin and batted her skimpy eyelashes at him. Was she flirting? Franklin D. and I traded smiles. He offered Oma his hand. "I'm Franklin D. Nice to meet you, Mrs. Friedman."

"Oma!" she cried.

"Oma," he repeated.

Her coy look switched to wariness. "Franklin Delano was chums with that nasty Winston Churchill."

"Well, actually, I was named after my great-grandfather, Franklin Douglas Schiller the Great."

Oma cocked her head. "You're a Jew."

"I told you he was Jewish," I said, embarrassed by her abruptness.

"So am I! I wear a Jewish star on my coat," she said.

Franklin D. seemed to take her dementia in stride. "I hear we don't have to wear those stars anymore."

Oma stilled like an animal hearing a lion approach through the weeds. "Quiet! The nasty bastards are coming."

"Who?" I asked.

"The ground is frozen, and my feet are bare, and that guard might pull out her whip." She reached under her sweater for the necklace and tilted her head. "Do you know where my shoes are, dear?"

"They're on your feet," I said.

"And my necklace? Have you seen it, Livvy's friend?"

"It's around your neck," I said, stroking her arm. "It's okay, Oma. You're safe."

"Not that one! The other one! My pearls. Where are my pearls?"

Oh no, not this again.

"What do they look like?" Franklin D. asked. I moved behind Oma and shook my head, hoping he'd get the message. *Don't ask, divert.*

"They sneak in during the night while I sleep," she whispered, her fingers clawing at the throw pillow. "They steal my jewels for money."

I shot Franklin D. a look. *What did I tell you?* Following Oma's logic was like trying to track a shooting star.

"What was it like in the concentration camp?" Franklin D. asked gently.

I winced. That kind of question could send Oma into a rage.

"I was in the hospital, and I was so sick." She grabbed her throat. The dramatic choking sounds sent Franklin D. from the room to retrieve a glass of water. Oma twisted her head away, refusing it. "Why is it so cold in here?" she asked him. "I want to live! But the nurse says, 'Take this food and eat it, or there'll be no prayer for you at all!' I have to listen to her, or I'll die, like that sweet little girl."

"What girl?" I asked. "Your sister?"

"There is no sister! We died a million deaths!"

Oma looked on the verge of collapse. Why had I brought Franklin D. here? But then she slid a hand around his arm and tried to pull Franklin D. toward the bookshelf. He glanced over his shoulder to let me know it was okay.

"Sorry," I mouthed.

Oma reached for the middle of the second shelf. She pulled out *The Hunchback of Notre Dame* and flipped through its pages, then discarded it for *Ivanhoe*. On the third shelf, she grabbed hold of *The Scarlet Letter*, shook it out like a towel at the beach, and threw it behind her. It hit the wall and slid to the floor, the spine broken.

"Oma, stop it!"

She started moving quicker, tossing books off the shelves. Franklin D. hopped out of the way to avoid being hit by a Dickens anthology. When Oma reached for *Sense and Sensibility*, her hand moving in for the kill, I grabbed her wrist.

"I have to find it!" Oma cried, ripping her hand free. She pulled *Wuthering Heights* off the shelf and sent it flying like a Frisbee. Dust flew out of its pages.

"Find what?" Franklin D. asked.

I pointed to the half-empty shelves. "Do you notice anything about these books?"

"Yeah, they're really old." He sneezed.

"Bless you. No, I mean the books were arranged in alphabetical order. By title. Well not anymore, obviously."

In a strange way, I found my grandmother's organizational system to be comforting. I had an overwhelming desire to protect the order of her world, even if Oma seemed intent on destroying it. I knew if it weren't for this disease, she'd be appalled at the mess she was making.

"Look for my journal," Oma pleaded to Franklin D.

I moved in front of the bookshelf, blocking her access.

"Gretchen's in my way, damn it," she said with a scathing glare that made me step to the side.

"You have a journal?" Franklin D. asked her. "Somewhere on this shelf?"

"The nurse hid them so no one will get in trouble," Oma whispered. "You're Jewish. I want you to take it back for me."

"Take it where?" he asked.

"Where it belongs!"

My eyes darted to the bookshelf. If a journal really existed, it could tell me things I'd thought were lost to time. I could learn more than the tattered scraps of the past that Alzheimer's had left behind.

Franklin D. said, "Sure, I'll look for you, Mrs. Friedman. Sorry, Oma, I mean." He turned away so he could wink at me without her noticing. "Excuse me, Livvy, I'm on a mission."

I moved out of his way, relieved that he was handling the situation. "Thank you," I whispered.

"Thank you," Oma echoed.

He pulled a book off the shelf and flipped through the pages for anything unusual. Oma tilted her head, gazing at him. On second thought, maybe it wasn't coyness. She looked like a kid who'd been caught with a hand in someone's wallet.

Franklin D. worked his way through the shelf, then moved on to the next one. He fanned through the pages of each book. Second shelf from the bottom, a scrap of paper floated out from *Pride and Prejudice*. Franklin D. handed the leather-bound book to me and bent down to retrieve the old page. I held the book upside down and three more sheets of paper slipped out into my hand, each a few paragraphs long and written in a foreign language. I went back to the beginning to check for more but didn't find any.

"Read it!" Oma's tone made the two innocent words sound like expletives.

"We can't read it," Franklin D. told her. "It's in another language."

"Dutch," Oma said.

"Can you read it to us?" he asked.

She stared at the papers in his hand, her lips pursed with disapproval. "Can't. Don't know how."

Alzheimer's, late stage. Loss of ability to read. Not the kind of fact I wanted in my head right now.

"My hair is falling out," Oma whimpered. "Soon I'll be bald. The lice will move to my armpits. Behind my ears. Irma says, 'Wash outside or you will die, dirty Jew!' She snaps her whip and calls her dogs."

"Who's Irma?" I asked. But this question, like all the others, earned me a blank stare.

"The war is over now," Franklin D. said.

"What if they come back?" Oma asked.

He turned his thumbs to his chest and sucked in air, puffing himself up like a superhero. "I'm a big guy, which means I'll kick their ever-hatin' Nazi butts, okay?"

I started to laugh but reeled in my reaction, reminding myself that it wasn't possible for Oma to find humor in the subject. To my surprise, she stayed calm, gazing at Franklin D. as if she was waiting for the next great thing he was about to say.

He laid the papers down on the desk beside her. She jerked back. "Take them away."

He picked them back up as his phone pinged. I glanced at the clock. It was almost time for him to go to the restaurant.

"My friend has to go now," I told Oma, wishing it wasn't true. Franklin D. was insta-Valium for my grandmother.

"Good-bye, Oma." He swept his lips across her cheek.

And there it was, Oma's smile, in all its glory. The sun breaking through the San Francisco fog. The sight of it stunned me into silence.

"I'll walk him to the door to say good-bye, but then I'll come right back, Oma," I said.

"Is it nap time already? Vickie says I need to take three a day."

Did she forget that she'd just woken up? "Not yet. Are you hungry?"

"I don't want your turnip soup. It's too watery!"

"Vickie told me that you had a quesadilla earlier. You don't have to eat anything else if you don't want to." I felt a twinge of empathy for Mom and all she'd gone through while taking care of Oma. Then again, she hadn't thought of me when she'd turned her back on sobriety. With that thought, the feeling vanished.

Oma's eyelids sagged. I grabbed her hand before she fell asleep standing up. Franklin D. waited by the front door as I led her down the hall to her bedroom. It was hard to tell, but it seemed like she was sleeping more every day. It was almost six thirty, which meant she'd probably go down for the night. I knew I should feel happy for the break, but I wasn't. It felt like another day lost.

When I came back, I said, "I'm sorry we didn't get to practice for the debate." It seemed like I was apologizing a lot these days.

"No worries."

We headed down the hallway. When I flipped the light switch, the overhead bulb flared, then went dark. I glanced over my shoulder, squinting into the shadows. *What if they come back?* Oma had said. I walked faster, eager to reach the light of the foyer.

At the door, Franklin D. glanced at the pages in his hand. "Do you mind if I take these with me? I bet there's a Dutch dictionary online."

"Yes," I said after a moment. "That's a good idea."

APRIL 1946

The tattoo parlor was at the end of a dark alleyway that stank of popcorn and urine. Though it was midday, the buildings blocked the light, laying shards of shadow at her feet. Adelle crossed her arms as she aimed for the wood door at the end, then thought better of the defensive posture. A woman alone in Manhattan could be easy pickings for a hooligan. She drew her shoulders back and tilted her head, leading the way with her chin.

A window from the back of an apartment, several feet above her, slammed shut. A bag of trash landed on top of a battered metal can, ejecting a jar of grape jam and a rotten cantaloupe. Within seconds, a stray cat showed up to investigate.

Adelle faced front again, walking as fast as her high heels would allow until she reached the entrance. A sweet, incongruous chime announced her arrival. The man, no older than her, perched on a stool beside the doorway. He shoved the girlie magazine in front of him under a small stack of old Time *magazines. With a shudder, she averted her eyes from the cover on top, a bloodred X stamped across Adolf Hitler's face, announcing the Führer's death.*

"I called an hour ago? About a tattoo?" she said.

He cranked an eyebrow, so she clarified, ". . . on my arm. Right here." She gave him the design. It wasn't art, but it didn't need to be. "This is what I want."

He glanced at it, then let his eyes roam up her blouse. It gave her the creeps. She knit her arms across her chest to block his stare. "That's it?" he asked.

"That's it exactly. Two inches long and one inch thick," she said, careful to keep her voice matter of fact. Her wedding day was in two weeks. There was little time to waste. She had a meeting with the florist at five, and after that, the caterer.

He laughed. "Sure thing, boss."

She reached into her handbag, pulled out the fee, and slapped the stack of cash on top of the magazines. There, now she didn't have to look at that horrible X anymore.

The man's laugh revealed crooked teeth stained from chewing tobacco. "I don't see too many dames. Sailors, Mafia, lovesick fatheads, yeah."

As he rambled on, preparing the tools, she thought of her fiancé. She imagined Herbert's face as he peeled off her wedding gown, seeing her tattoo for the first time. The sacrifice was more than a declaration of the past; it was necessary for love, a reminder that there need only be a present and a future to ensure happiness.

"You know this is gonna hurt like the dickens, right, sugar?"

He was seeking a reaction, but she had no intention of giving it to him. "Get on with it, please," she instructed, rolling back the sleeve of her blouse to offer her arm.

SIXTEEN

At eight on Saturday morning, Vickie finished her shift. The front door slammed, which was her way of letting me know it was my turn. I pulled up on my elbows, listening for Oma. Whew, she'd slept through Vickie's wake-up call. I dropped my head back onto my pillow. I should get up to make breakfast—Oma liked her eggs soft-boiled—but I couldn't pry myself from bed.

My phone rang, startling me. I rolled onto my side and squinted at a familiar number on the screen. "Hello?" I croaked into the receiver.

Franklin D. said, "I figured you were up."

"Sort of. Isn't eight kind of early to call?"

"Twelve minutes after eight," he clarified.

"I hope you're not worried about the debate. We did fine, considering we didn't have much time to practice. That was my fault. Sorry."

"No, it's not that. I need to talk to you."

I pulled back up to a sitting position and leaned against the headboard. "I'm listening."

"Actually, I'm in the area. Like on your porch. I didn't want to ring the doorbell in case your grandma was still sleeping."

On the porch? Geez. I ran my fingers through my hair. "I'll be right out."

The door wasn't even fully open when Franklin D. blurted out, "Online translators are modern torture devices, so I asked around. Turns out my uncle's mechanic speaks Dutch. I was going to see if you want me to ask him to interpret the journal . . ." He shifted from foot to foot like it was cold out. It looked to me to be a gorgeous October morning. The sun, peeking over the apartment buildings, promised T-shirt temps.

He followed me into the living room so we wouldn't wake Oma. "I was able to figure out a few words on my own," he told me. "About two-thirds down the page on one of the entries, it said, '*De meisjes van Frank.*' I'm butchering the Dutch, but—"

"What does it mean?" In the shadowed light, the old room felt like a fragment of the past being kept on life support. I parted the drapes to let the sunlight in, even though Vickie would close them as soon as she got the chance.

"According to the dictionary, 'Frank girls.'"

I turned around to stare at him. "Frank girls?" For all I knew, there were many Franks at Bergen-Belsen. But girls? Frank girls couldn't be nearly so common. "You think it means Anne and her sister, Margot? They died right before Bergen-Belsen was liberated." It was clear from his expression that Franklin D. had already made the connection. His point slammed into me full velocity. "You think that Oma knew them? That she actually wrote about them in her diary?"

"If this mentions Anne Frank, it could be an important document. Like historically important," he said. "As in, the entire world may be wholly interested."

"Are they mentioned in more entries?"

Franklin D. shrugged. "Can't tell. Whoever wrote this used first initials instead of names, probably to protect people's identities in case the pages were found. But there are some that start with an A, and a few with an M, I believe."

"That's not exactly proof," I said. "I mean, there's Adelle and her sister, Margaret, for example." I was struck by the coincidence. My grandmother and her sister shared the same first initials with the Frank sisters. Maybe that had been enough to bond two pairs of sisters.

"I thought your mom said that Oma only had a brother," Franklin D. said.

"Yeah, well, she also said that my grandmother was dead. Hey, what's that mechanic's name, the translator guy?"

"Dan."

"I think you should put Dan on the job," I said. "Right away."

He grinned sheepishly. "Already have. Figured you'd say that." He peered at me through lashes a shade lighter than his eyebrows. The early morning sun deepened the soft brown in his eyes. They were the color of the mahogany vase sitting on Oma's kitchen shelf. Wait, why was I thinking about Franklin D.'s eyes?

"I'm glad you went ahead." My voice squeaked. What was my problem? This was Franklin D., king of goofiness. "How could Oma have kept a diary in Bergen-Belsen anyway? I don't think that was a Nazi-approved activity."

"I had the same thought," he said. "But a woman named Hanna something or other wrote a diary, and I think there were a few others, too."

"If only I could ask Oma about this." If only she could be lucid for more than a few seconds.

"Dan says he might be done by next weekend."

"Why don't we go see him now? Maybe he's had a chance to translate the first entry by now," I suggested.

"He says he won't have time for a few days."

A piercing call came from the hallway. "Where is everybody? Did I die and go to hell?"

"Most people say heaven at the end of that phrase," Franklin D. said.

I shouted back, "Be right there, Oma."

"Quack, quack!" Oma called from inside the room. She sounded more like a barking seal than a duck.

The disease made her do silly things sometimes, but I didn't mind. The silliness made her seem younger. Spirited. I couldn't help but smile. I opened the door, glad I felt comfortable having Franklin D. around this time. Oma stepped forward, folding her arms around my waist. I hugged her back and thought about my mother's comment: *She can't even remember what a rotten mother she was.* Maybe so, but she wasn't a rotten grandmother.

Oma eyed Franklin D. "What's that boy's name? I like the looks of him, but he doesn't have a name."

"That's my friend, remember? Franklin D. Sch—"

I stopped, not wanting to go through the "Is he Jewish?" conversation again.

Franklin D. spread his arms out. "Ready or not, here I am!"

I laughed, recognizing the dorky phrase he'd used on me a few times.

"You're a chatterbox!" she said, nudging him in the side with her elbow.

"I've been accused of worse."

It seemed that Franklin D. genuinely liked her. That wasn't a huge surprise. He preferred people who were different from everyone else.

"Hey, you're still in your pajamas," I said to Oma. "Why don't I help you—"

"Don't touch me!"

"Oops—I forgot. She never lets anyone help her," I told Franklin D., forcing a smile for Oma's sake. I didn't want to start the morning out wrong. "She gets dressed by herself."

"Nothing wrong with that. I always insist on dressing myself, too," Franklin D. said.

"Maybe we shouldn't encourage her," I whispered.

Oma tried to toss a pillow at me from where she sat on the couch. It fell short. She braided her hands in her lap, chin jutted in mounting defiance.

"Don't worry. I won't touch you," I said nervously, bending over to get the pillow. I didn't expect to be whacked in the back. I spun around, greeted by Franklin D.'s grin. The pillow from the window seat lay at my feet.

"I got her for you, Oma," he said.

My eyes skipped back to my grandmother. The rage melted off her face, replaced by a twitchy smile. I couldn't believe it. Oma hiccupped, except it wasn't a hiccup. It was a laugh—timid but real—a sound so rare that I felt compelled to keep the game going.

"Revenge!" I yelled, scooping up the pillow and smacking Franklin D. on the thigh, which made Oma hiccup even louder. Franklin D. snagged the rose afghan off the trunk. He darted around the room, fending me off like a bullfighter with a cape. Oma pressed her hands to her mouth as if giggling was against the rules.

We fell onto the couch beside her, both of us panting heavily. Oma scooted closer until she was almost in my lap. She grinned up at me. "Isn't my girl marvelous?" she said, dropping her head on my shoulder.

Franklin D. nodded. "Definitely."

I shook my head like Oma's offhanded remark didn't mean anything, but I slid my hand on top of hers. She yanked her fingers free, then curled them around my wrist as if she didn't want me to leave.

"Livvy . . ." The air escaped her lips, a breeze on my cheek.

My name had never sounded better. I'd been Gretchen for most of last week. Sometimes she failed to pull a name out at all. The day was coming when she'd stop remembering me altogether. But today? Today was good.

"I want to watch a movie," she said.

"But it's early. You haven't had breakfast yet," I said.

"How about the Lord of the Rings trilogy?" Franklin D. suggested. "We can see part one, two, or three, but *Fellowship of the Ring* is the best one. The computer technology is downright awe-inspiring."

"Nerd," I stage-whispered to Oma.

Franklin D. feigned offense. "I most certainly am *not* a nerd. I'm a geek. A geek is a nerd with social skills, thank you very much."

"He said thank you," Oma said. "That's nice to say in polite company."

"See? *She* appreciates my social skills," Franklin D. said.

Oma launched into her favorite song, "Animal Crackers in My Soup." "She wants a Shirley Temple movie," I told him. "My mom found this DVD set at a garage sale. Oma's seen them all at least twice."

"I'm embarrassed to admit that I've never had the pleasure of viewing Shirley Temple," Franklin D. said, already on his feet. "Sounds like movie time."

"Movie time!" she echoed.

In Oma's bedroom, the three of us lined up on the small love seat next to her twin bed. She chose the 1938 film *Rebecca of Sunnybrook Farm*. We watched ten-year-old Shirley, adorned in soldier regalia, tap her way up a staircase.

An hour later, Oma was back asleep. Her face relaxed, smoothing out the frown lines that had seemed etched in place. Franklin D. helped me move her to the bed.

"She's a sound sleeper," I told him as I turned off the TV. "Do you think it's normal for her to nap this much?"

"It's definitely not normal to zone out in the middle of such an exhilarating tap sequence."

We heard a chirp. Franklin D. glanced at his phone, but there wasn't a text. As I gently rose from the bed, Oma cuffed her fingers around my arm. She wouldn't let go. I sat back down.

"Did you know Shirley Temple Black ended up as an ambassador to Ghana in 1974 and Czechoslovakia in '89?" I whispered to Franklin D. as Oma's eyelids fluttered closed again.

"Fact source?"

"*People* magazine, orthodontist's office, last March."

Franklin D. caught my expression—a murky mixture of shame, guilt, and pride. "Aha! I knew it!" he said. "You're more than a fact junkie. You have a magnificent memory, too."

I flinched. "Only about stuff that interests me. The other crap goes in one ear and out the other."

"Still normalizing, aren't you?"

I didn't know what he meant. At least I pretended that I didn't.

"Can you show me how your prodigious memory works?" he asked. "Let's see. How about the third page of chapter three in that textbook over there."

I glanced at the algebra book I'd left by the lamp last night. I pretended to consider his request. "No."

"Livvy, do you have any idea how absolutely friggin' cool to the nth degree this is?"

"Not everyone feels that way. My friends back home wouldn't think it was cool."

"Why not?"

"They thought I was cheating because I didn't study for tests. They didn't think it was fair that I got perfect grades."

"But it was your memory," Franklin D. protested. "You couldn't help it."

"They didn't exactly know that part," I admitted. "Look, I saw how they reacted. That was bad enough. So I fixed the problem. I missed a question here and there." I didn't like the way Franklin D. was looking at me, as if I was weak, instead of smart enough to make everyone happy—including myself.

"I still got A's, but it got them off my back. They weren't suspicious anymore."

Franklin D. considered this. "These are your *friends?*"

"They were fun. We had parties almost every weekend."

He looked unimpressed. "Some people see the beauty in differences. If we had the same sunset every day, would anyone even notice it?"

I agreed with him in theory, but I was more pragmatist than philosopher. There were plenty of people who tore apart others' differences. This was a fact. Even so, I changed my mind and decided to take him up on his challenge. "Third page, chapter three, um, third paragraph down, for alliteration purposes. It's a complicated definition for the term "division algorithm." I didn't bother to share with him the artwork someone left on the bottom left-hand corner—a highly inaccurate depiction of an anatomical part belonging to the male gender.

"I'll assume I don't need to check," he said. "Thank you for sharing."

His admiration, direct and intense, caught me off guard. My cheeks flamed. "You better never tell anyone about this," I warned.

"It's not my good news to share."

There was another chirp. Franklin D. looked around, zeroing in on the source. "I think this thing needs new batteries." He picked up the baby monitor tipped on its side behind Oma's alarm clock. "Why is there a walkie-talkie in your grandmother's bedroom?"

"It's a high-tech device for the super paranoid," I told

him. "Vickie keeps the receiver in her apartment on the other side of this wall."

It occurred to me that she might be listening to us right now. I gave it a second of contemplation, then decided I didn't care. "It's so she'll hear Oma if there's a problem that I don't catch." I switched the monitor off. "She can transmit the other way, too. That way she can say, 'Don't you know it's time for some wink-eye, sweet thing?'"

"She talks to your grandma that way?"

"I think her caregiver manual got old age and toddler care reversed."

Franklin D. turned the monitor back on. "Oh, Livvy, stop doing that. You're driving me crazy." His hoarse stage whisper made him sound like a dirty old man. I bit my lip to keep from laughing and snuggled in close, my mouth near his. "I live to drive you wild, Franklin D. Schiller."

I must've been good at pretending, because his lower lip went slack. He stared at my mouth. I cleared my throat and pulled back.

Franklin D. glanced down at his watch with sudden interest. "I have to go. My carriage turns into a pumpkin at ten forty-five."

"Carriage?"

"Otherwise known as the last Muni bus that gets me home before noon. I have to finish a gruesome essay on sexually transmitted diseases."

I was sympathetic, having suffered through health class in Vermont.

Oma lifted her head from the pillow, startling us. "Good-bye, my Jewish friend. Do come again."

"I will," he promised.

Oma's eyelids snapped shut.

When I caught up with him in the hallway, I said, "I think she likes you better than me."

"That's true!" she called from inside.

I laughed, not feeling at all offended. If I were Oma, I'd like Franklin D. better, too.

I walked with him to the front porch. "That's strange," he said.

"What?"

"The mezuzah's on the wrong side."

"Does it matter?"

"It's supposed to be on the other side of the doorframe. This one's on the left."

"Maybe she didn't know."

"If she's been Jewish her whole life, she'd know," he said. "Even if she converted, she would've learned that."

When *had* Oma put up the mezuzah? I wished I could ask Mom more questions, but she was off-limits for another eighteen days according to the countdown app on my phone.

Franklin D. shook his head. "Well, I'm going to have to fix that. It's wrong there."

"Okay, you do that," I said. "Still trying to get in good with Oma, huh?"

"No need. She adores me."

"Listen, when you get the translation back from your uncle's friend, come over. I'll make you dinner," I said.

He wagged his eyebrows. "That sounds suspiciously like a date."

"On the other hand, maybe I'll buy you a Happy Meal."

He opened his mouth, then shut it, then opened it again. "Livvy, I really . . ." He sighed. "Never mind."

"Look at that. Restraint, coming from you," I joked, but secretly I was glad that he hadn't finished the sentence.

"Restraint's overrated," he said with an exaggerated frown. His forehead moved closer to mine. I froze, a mass of indecision and confusion. He took a step backward, studied me for a moment, and waved good-bye. I waved back, too perky, and went inside.

SEVENTEEN

"WHY ARE THERE BOOKS ON THE LIBRARY FLOOR?" VICKIE asked the next afternoon when I came into the kitchen for a homework-sustaining snack.

"Oh . . . um . . . Oma was looking for something on the bookshelf the other day," I said, then added, "I've been picking them up, but I keep getting sidetracked. I'll do the rest later." I didn't tell Vickie that I was only a third of the way done—putting the books back in alphabetical order took a long time.

I was afraid our conversation would remind my grandmother of the journal, but she seemed more interested in rolling her soft-boiled egg around her plate. I frowned at the bib that Vickie had tied around her neck.

"Actually, I'll do some work in the library now, before my shift starts," I said. I opened the fridge but found little inspiration in cottage cheese and carrot sticks. I pecked Oma on the forehead and sped out of there.

In the library, I reached for *The Canterbury Tales*, put it back on the shelf, and searched for the next title. The importance of getting the order right didn't matter anymore, I knew that, and yet I felt compelled to return the library to its pre-Alzheimer's state.

While I shelved, my mind wandered to the awkward good-bye with Franklin D. yesterday, not to mention the forlorn look he'd given me as he'd left. The thing was, Franklin D. wasn't my type. He was an extreme extrovert with a faulty brain-to-mouth filter. Eccentric, silly, awkward as hell—but loyal, that couldn't be denied. True, smart was on my list. Anyone who could annoy teachers with his philosophical ramblings, while maintaining a 3.87 (unweighted) GPA, had to be intelligent. But a lot of people had brains, not just Franklin D.

I shrugged off my circular thoughts and focused on the task before me. The book in my hand, *The Diary of Anne Frank*, was a rare post-Edwardian addition to the library. I considered the poem Oma had written about the chestnut tree. It made sense that my grandmother would own the diary. But could there be more to it? The journal's reference to the "Frank girls" made me question again if Oma had crossed paths with Anne or Margot Frank in Bergen-Belsen. I held the book in my hand, staring at it, hesitating. Instead of shelving it, I put it on the desk behind me.

An hour later, I added the last book—*Vanity Fair*—to the bottom shelf. I stepped back to admire my work, then reached for *The Diary of Anne Frank* again. I studied the cover. Anne was younger than me when the picture was taken, but we looked a little alike. Not the hair but the smile, broad and thin-lipped. Anne was skinny, not as curvy as me, but both our chins were, depressingly, on the pointy side. With my blond hair, I looked more German than Anne had, even though the preface explained that she'd been born in Frankfurt before her family moved to Amsterdam. It didn't seem to matter if people had been German citizens their whole lives; if they didn't fit Hitler's definition of Aryan, they became scapegoats for everything that was wrong with the country.

If I'd been alive back then, would I have used my blond, blue-eyed looks to hide my identity? Definitely. Being a proud Jew seemed like an automatic death sentence, from what I gathered. But somehow I knew that Franklin D. wouldn't have hidden who he was, no matter what the consequences. I didn't understand that kind of thinking. Why not try to save yourself? I was glad that he'd been born in a different time and place.

I sat on an uncomfortably hard armchair, turned to chapter one, and read by the overcast light slanting through the wooden blinds. This time, I noticed how different the diary was from others that I'd seen. It had dialogue, and even fake names, which Anne had made up. I knew she'd rewritten her diary in the hopes that she'd get it published one day. "I want to go on living even after my death!" she'd written. How ironic that she had to die for her words to make an impact.

I read for nearly an hour until Vickie's knock on the door let me know it was time to take care of Oma.

. . .

The next Sunday, Franklin D. and I headed to the Palace of Fine Arts. The sun shone down on the building, turning its domed top a peachy orange. We sat by the lagoon, next to a guy with a pastry in one hand and the *San Francisco Chronicle* in the other. Through the trees, a pink-tinged fog drifted lazily out to the bay.

All of a sudden I got it. Why people loved this city. When San Francisco was on, it was really on.

"I have a gift for you," Franklin D. said. He handed me something soft and red, rolled into a sausage and tied with a thick blue ribbon.

I unfolded the T-shirt, which read, *Statistics Is the Art of Never Having to Say You're Wrong.* It was geeky as hell, but it captured me perfectly.

"It was too small on me," Franklin D. said. "I suspected it would look better on you."

A part of me hoped this was a hand-me-down, not something he'd bought. Gifts required planning and thinking about someone. I held it up to my body. It was the right size. "Thanks," I said.

"Try it on," he urged.

I wiggled my way into the shirt. Franklin D. stepped in close, lifting his phone to get a photo of us. I ducked before he could take the picture.

"I love it," I said, pulling it off. "Hey, did you see that Thurmond finally posted our debate grade?"

"Yeah, she gave me a lousy B as in buffalo buttocks." Franklin D. took a noisy sip of his tofu shake.

Ms. Thurmond said that Franklin D. tended to lose perspective in the throes of passion. Sounded like she was teaching Sex Ed. She'd called me the Queen of the Fillers, even though I couldn't remember saying a single *uh* or *um*. "Yeah, I got a B, too," I told him.

Franklin D. groaned. "I'll have you know I thoroughly enjoyed your description of the evil relatives pulling the plug." He glanced at his phone, at the photo of himself, at the top of my head, mostly out of the frame. "Something's missing," he said after a moment. "Can't quite put my finger on it."

. . .

After a cupcake stop on Union Street, we hiked up Fillmore. The hills, I'd come to appreciate, were a free gym membership. My calf muscles were rock solid.

When we reached Oma's porch, Franklin D. insisted on fixing the mezuzah. I went to the garage to get a hammer. A few minutes later, the mezuzah was on the side of the door that God recognized.

Once we were in the house, Franklin D. waited in the living room while I got us a snack. Vickie was sautéing vegetables. Oma swiveled around in her chair, snatching glimpses at the TV. Canned laughter erupted from *I Love Lucy*, followed by a three-second delay before Oma echoed the fake chortles. She wasn't getting the jokes, only imitating sounds. Despite the laughter in the kitchen, I felt an almost unbearable sadness.

I spotted a bag of pretzels on a high shelf and jumped up to get them. As the bag came down, a grocery receipt fell to the floor. I bent down to retrieve it.

Vickie, at the stove, raised an eyebrow. "What's wrong, Liv?"

I eyed the long stretch of paper. "Well, it's just . . . this is a lot of food. I mean, the bill's over four hundred dollars."

"I only go shopping for your grandmother once a month." Vickie took the receipt before I could take inventory. "I'm so glad you found it," she continued. "I have to expense it to Mr. Laramie, and I thought it was lost."

"Why's it so much?"

Her smile dimmed. "Your grandma likes brie, smoked salmon, chocolate, gelato . . . She has enough going against her, so I like to indulge her cravings every now and then. I'm sure you, of all people, can understand the soft spot I have for her." Without glancing at the receipt, she said, "Of course, this is a month old. I hope it's not too late to submit."

Her soft spot, it seemed, didn't extend to her own wallet.

Oma's eyes were glued to *I Love Lucy*. I stepped in front of the television. "Do you like brie, Oma?"

Oma cocked her head, thinking. After a moment, she muttered, "No one's free."

Vickie laughed. "That's asking a bit much from our gal, don't you think?"

I crossed to the door, feeling drained. "I'll be with Franklin D. if you need me."

"You're not on duty yet. No need to report to me."

"Well, just saying, I'm around in case of an emergency or something." The pretzels clamped under my arm had to be pulverized by now.

When I returned to the living room, Franklin D. took one look at my face and said, "Good old Vickie, eh?"

I tossed the bag to him. He caught it and tore it open. "She gets under my skin, that's all," I said.

"Like how?"

"Like she's always Skyping with this guy on my grandma's laptop when she's supposed to be with Oma. As soon as I come in, she shuts it off."

"Whoa, Vickie's got a boyfriend?"

I laughed. "I know, right?"

A few days ago, I'd asked her what she did on Oma's laptop all day. Shockingly Vickie opened up a bit. She mentioned a long-distance relationship with someone named Ryan who lived in the Midwest.

"So how'd you meet him?" I'd asked.

"Do you know why they call it a personal life, Livvy? I'm sure you can respect my need to keep work and private separate." As if I'd forced her to talk about her love life.

Franklin D. threw a pretzel in the air and ducked under it, catching it with his tongue. "Guess that proves there's someone for everyone," he said, crunching away.

I picked up *The Diary of Anne Frank* and flipped to the earmarked page. "So, remember the other day when Oma was acting like a duck?"

"How could I forget?"

"Before the Franks went into hiding, Anne got into trouble for talking too much in class, so her teacher assigned her an essay as a punishment. Anne wrote a short story called '"Quack, Quack, Quack," said Mrs. Chatterback.' Look, she writes about it here, in her diary."

He leaned in close, his soft curls sweeping across my cheek. I waited as he read about how she'd turned the story into a joke to get back at a teacher who accused her of being a "chatterbox"—a word I remembered Oma using. She'd described Franklin D. that way.

"I have a thought—maybe it's crazy—but it's about how my grandma met Anne Frank," I started. "You see, a few years ago, this woman who survived Bergen-Belsen wrote a book claiming that Anne used to tell stories to the kids in the camp to keep their spirits up. It seems like something she'd do, doesn't it? If it's true, then she probably retold the ones she wrote before the war, right?"

Franklin D. nodded slowly. "Didn't your grandma say something about a hospital the day I met her? She was sick, I think."

"Exactly. If she was one of those kids who listened to Anne's stories, that would explain why it stuck in her head." I pictured a group of emaciated kids huddled around a girl almost my age.

"How old do you think Oma is?" Franklin D. asked.

I shrugged. "I've asked her four times, but I think she forgot."

"Let's say she was ten in 1944. That would make her about eighty now . . ."

"Eighty-three," I corrected. Annoyed by my left-brained self, I added, "Sorry."

"She kind of looks older," he pointed out.

"That makes sense, after going through all that."

"Yeah, probably." His phone rang. He glanced at the screen, then answered, mouthing "Dan" to me. I waited. He listened for a bit, then said, "No, that's not right. We agreed on . . . yes, I know, but they're short—only a page each. Hold on, would you?" He pressed the phone to his arm and whispered to me, "There's something I didn't tell you. When I called Dan to see if he'd help us out, he asked for fifty bucks for the translation. I gave it to him, but now he's saying it's more work than he thought, and he wants a hundred."

"Are you *kidding*?" That wasn't right. Dan should do

the work for the agreed amount. At the same time, I really wanted to know what the entries said. *It's only money*, I told myself. It wasn't like I had a group of Dutch translators at my disposal or anything. "I guess we could—"

Franklin D. put the phone back to his ear. "My friend says seventy-five is as high as she'll go. That's our final offer. If you can't do it for that, then the deal's off. I can stop by right now to pick up the pages if that works for you."

I winced, afraid of Dan's reaction, but seconds later, Franklin D. said, "Good. I'll come by to get the first two then. When will you finish the rest? . . . Okay, fine." He hung up, then growled under his breath like a dog that hears someone fiddling with the doorknob. "I'm going over right now, even if he isn't done with them all."

"I'll pay you back." My first paycheck from Mr. Laramie had come on Friday. For a few seconds, I'd been happy to get the money, but the feeling hadn't lasted. I was Oma's granddaughter—I should be taking care of her for free. In the end, I deposited the check in the bank, telling myself that I needed every cent to pay off Mom's DUI fines.

"My treat. I have some bar mitzvah money that I've been saving to spend on the perfect girl with a compelling mystery," Franklin D. said.

I laughed to hide the unexpected impact of the words. *Perfect girl.*

"I'll be back with the entries, as fast as a blur," he said.

He darted out of the house before the *thank you* could form on my lips.

. . .

186

Two hours later, he handed me a flyer advertising an eighty-dollar rebate on a set of Goodyear tires. On the back were Dan's notes, slanting down the unlined paper.

"I had a bad feeling about that dude the first time I called him on the phone," Franklin D. said. "I wouldn't have given him the job if I knew someone else who spoke Dutch. Before I even met him, I was obsessing that he might try to sell the pages if they had anything to do with Anne Frank."

I hadn't considered that. Would an unscrupulous private collector be willing to pay Dan for a few pages that mentioned her?

"So I made copies and kept the originals safe and sound right here." He patted a green folder beside him.

"Oh, I get it. The age of the entries can't be proven with a copy. It could be a forgery that someone made last week," I said.

Franklin D. grinned.

"You're really smart, you know that?" I inched closer, eager to decipher Dan's lousy handwriting.

The door swung open. Oma stood there, wagging a wooden spoon at us. "Who ate my goddamn cookies?"

The last thing I needed was a meltdown. "Not us, Oma, but I'll make you some more later, okay?"

"It was the Jews! They'll eat anything, even bread made from sawdust."

I cringed. Vickie ran into the room, drying her hands on her pants. "Oh, there you are!" she said to Oma. "I can't even go to the bathroom without you causing trouble."

"She wasn't causing trouble," I said.

Vickie's gaze landed on the translation. Franklin D. shifted to block her view.

"Did you steal my cookies?" Oma accused her.

Vickie plunked a hand down on her shoulder. "Don't be a silly goose." She led Oma out of the room. We heard her say, "You can forget about the cookies. Next time, stay in bed, or else . . ."

Free from prying eyes, we returned our attention to Dan's translation. The auto mechanic's handwriting looked like a seismograph reading of a 7.2 earthquake. I drew in a tight breath and began to read.

CHAPTER

EIGHTEEN

WHILE DECIPHERING THE PUZZLING INTERPRETATION,
I tasted blood. I hadn't realized I'd been gnawing at the
chapped skin on my bottom lip. I wiped my hand across my
mouth and stared at Dan's notes.

"That train trip from Auschwitz to Bergen-Belsen . . ."
I stopped, dizzy from an assault of emotions. Reading this,
I couldn't help but imagine myself on the transport in a
crammed freight car, where everyone—men and women
together—shared latrine buckets. The words "retching" and
"smells" were enough to make something unmentionable
climb up my throat. That wasn't the worst part, though. Dan
had scrawled a series of disjointed words on the page: *Train
halt. Dead bodies. Dragged/dumped/thrown away.* When Franklin
D. left to get a glass of water, I pulled out my phone to research.
Yes, the trains had stopped multiple times, always for the same
purpose. Friends, relatives, lovers—dead from suffocation or
exposure to the elements—tossed out like trash.

"I wish these notes made more sense," Franklin D. said.

In a way, I was glad that Dan could only pluck individual
words from the entry. Whole sentences might do me in. I saw

it all through Oma's eyes, making each word more intense, more real.

The first entry ended with the train's arrival at the camp. The barracks were full, so the Nazis moved the women to a tent. They slept on hay and mud, huddled against the cold German November. Bergen-Belsen seemed no better than a chicken factory, overcrowded and unsanitary.

"What's this part about the stars?" Franklin D. asked.

Dan had written, *M. says imagine stars above us.*

"I'm not sure," I said. "But I don't think pretending helped."

Franklin D. rifled through the folder and pulled out an original entry. "Do you think we should try to find a sample of your grandma's handwriting?"

"Okay," I said, though it seemed obvious to me that Oma was the author of the diary. I'd found it in her house. But I led the way to the library and went to her desk.

"Is everything all right, Livvy?" Vickie called from the kitchen.

"Just doing homework." It was Saturday night. I never did homework then, but she didn't know that.

In the middle drawer, I found an old shopping list.

> *bread*
> *eggs*
> *cheese the orange kind*
> *lima beans*
> *canned chili*
> *mashed beans in a can*

The letters on the list were more upright than slanted, written with a shaky hand. I tried to focus on the handwriting, but all I could think about was Oma's dementia. When she'd written this, she'd already forgotten the words for *cheddar* and *refried beans*. The writing on the entry was more compressed. I pictured a younger version of my grandmother trying to cram her thoughts on the scrap of paper.

"I'm no handwriting expert, but they look a little different," Franklin D. said, watching me carefully.

"Of course they would. That was over seventy years ago. Time changes everyone's writing, especially with Alzheimer's."

"Yeah," he said after a moment.

"It affects fine motor skills," I added.

We returned the list to the drawer and stepped out into the hallway. Vickie stood by the kitchen door, phone to her ear. She watched us walk into the living room.

Back on the couch, Franklin D. took out Dan's translation of the second entry, also from November 1944. I ignored the lump in my throat and began to read about a storm that had barreled through Bergen-Belsen one night. Oma had been too scared to go inside the tent, but her sister made her. It "groaned" in the wind, Dan wrote. And then the unthinkable happened. The whole thing collapsed. Women screamed. People tripped over one another, blindly pushing toward the exit.

Here, Dan interpreted a full sentence: "Someone called, 'Frank girls, over here!'" The sisters had followed the voice to the exit, clinging to each other.

After that, there was a string of question marks. I swallowed my annoyance at our interpreter's laziness and moved to the next part. A guard named Irma had a dog, a half-starved animal that Dan wrote "liked the taste of human flesh." I wondered if it had been Irma who'd led the drenched women to a barrack that night, where they slept for a single hour before being woken for roll call.

My eyes reversed a few lines, reading the two words Franklin D. had found before: *Frank girls*. The meaning hit me like a dodge ball to the head. "You want to compare the writing to Oma's because . . . because you don't think my grandma wrote this at all. You think *Anne Frank* did?"

It was hard to wrap my mind around it. This was my grandmother's journal. In Oma's house. On her bookshelf. *You have to find my journal!* That's what she'd said.

Franklin D. confirmed my thought with a nod.

"Maybe someone called out to the Frank girls, but it was Oma and her sister who followed the voice," I reasoned.

He took a folded piece of paper out of his pocket. "I printed a sample of Anne Frank's handwriting that I found online. We didn't have the translation back yet—but . . . well, just look."

I stared at the bold, determined strokes. The way the G's and the Y's dipped down, pulling to the right as if the words were in a race to make it off the page. I turned back to the original entry. I had to admit, they looked similar.

Franklin D. covered my hand with his. "I know you were hoping to learn about your grandmother."

The unexpected sympathy brought tears to my eyes. "No,

I'm okay," I said, shaking off disappointment. "I mean, this is unbelievable." I took a moment to let it sink in. If this really *was* Anne Frank's concentration camp diary, it would be an incredible find. Not just for us, but the world. That definitely outweighed learning more about my grandmother's past.

"When I first tried to translate them myself," Franklin D. said. "I checked if there were names on the four pages. I found mostly initials, but there was one that was interesting . . ."

"What?"

"Pim."

Chills spread up my arms. "Anne's nickname for her father." A thought wormed its way into my head. Franklin D.'s photocopy would stop Dan from selling the journal if it belonged to Oma, but not if Anne Frank had written the entries. "Dan could still sell them!" I blurted out. "He won't get as much as he would with an original, but he could still use the handwriting to prove that Anne wrote it . . ."

Franklin D. cupped his fingers behind his head. He smiled, slow and knowing. "Too bad he doesn't have her handwriting."

I looked at him, lost.

"Like I said before, I was on my way to see him when it dawned on me that it was a stupid idea to give him the originals. Unfortunately I'd left my portable copy machine in my backpack, so I had to write them out by hand." He took out the version he'd shared with Dan. Franklin D.'s handwriting looked different from either Oma's or Anne's.

I was impressed. "Wow, it must've taken you forever to write those pages out."

He looked at me in the strangest way as if I was a new breed of animal at the zoo. Feeling self-conscious, I tightened my ponytail.

"The entries were short, but it was pretty hard to write a foreign language," he admitted. "I guess it's not Dan's fault that he couldn't translate some of it. My handwriting doesn't just suck in English, apparently."

"Well, I think you're brilliant," I said. Before I knew it, my lips were against his cheek. His hair smelled like the beach. I pulled back, laughing to hide my embarrassment.

He lowered his hands to his lap and studied them. "I like how you say thank you."

I picked up the throw pillow and clasped it to my chest. "Here's something I don't get: Why would Oma have Anne Frank's concentration camp diary in the first place? It doesn't make sense that she'd hide it from the world for seventy-three years. If it belonged to Anne, Oma would've given it to Otto Frank as soon as she found out he was alive."

It dawned on me that if this went public, people might be angry that Oma had kept it for so long, no matter what her reasons. Alzheimer's couldn't explain the decades that had passed.

Franklin D. shook his head. He didn't have answers, either. If only I could ask Oma. I studied the rug in front of the armchair: an intricate display of swirls and flowers trapped inside a dark green border. Once again, I felt defeated by my grandmother's disease.

"I better put the originals back in the library for safe-keeping," I said. But not in the books. Oma might dump them on the floor again.

We heard a noise out in the hallway. I looked at Franklin D., then crept to the door. When I opened it, Vickie stood there, crystal pitcher in one hand. She almost dropped the two glasses with handles that were hooked on her pinkie. "I was about to knock," she said. "I wanted to apologize for being short with you before. It's been a lousy day of fending off bill collectors. I thought I could make it up to you with some lemonade. Any takers?"

"Thanks, but . . . ," I started, my voice unsteady.

Franklin D. moved beside me, his hand molding into the curve of my back. "We'd love some. Thank you." He took the pitcher and cups and smiled. But I knew him by now. When his smile petered out before reaching his eyes, something was wrong.

Vickie excused herself and left. Franklin D. waited, listening for the kitchen door to shut. He stood there until he heard her turn on the faucet.

"Do you think she was spying on us?" I whispered.

"I don't think so," he said, heading back to the couch. "Or if she was, I don't think she could have figured out what we were talking about." I noticed that he left the door open so we would know if she came back.

I considered what had been said, what Vickie might have heard. The translation notes? Our conversation about who wrote them? Maybe she was bringing us lemonade, like she said, and hadn't heard anything at all.

We returned to Dan's notes. Franklin D. inched closer to me, reading them again. I tried not to focus on the hairs of his arm, which tickled mine.

"Irma," I said after a moment.

"What?"

"First, Oma mentions that name, and then it's here, in this entry." I pointed to the laptop on the mantel. "Let's see what we can find out."

Franklin D. went to get the laptop and plopped down beside me, closer than before. A tap on the space bar raised the password prompt.

"You have to go to my login, not hers," I said, showing him where to find it. "My password's twenty-three Dogwood. That's my old address in Vermont."

"Why do you and Vickie have separate login screens?"

"Because her 'work and private life must be kept separate,'" I said, exaggerating Vickie's twang.

From another room, we heard Oma shout at the neighbor's dog. Peeing on the tree again, no doubt. I heard Vickie tell Oma to calm down in a voice that was decidedly uncalm. I turned back to Franklin D. "The irony is, I know her password anyway."

I hoped Franklin D. didn't think I'd been spying on Vickie. When I passed by her the other day, I caught the string of numbers. They weren't hard to see. She pecked so slowly that I considered buying her the SpongeBob SquarePants typing program for Christmas.

"I can't turn off my kind of brain," I told him. "Especially numbers. They burn into my memory."

"So what are you waiting for? Spit it out."

I laughed. "I might've missed one."

"Let's try and see."

"The first three digits match an area code in Michigan." I pointed out. Vickie says her boyfriend lives in the Midwest, so maybe it's his phone number, but I only saw nine numbers."

Franklin D.'s lips curled into a mischievous smile. "Seems to me there's only one way to find out."

I balked. "It's her password! And besides, I don't care to know more about her."

"I have no interest in reading Vickie's lovestruck e-mails. I'm fascinated by your mind. It's damn sexy."

To be honest, I was curious if it would work, too. I rattled off the numbers.

"Whoa, slow down."

I repeated it. Sure enough, Vickie's desktop pulled up on the screen. Franklin D. grinned. "I'm just curious. How many numbers of pi do you know?"

"Well since you asked, I memorized the first twenty-three in elementary school, but then it got boring, so I moved on."

He laughed. I nodded to the screen. Franklin D. typed *Irma* and *Bergen-Belsen* into the search engine. Images of the female Nazi warden made my heart stutter. The woman's cold eyes focused to the side like she was drawn by something shocking. Her expression was as stiff as the collared shirt that protruded from her knitted vest. Even the ringlets in her hair looked rigid as metal pipes.

Franklin D. switched to the Jewish Virtual Library website. He clicked on a link that described the "most notorious of the female Nazi war criminals" and how she beat women prisoners to death with a plaited whip.

"'Acts of pure sadism, beatings and arbitrary shooting of prisoners, savaging of prisoners by her trained and half starved dogs,'" I read out loud, choking on the description.

I wondered if Franklin D. remembered Oma's exact words: *Irma says, 'Wash outside or you will die, dirty Jew!' She snaps her whip and calls her dogs.*

"She was executed a few months after the war ended," Franklin D. said.

Irma Grese was twenty-two when she died. In the photograph, she looked twice as old. Hate and evil had a way of aging a person.

As Franklin D. cleared the history and shut down the computer, I thought of Vickie's expression when I'd opened the door earlier. Now I realized she looked a little like Irma Grese in this photo, staring with disapproval at something happening outside of camera range.

NINETEEN

I CARRIED THE FOLDER WITH THE PAGES, REAL AND
fake, to school with me on Monday. I wasn't ready to let it
out of my sight.

After a quiz, or when a teacher gave extra class time for
homework, I read Dan's notes again.

My grandma's past was as much a mystery as it had ever
been. I wondered if she'd suffered through the same storm
that had collapsed Anne and Margot's tent. Maybe Oma had
been bunkmates with the sisters in the women's barrack?
They might have become friends. Anyway, I could still learn
a lot about my grandmother through Anne's words. Having
decided that, I could hardly wait for the last two entries from
Dan.

After school, I made sure Vickie was occupied before
ducking into the library to hide the folder. After dismissing
the too-obvious desk drawers, I considered the file cabinet.
Oma would have to slide the knob to the right while pulling
the drawer at the same time. She couldn't pull off the
coordination, I was sure of it. I sandwiched the folder behind
the gas and electric bills from August 2001, the month and

year I was born. It would be safe there. A person would need an asthma inhaler to survive the dust cloud.

As I was closing the cabinet door, I spotted a folder marked PUBLISHER that I hadn't noticed before. Inside were two letters. The first was dated March 22, 1987.

> *Dear Anonymous,*
>
> *Per our phone conversation yesterday, we are pleased to publish your memoir titled* Bergen-Belsen: An Insider's Account *for our Spring 1989 list, under the pseudonym "Anonymous."*
>
> *Our committee feels that this is an important work with a voice and perspective that will intrigue a wide readership. A contract will follow shortly, as well as an editorial letter sent to the post office box provided.*
>
> *As discussed, in order to assure an appropriate level of privacy, and for your own safety, please provide a bank account number so that the advance and any future royalties may be deposited in a prompt and secure manner.*
>
> *Thank you again for permitting us to take a role in bringing this important work to light.*

A memoir! All my questions about Bergen-Belsen and Oma's life could be answered within the pages of that book. It was probably out of print by now, but there had to be a copy somewhere. I'd pay anything to fill in the blanks. The memoir might even give a hint as to why my grandmother had Anne's camp diary.

I pulled out the next letter.

Dear Marla,

I deeply appreciate your devotion to my Bergen-Belsen memoir. It takes courage to publish such a perspective, one that could cause an unknowable disruption to both publisher and author. It is for those reasons that I have made the difficult decision to pull it at this time. I know it is highly irregular at this stage of development, but I fear the attention it may bring us all. I am returning the advance to you, in its entirety, along with my most sincere apologies.

There was no signature, but the meaning was clear: Oma had chickened out. I didn't get it. This letter was written in the 1980s, long after the war was over. So much about the Holocaust had already been said. I pushed my sleeves up and studied the letter a second time. Why would Oma want to be anonymous, anyway?

My imagination kicked into gear. What could she have done that would cause her to pull the project? Perhaps something scandalous had happened, like she'd had an affair with the enemy. Could my grandmother have killed a Nazi officer? That last one would make her a hero in some people's eyes, but others might not see it that way. I wondered if she'd feared retribution.

All I knew was that I had to find the memoir. My grandmother's story was probably in the house, but where? Maybe it was with the missing photo albums. Oma had trashed the library in a frantic search for the journal pages. I hoped she hadn't thrown the memoir out after retracting it from the publisher. I honestly couldn't tell how much of her volatile behavior was brought on by the disease, or if she'd been this way her whole life.

I searched through the library again, but gave up a half hour later. I wanted to check the rest of the house, but I couldn't—not as long as Vickie was around.

As I reached for the edge of the bookshelf to pull myself up, I noticed something strange. *Vanity Fair* beside Oscar Wilde's *The Picture of Dorian Gray*. I looked at some other books: *Dracula*, *Anna Karenina*, *Oliver Twist* . . . all shelved in the wrong spots.

Oma couldn't have been the one to move them—she would have just dumped the books on the floor. That left one person. I remembered Vickie's gasp as I'd opened the door yesterday, the pitcher trembling in her hands. Had I mentioned putting the pages back on the bookshelf?

The file cabinet didn't seem like a safe place to hide the journal anymore. I studied the room for a few minutes before finding a solution. Flipping the couch cushion over, I ran my fingers along the seams until I hit the invisible zipper. Then I buried the file—Anne's entries and Franklin D.'s handwritten copies, along with the translation notes—in a sea of foam pellets.

. . .

When Vickie and I changed shifts an hour later, I told the lie.

"Did you know Oma wrote short stories?"

Vickie moved the Dell over to make room for my plate of chocolate chip cookies. I took a sip of milk and continued. "I found something that Oma wrote a long time ago."

202

Her eyes stayed on me like a hawk watching a mouse. "I thought she was a poet."

"I guess she dabbled in other stuff. Like, she wrote this amazing story about Anne Frank's diary. You know, what it might've said if Anne had written it in a concentration camp. It was pretty creative, actually."

"Can I see?" Vickie said. "I'd love to read it. It's always nice to know something about the people you take care of. It's a reminder of their human side."

My stomach turned. I stuffed a cookie in my mouth, chewing slowly, to give myself time to think.

"I wish, but I took it to school. Bonehead move. A friend of mine spilled chocolate milk on it, and I had to throw it out. There wasn't much to it, anyway. Only a few paragraphs."

"Oh," Vickie said, looking disappointed.

The story felt weak, but it was all I could come up with under pressure.

Vickie logged off the laptop and stood up. "I didn't get a chance to feed your grandmother before she fell asleep. There's broccoli and chicken pasta in the fridge from a few days ago. Should still be good."

Leftovers more than a day old turned my stomach, but I nodded, fixing a smile on my face. "Got it. Thanks."

"You're welcome. See you tomorrow morning."

I listened as Vickie dropped off the computer in the living room, then clomped to the front door with no attempt to be quiet. My grandmother's naps were only important when they made her shifts easier.

I texted Franklin D.: *Looks like I'm as good a liar as the rest of my family.*

When Vickie left, I searched the rest of the house for the memoir. Nothing. Exhausted, I fell onto the living room couch and used the computer to search for Anne Frank facts. I was soon caught up in what had happened to the eight residents of the "Secret Annex" after they'd been arrested. First they went to Westerbork, a "transit" camp in the Netherlands where they had to break apart dusty batteries. A month later, they were sent out on the last train to ever leave Westerbork. If only they'd been able to hide in the attic for a little longer, they would've spent the rest of the war at the transit camp—a much safer place than Auschwitz, which would one day be called "the world's largest grave."

After arriving in Auschwitz, the men and women were separated. That was the last time Anne and Margot Frank saw their father. Two months later, the sisters were transferred to Bergen-Belsen, this time without their mother. They did end up traveling with one original resident. As I read his name, I thought about one of Dan's notes that I hadn't understood the first time. He'd written, *they took v.P. away.*

In the annex diary, Anne had referred to him as "Van Daan" to protect his identity, but the man's real name had been Auguste van Pels.

Finally I checked out the separate living sections in Bergen-Belsen. About three thousand women, most of them arriving from Auschwitz, were immediately shuttled to temporary housing. Tent living was worse than I'd gleaned from the entry. No electricity, water, heat, or toilets.

These prisoners were sent to Bergen-Belsen to die.

TWENTY

I WAS LYING ON MY BACK, WATCHING THE ICICLE-drop chandelier throw rainbow darts on the wall, when Mom called.

"Hi, sweetie," she whispered.

I bolted upright. "Mom! I thought it was against the rules to call me."

"I borrowed a friend's phone, but they're giving mine back soon for good behavior. Anyway, I miss you so much that I had to call and say hi."

"It feels like you've been gone for so long."

"I know, but I'm almost done. I'm flying back a week from tomorrow. My flight gets in at two fifteen on Friday."

I wanted to ask how rehab had gone. Had it helped? Would it stick this time? "That's great, Mom."

There was an awkward silence. I tried to come up with something neutral to say but drew a blank. Finally Mom asked, "How was your Halloween?"

Yes! That was a safe subject. "One of my friends, Elizabeth, was a singing water bottle—she just got the lead in our school musical—and I was her sidekick, a recycle bin. You know Kermit's song, 'It's Not Easy Being Green'? Elizabeth sang it all over school, only she gave it a cool environmental twist, and I danced around—well, as much as I could in a trash can costume." I ran out of air and had to take a breath. "We actually raised one hundred and three dollars and forty-two cents for the Trash Museum in Berkeley," I finished.

"I'd love to meet her. She sounds great."

"I'd like that, too," I said, thinking how Mom would love Franklin D. and his outspoken personality. I almost told her about him but didn't. I couldn't handle a ton of nosy questions right now. "So, what's it like in Vermont?" I asked.

"Gorgeous. The leaves look like they're on fire. The best part is, I don't have to rake them."

I was the one who'd done the raking. "Can we afford this place? Evergreen, I mean."

"Mr. Laramie's arranged everything. It will come out of my trust."

"But you haven't gotten it yet." I didn't like to think about that part, no matter how it would make our lives easier. Getting that money would mean my grandmother wouldn't be around anymore.

"This is an advance." Her businesslike voice brought back the pathetic relationship between her and Oma. I thought about all Mom and I had gone through in the past month— the vodka bottle behind the armchair, the harrowing ride through Pacific Heights, her arrest. Her drinking problem didn't have to ruin us. I couldn't let our relationship turn out like theirs.

"This place would be a perfect vacation if it weren't for all the work they make me do," she said.

"They make you work?" I pictured Anne Frank's family, hands black from grimy old batteries. I shook my head, wishing the images would leave me alone.

Mom giggled. "On myself, silly. Therapy's a bitch."

"Oh."

"So how's it going on the West Coast? Are you managing?"

"It's okay." I filled her in on Oma's condition, how she'd lost some agility and balance. I explained how she never let me dress her, even though it took her a half hour to put her blouse on.

"Liv, I just want to say thank you for all you've done. For her, for us. I know it hasn't been easy."

The worst part was watching Oma deteriorate. But I knew Mom saw it through a different lens, and the last thing I wanted to hear right now was how it would all be better soon. "Everything's fine," I said.

Mom heard someone and gave a clipped good-bye. A second later my cell rang again. I propped myself on an elbow and switched the phone to my other ear. "Hello?"

"Dan dropped the rest of the translation off. It's killing me not to look."

"Don't you dare!" I told Franklin D. "I want to see it with you."

"Then I'm coming over right now."

"Don't your parents wonder why you're at my house so much?"

"I've found a way around that problem. I said I was dating a Jewish girl, so now my mom's willing to drive me anywhere, anytime."

"You didn't!"

"Yeah, um, I kind of did. They were thrilled, Liv. You won them over at Shabbat."

I paused. "Now I can't come to your house without them thinking . . . well, you know."

"Is that so bad?"

That stopped me. Was it? I didn't know.

"I'll bring the entries over right now. See you soon." He hung up before I could think of an answer.

I heard Vickie rustling in the hallway, getting ready to leave. At least I wouldn't have to worry about her big ears when Franklin D. and I looked over the new translation. The reshelving of the books still bugged me. It had to have been her—who else?

When I came out of my room, she was zipping up her coat. "So, what are you up to tonight?" she asked.

My first instinct was to lie, but there was nothing to hide. "Franklin D.'s coming over for a while."

Her mouth puckered in disapproval. "Did you tell your mom that you have a *guy* coming over all the time?"

Why did it feel like Vickie was looking for ways to get me into trouble? Did she really think that because my mom wasn't around, Franklin D. and I were going to act like animals in perpetual mating season? "Not yet. But Mom has bigger issues to deal with. Besides, she trusts me."

"Well I left the laptop in the living room so you and Franklin D. can work on your homework."

"We're just friends, Vickie."

"Very, *very* good friends," she said, imitating Franklin D.

When she strode out the door, I kicked it shut behind her.

. . .

The temperature outside had dropped in the past week. Now it was drizzling. Drops of water beaded in Franklin D.'s hair, capturing the porch light.

We put Oma to bed, and then I went to the kitchen to make us hot chocolate, leaving Franklin D. to light a fire in the fireplace. When I came back, I handed him today's newspaper from the recycle bin and watched him stuff sections under a log. I wasn't sure how to make a fire, having grown up with the electric variety. Our old fireplace was a lot easier to operate, though I loved the smoky wood scent that floated through Oma's living room.

Franklin D. was about to crumple up the front page of the *San Francisco Chronicle* when he said, "Did you see this?" He handed it to me.

I read the headline. Startled, I shook my head.

"Swastikas were painted on the walls of two synagogues in the Sunset district," he said. "Another one on the Jewish Community Center."

"You think it might be a prank?"

"Joke or not, it's anti-Semitic. I hope they nail the bastards."

"But neo-Nazis . . . in San Francisco?" I said. "I picture them hiding in the backwoods somewhere, not hanging out in the most liberal city in the United States."

"Even assholes take vacations," Franklin D. said. I couldn't tell from his solemn expression whether he was kidding or not.

He tossed the rest of the newspaper into the fire. I was glad to see it burn. We moved to the couch, where Dan's new notes waited, this time scrawled on the back of a junk mail envelope.

"For seventy-five bucks, you'd think he'd at least spring for some notebook paper," Franklin D. said. He rested his head against the unyielding cushion and shut his eyes.

I took a moment to prepare myself before we read the next entry, dated February 1945. It seemed that "A" had found an old friend. This was the same entry Franklin D. had mentioned earlier—the one with Anne's nickname for her father. She mentioned Pim when she told her friend about the deaths in the family

I sagged back on the couch, dropping my elbows to my knees. Franklin D. laid a hand on my shoulder.

"If only she'd known her father was alive," I whispered. "She might have fought harder to survive."

I knew how naïve that sounded. Typhus was a powerful disease. Stronger than willpower. The fact was that thousands of people had died during the epidemic, despite thousands of reasons to live.

Franklin D. was kind enough not to comment.

From there, the notes touched on Margot's illness. Dan had translated an entire sentence: *If she dies, I will be all alone in the world.*

In several places, Dan had crossed out his first guess and written a different interpretation above it. I gathered that Anne had returned to meet her friend. The girl brought extra rations for Margot, but another prisoner snatched the package and ran off, leaving Anne empty-handed.

I cringed. I could only imagine how desperate Anne had been to help her sister.

I looked at Franklin D., glad to have finished the page, though I knew there was more to go. "I can't stand reading this, knowing how it will end," I said. Dan's translation of the last entry wasn't dated. "You read it." I thrust it at him.

Franklin D. began to interpret the skeletal outline. "I think this is the part where her sister dies," he said. "She just fell out of the bunk, dead on the floor, and the 'vultures'"—he looked up—"I'm guessing that refers to some prisoners. Anyway, they grabbed Margot's shoes and a heel of bread under her pillow." It took two roll calls that day before the head count matched the roster.

I skipped ahead to some words Dan had written in quotes. "What does that say?" My eyes were too blurred to read it myself. Also, it seemed less frightening when sifted through Franklin D.'s voice.

He took a deep breath. "It says, 'I asked everyone, *Have you seen my sister*? I asked again and again, despite getting the same answer each time.'"

I was silent as Franklin D. kept reading.

"She's not well," he told me. "She says she wants to be remembered for more than the numbers on her arm."

I brushed my fingers up my own arm.

"Wait a sec . . . ," he said, a spark of hope in his voice.

"What?"

"Hold on." I watched his eyes skip back and forth over the same sentences. "She might get on a train. I think she has a new friend. Maybe from the infirmary, because she's sick now. She's telling the friend that the train is her last hope, only . . ."

"Only what?"

Franklin D. looked up at me, the hope stamped out. "Dan doesn't say."

"Oh my God," I gasped, flipping the paper over. "Where's the rest? Where is it?" I searched Franklin D.'s eyes for the unanswerable.

Unanswerable, because there wasn't any more.

This was all there was.

TWENTY-ONE

At noon on Sunday, Franklin D. and I met at the park by his house. I knew he expected me to climb off the bus near the playground where we were supposed to meet, but I walked the three miles instead. I needed time to sort the chaotic thoughts competing in my head.

I had to bring sense to an insensible theory.

By the time I got there, I was ready.

. . .

The park was empty except for a border collie that appeared on the hill behind us. The dog retrieved his ball from a flower bed and vanished into a row of bushes.

I sat down on the swing, Franklin D. beside me. "Did you know that *The Diary of Anne Frank* has been published in at least sixty-seven languages?" I said.

"Nope, can't say that I did."

"In 1955, they made it into a play. It won the Pulitzer Prize." I pushed off the ground, pumping my legs, rising higher. "Four years later, it became a movie. It won three Academy Awards, and Shelley Winters got an Oscar for Best Supporting Actress, which she donated to the Anne Frank House in Amsterdam."

Franklin D. sat motionless, mulling it over, as I flew past him. Finally he said, "Are you aware that you rely on facts when you're feeling emotional?"

I dug my heels into the dirt, jerking to a stop. "So, what's wrong with that? Facts tell the truth better than feelings."

"I disagree," he said. "You need both."

He sounded like my mother. "I'm not talking about *me* here. I'm talking about a book that's impacted millions of lives. A diary that symbolizes almost six million Jews who died during the Holocaust."

"*Almost* six million?" Franklin D. teased.

"Technically, 5,860,000, but *normal* people round it up for ease."

"I hate that word."

Ironically I wanted to say something *not* so normal. What I was thinking was completely unfactual, irreverent, so outlandish as to be potentially disrespectful to Anne Frank's memory.

"There were thousands of people on the last three transports out of Bergen-Belsen," I said. "Almost all of them were Dutch citizens. Prisoners of political consequence to use as barter for captured Germans. The thing was, Anne's father was in charge of a successful company. She should have been on that train, but no one knew that. Her father wasn't with her anymore. She was alone, with no one to help."

I slid my hand into my pocket for an article by Rabbi Joseph Polak. I handed it to Franklin D. I was impatient as he read and interrupted, "The first train—the one Anne mentioned in her pages—traveled for six days before it was liberated by the Americans." I guess I was as ready as I was going to be. "But what if Anne got on the train somehow? What if she was so sick that when it finally stopped, she wandered off, and someone took her to a local home to recover?" I summed up the last paragraph for him. "Most of the passengers said the trip was a haze."

I shut up so he could read the article again in peace.

"It doesn't mention Anne Frank at all," he said a minute later. "I don't get why she'd be on that transport, anyway. I can see why she'd *want* to be on it, but she wasn't from the barrack where most of the prisoners came from."

"Sternlager," I offered, recognizing that I was straddling the line between knowledgeable and know-it-all. "It was where important Dutch citizens lived. If her dad had been at Bergen-Belsen, that's where they would've stayed."

Franklin D. let out a whispered sigh. "The history books say Anne died in March. Maybe even February, a month or two before Bergen-Belsen was liberated. Didn't some women in the barracks say they thought Anne had died a day after her sister?"

"This magazine I read, *Scientific American*, says eyewitness accounts are highly unreliable. Especially under stressful circumstances." A wet tennis ball skipped over my foot. I kicked it down the hill, and the collie bounded after it. "Look, there isn't proof that it happened. But there isn't proof that it *didn't*, either. Like I said, facts tell the truth better than feelings."

"A barrack leader said she saw Anne in a coma."

"What if she was confused? What if she just *thought* it

215

was Anne?" I said. "People died all the time, every day. Even if it was her, someone might have taken her to the hospital. What if she got better?"

"She had typhus, Liv. It's a deadly disease, especially if a person's not eating decently and living in dirty conditions. Anne's sister died of it. They were both buried in a mass grave."

"But did anyone see their bodies?" I knew the answer because I'd researched it.

"A lot of people were buried in those graves. Just because they weren't identified doesn't mean they didn't die." His voice was soft, as if he wanted to be respectful of my new way of thinking, even if he believed, deep down, that it was crap.

The sun ducked behind the clouds. I tucked my hands under my armpits to keep warm. "I'm just saying . . . oh, never mind."

Franklin D. studied me for a moment. "No, wait. Let's talk this out. If Anne *had* survived, wouldn't she have run to her father as soon as she learned he was alive? She loved her dad more than anyone."

"People don't look for relatives they think are dead. Not to mention, she was near death herself. It probably took her a while to recover."

"But she would have found out he was alive when her diary was published."

"Maybe she *did* go see him. What if they decided together that she should stay underground? I mean, by that time, the world had put her on a pedestal as a symbol for the Holocaust, right?"

"Interesting," he admitted. "As a Jew, I get that. It wouldn't

216

be easy for her to say, 'Hey, everybody, look at me, I didn't die after all.'"

"The book, the play, the movies . . . Anne Frank was arguably the single most important connection that people had with the Holocaust," I said. "If it were you, wouldn't you have asked, What has more impact, my death or my life?"

"Maybe," Franklin D. conceded.

This wasn't the wildest part of my theory. Not even close. "Last night, I woke up at three in the morning. The word *chatterbox* was stuck in my head. I wondered if Oma had used it for a more logical reason than because she heard Anne Frank tell a story in the hospital."

Franklin D. saw where I was going with this, I could tell. He answered my question, but not in the way I expected. "The chatterbox story is in the attic diary. Anyone could have read it there."

Defending wacky theories was more his style than mine. Still, I had to see this through. "Oma once said something about a 'last train out.' I thought she meant the one my mother got on, which was the last time my mom came to San Francisco to visit her, but now I'm wondering if she meant something else." My words filled the space around us, blocking out the street sounds.

"What exactly are you saying, Liv?"

Franklin D. was going to make me say it. He was going to make me claim a theory that no one else in the world shared. I couldn't shake a fear that once it was out, it couldn't be taken back.

I did it, anyway. "I think my grandmother is Anne Frank."

TWENTY-TWO

WE CREPT INTO THE HOUSE AND VEERED RIGHT.
Franklin D. waited in my bedroom. I headed to the kitchen
to pour the gallon of milk down the drain. Step one in my
plan.

I found Vickie in Oma's room, tucking a sheet around
my grandmother's legs. Oma's eyes were closed. She had the
sweetest smile on her face, like she was dreaming wonderful
things.

Vickie noticed me standing by the door. She pressed a
finger to her mouth. I waited for her to finish, then trailed
behind her to the kitchen, where she snapped, "Yes?"

"We're out of milk."

"That's not possible. I just bought some two days ago."

I shrugged. "Oma's been drinking a lot of it lately."

She looked into the fridge and frowned. "You know I
need milk for my coffee, Livvy. Didn't I ask you to tell me if
it's running low?" She pulled a wad of cash out of her wallet,
peeling off a ten-dollar bill. "Please bring me the receipt so
I can expense it."

"I have homework. I'll get it later."

She gave a dramatic huff. "Fine, I'll go. But you'll have to watch your grandma until I get back."

My smile was so warm, it could start a fire.

After Vickie left, I darted down the hallway and flung open my bedroom door. Franklin D. followed me to Oma's bedroom. She was in the same position Vickie had left her, flat on her back. A snore rumbled in her chest. Franklin D. and I nodded at the same time. I leaned over my grandmother and inched back the sleeve of her blouse, as gently as if I were removing a bandage from a burn wound. Oma didn't move, didn't stop snoring.

When we were in the park, we'd used Franklin D.'s phone to look up Anne Frank's tattoo number on the U.S. Holocaust site. The exact identification record hadn't been preserved, but the site listed a range of possible numbers. Franklin D. started to write them down, but with me around, it was pointless. The facts lodged in my head, an endless reservoir for details that kept to themselves most of the time, but surfaced with random thoughts to remind me of their existence. For as long as I lived, I would never forget that Anne, Margot, and Edith Frank had been inked with numbers that fell between A-25060 to A-25271.

Now, with Oma's arm exposed, we saw the tattoo. Only it wasn't what we expected. An inch-thick black line covered whatever numbers had once existed. The name HERBERT floated above it.

. . .

With Vickie at the store, Franklin D. and I checked that the papers were still hidden in the library. The zipper was in the same position as I'd left it. As I closed the cushion back up, I twisted the tab until the teeth bent. Now it would take scissors to open it. Vickie was a snoop, but she wouldn't destroy furniture to feed her curiosity.

We searched in the kitchen for the memoir. My best guess was that my grandmother had shed her identity after the war, shutting out her child, and maybe even her husband. I was more determined than ever to find the answers that she wouldn't give when she was younger and that she couldn't give now.

"I'm sure she put that tattoo over her camp numbers," I told Franklin D. as I pushed a waffle iron to the side to search the cabinet. I had looked for the memoir there before, but I couldn't rest until I double-checked every inch of the house.

"Don't get ahead of yourself." Franklin D. climbed up on a chair to look on top of the fridge.

I turned to face him. "What do you mean?"

"Granted, it's a compelling idea, but it goes against historical fact."

"You always said facts aren't everything."

"I think it's too early to jump to conclusions." He stepped off the chair and crouched down, peering into the bottom cupboard.

I kneeled beside him. "Anne was born in 1929, which would make her eighty-eight now. Remember when I suggested that Oma had been a kid, listening to Anne's stories, and you said she looked too old now to have been that young? But she could be in her late eighties, right?"

"Doesn't your mom know how old she is?"

"She said Oma pretended to be thirty for a really long time."

Franklin D. laughed. "Sounds like her."

"So?" I waited expectantly.

"Do you think she looks like Anne Frank?" he asked.

I shrugged. I still hadn't found any of her photo albums, and it wasn't easy seeing similarities between a teenager and an old lady. I told him this. "Don't you think it's possible that she might have done something to change her appearance anyway? If she was Anne, people would recognize her after the diary became a best seller."

"What do you mean, like plastic surgery?" Franklin D. asked. "Did they even do that back then?"

"Actually, I read there was an increase after World War II." I'd done my research, and I wanted Franklin D. to know every bit of it. "When the injured soldiers stopped coming in, the doctors targeted women to keep their practices going." I saw the skepticism on his face. "What? You think this is crazy?"

Franklin D. shook his head. "Just playing devil's advocate here."

Well, don't, I thought.

"If the average life expectancy of an inmate at Bergen-Belsen was only nine months," he continued, "and in March, alone, 18,168 people died . . . it would take a miracle for a girl as sick as Anne Frank to have survived."

It was both sweet—and frustrating—that he'd memorized facts to persuade me.

"Let's keep looking for the memoir," Franklin D. said when I didn't respond. "Why don't you check the pantry? Didn't you say your mom found some stuff that Oma had put in there?"

"Yeah, her purse," I said.

I looked behind the boxes of cereal. Most were open and long expired. I started to chuck them, but Franklin D. stopped me. "Vickie has to find things exactly the way she left them."

We moved into the living room next, even though we'd looked there many times before. I peered under the couch, hoping to find a manuscript obscured by dust. Franklin D. lifted the heavy drapes off the floor, searching for a hiding spot within the folds of velvet.

"It's not in this room," I said. I crossed the floral rug to the porcelain Siamese cat, staring haughtily at us from the fireplace hearth. I gave a cursory glance behind it and froze. Franklin D. came to my side. A tiny green dot glowed on the baby monitor. I turned it off. How long had it been there? And why?

We heard a click at the door. I barely had time to step back from the hearth when Vickie walked into the room, holding a gallon of milk. "I'm back. I'm going to go put this in the fridge." Her eyes swung away from me, narrowing for a flash before her lips curved into a smile. "Hello, Franklin."

D. I thought to myself. *Franklin D.*

"Hi, Vickie," he said.

"Listen, since I have you both here, I want to extend the olive branch. I know it's been a stressful time since Gretchen left. For all of us. Livvy, I know you've gone through a lot since moving here. As for me, it's been hard to make ends meet on a caregiver's salary, but the job market's horrible right now."

I wanted to see how Franklin D. was reacting to her sob

222

story, but I didn't dare take my eyes off Vickie's face.

"Anyway, I won a gift certificate to a restaurant through this radio contest," she continued. "It's a good place, right downtown, but definitely a steak and potatoes joint. I'm thinking about going vegetarian, so I thought you might want to have it. It's worth a hundred dollars. You can have a good meal for that. Oh, and I hear it's a nice place for couples." She winked at me, which made me want to bend over the settee and throw up. "It has to be used this Tuesday, though."

"My shift starts at five," I said.

She shrugged. "It won't kill me to work a few extra hours. You can owe me the time."

"Thanks," Franklin D. said, his voice flat.

Vicky pulled the certificate out of her purse. She handed it to Franklin D.

"Yeah, thanks," I repeated.

"You're welcome. I just hope you know that when your mother gets back on Friday, the three of us will make a great team for your grandmother."

When she left, Franklin D. switched off the monitor. "I think she's been listening so she can catch you doing something irresponsible, like making out with me on your shift," he whispered. "Then she can tell Mr. Laramie and get you out of the picture."

"If she's out to get me, then why would she give us her gift certificate?"

He grinned. "Who knows, but a free meal's a free meal."

I smiled uneasily.

"You know, I bet she's worried about job stability with your mom coming back," he mused. "You heard what she said about the three of you making a great team, right? She's keeping her options open. If she can't get rid of you, she wants to join you."

I rolled my eyes. Fat chance of that.

I looked behind the porcelain cat again, verifying that the green light on the monitor was still off. "Could Vickie know about the diary pages we found?" I whispered. Between the reshelved books in the library and the hidden monitor, the possibility seemed more likely than ever. But it wasn't as if she needed to send us away somewhere to look for the diary. I was at school eight hours a day. She had more than enough time to search the house.

I was glad that Franklin D. and I had discussed the wildest part of the theory at the park, away from Vickie's spy setup. Then again, I couldn't be sure how long the baby monitor had been recording our conversations. Even if Vickie only had part of the story, the fallout if she blabbed would be major. If Oma really was Anne Frank, a lot of people could be furious that she didn't come forward. Everything she'd sacrificed for the good of society might come back to haunt us. And what about the revisionists that Franklin D. had mentioned that first day in debate class? Would they claim that Anne Frank's "lie" about her death proved that the Jews had also lied about the Holocaust?

"Remember when I told Vickie that Oma had written the entries as a short story?"

Franklin D. nodded. "You said you weren't sure she bought it."

"Well, I'm thinking now would be a good time to re-inforce it."

224

TWENTY-THREE

AFTER A FEW WHISPERED REHEARSALS IN MY ROOM, we returned to the living room. Franklin D. switched the baby monitor back on.

"Look what I found," I began.

"What?"

"I told you those entries were fiction. Here's a letter to Oma from some publisher." I cleared my throat and read from the script we'd prepared. "Thank you for the short story you sent us about Anne Frank's diary from Bergen-Belsen. Unfortunately, at this time, we are going to pass. Though the imagery and imagination of the piece are strong, we are hesitant to publish a fictional account of this well-known historic figure."

"What happened to that story? I thought it was pretty good," Franklin D. said.

"Oh, Elizabeth spilled milk all over it. I had to throw it away."

"Too bad. Oma was a decent writer." He waited a second. "Hey, you got any food around here? It's been at least an hour since I last ate."

I laughed. "Yeah, sure. Come on."

When we got to the kitchen, Vickie was typing on the laptop, the baby monitor on the ledge beside her. Franklin D. and I traded looks, then headed to the refrigerator for an afternoon snack.

. . .

On Tuesday, I went directly from school to my room to avoid Vickie. I wanted to get ready for my dinner out with Franklin D., even though the reservation wasn't until six thirty. I'd already looked at the menu online, and I had my order memorized.

Appetizer: Pumpkin, Squash, and Apple Puree Soup
Entrée: Grilled Salmon with Meyer Lemon Relish on a bed of Mashed Potatoes
Dessert: Molten Chocolate Lava Cake

At four, I put on makeup. I'd lightened up on it since coming to San Francisco. But tonight was special. Not because of who I was going with, I told myself, but because I hadn't had a decent restaurant meal in months.

With painstaking effort, I applied foundation, powder, and blush. Even brow-setting gel—I don't know, in case a hurricane blew through town and tried to take my eyebrows with it. When I finished my second application of mascara, I looked in the mirror. Not bad. Except I still had an hour and a half until it was time to go. A little before five, I touched up my lipstick. As I reached into the front pocket of my backpack for passion fruit lip gloss, my hand brushed over the science test I'd gotten back today. I took it out and looked again at the large A+ and the *WAY TO GO!* that Mr. Karnofsky had written on the page. I started to put it back but changed my mind. It didn't deserve to be buried in my three-inch binder. I propped it against my alarm clock where I could see it.

A minute later, Franklin D. called. "I got us a cab since we're living the high life tonight. But man, this driver dude drove like a maniac, and I'm outside your house already. Hey, did you get my text?"

I glanced down at my phone. Sure enough there was his message that he might be getting here "a tad" early.

"Any chance you're ready to go, like, right now?" he asked.

I glanced in the mirror. "Uh, yeah, just about." I checked that my lipstick hadn't smeared.

"Ah, Livvy, you're already beautiful. You don't have to do anything." He let out a sigh. "What was I thinking? You're right. Girls have to do girly things. This is *so* not cool of me. I guess I'm just enthusiastic, that's all." He seemed sincerely apologetic, which was rather charming. "When you're ready, we can go and wait for our reservation at the bar. We'll order Shirley Temples, in honor of Oma."

I laughed. "Sure. I'll be right out."

I straightened my dress and crammed my feet into my favorite pair of killer high heels. Then I slipped out the door, shutting it softly behind me.

. . .

The hostess said she could seat us early, so we followed her to a private corner, carrying our Shirley Temples with us. A red candle glowed in the middle of our table beside a miniature glass vase with a pink-and-white striped rose, snipped below the bloom.

"Wow, this is, uh . . ." Franklin D. struggled to find the word.

"Nice?" I suggested.

"Romantic," he said.

Oh. "It's, um, pretty, too."

We stole peeks at each other as the waiter took our order. I couldn't help but notice that Franklin D. looked handsome in a charcoal-gray jacket, a blue button-down shirt, and khakis. I checked out his shoes, expecting to see sneakers, but his dress shoes shone like black licorice. His unruly curls were tamed, framing his face. Funny that I'd never noticed his chin before. It was strong and square—the kind that's called chiseled when you see it on a male model, which Franklin D. wasn't. But he did have a masculine chin, I'd give him that.

When the waiter brought our soups, we stared silently into our bowls. This place was way too romantic for comfort.

After our entrées came, Franklin D. spun his fork in his pasta and offered me a bite. "Want some?"

"No, thanks."

We debated who had the best meal until the waiter asked if we wanted dessert. "Share?" Franklin D. asked me. "I'm too stuffed to eat one by myself."

"Can you divide a molten lava cake?" I asked the waiter. There was something too intimate about sharing a dessert plate.

"I recommend an *intact* dessert," the waiter said, looking mildly offended. "If we cut it, the chocolate will spill out."

"I feel a tickle in my throat," I lied. "I should probably have my own." The waiter nodded once and walked away.

"I don't want you to get sick because of me," I added lamely.

"No problem," Franklin D. said.

I opened my purse and took out Oma's poem from the

anthology, glad to have something to talk about other than us and this place where people came to propose or celebrate anniversaries.

"Oma wrote this before she was diagnosed with Alzheimer's. It's called 'Anne Frank Kastanjeboom,'" I said. The poem had been one of the earliest clues about my grandmother's identity, I now knew. I'd wanted to share it with Franklin D. before, but the moment hadn't felt right until now. "*Kastanjeboom* means 'chestnut tree' in Dutch," I explained.

Franklin D. was watching me in a way that made my heart flutter like a moth against a window screen. I licked my lips, trying to focus on the page in my hand. "The tree helped Anne feel hopeful when she was in hiding. I mean, it made *Oma* feel hopeful."

The light from the candle flame climbed up the paper as I read aloud.

> *"Stealthily, the blight moves in*
> *rotting the core*
> *from inside out*
> *The spine sways and saps the strength*
> *Leaves decay and*
> *drift down, to the ground*
> *one*
> *on*
> *top*
> *of the other*
> *in heaps, swallowed by the earth.*
> *Still it stands, this chestnut tree,*

reaching up
with tired arms
that creak at night,
but it
doesn't
give in
Hope rests in its boughs.
The boots of the storm
march in, march out,
rocking the tree
to its roots.
Kicking it when it's down.
It lies, a mound
of crippled wood."

For the first time, the poem's meaning, in all its shades, rose to the surface. There were still two stanzas to go. I took a breath, glad I didn't have to hide my sadness from Franklin D. Tears rolled down his cheeks, too.

"An evil wind
that peels the bark, and
shreds the clothes, and
drives bare that which
was beauty.
Hope ends,
a barren place,
toppled down and left to memory
like the others, that came before."

"The first time I saw this, I thought it was about a tree," I said. "A tree that symbolized hope until it fell in a storm many years later. But it's about so much more than that."

"It's a metaphor for the people who were killed in the Holocaust," Franklin D. said, so softly I almost couldn't hear him. "It's a beautiful poem. Beautiful and catastrophic."

I put it back in my purse and looked at him. Really looked at him. People looked different, depending on how you felt about them. For weeks, I'd been watching Franklin D. through a microscope, deconstructing his personality into categorical detail: nerd, goofball, Dungeons & Dragons type. But now, I zoomed out. I could see all of him. The complete deal. And the weird part was, Franklin D. wasn't half bad. Actually he was kind of cute.

I closed my eyes, feeling the heat of Franklin D.'s gaze on my lids. His fingers slid over my hand, and my eyes flew open. Friends didn't think this way. Friends didn't slide hands across the . . .

My thought went unfinished because he leaned forward, mouth close. Then closer. Until he stopped and fastened his eyes on mine, seeking permission. I couldn't look away. I couldn't blink. All I could do was observe the green flecks shooting like rays from the center of his eyes. They were hazel, I realized. Not just brown. My heart was everywhere—in my chest, my throat, my ears, dulling the restaurant noise.

And then my body grew tired of us researching the hell out of each other, measuring if the cliff was safe enough to dive. I reached behind his head, my fingers in his curls, and pulled him to me. His lips were soft and tentative at first, and then resolved. My mind shut down, lost in a moment that was so much more than I'd ever had before. Oh, God, I wanted to keep kissing him forever.

Finally we pulled back to catch our breath. "Where did you learn to *kiss* like that?" I said.

Franklin D.'s voice was a husky whisper. "Dora. Shakespeare Camp. She gave me lessons in exchange for the contraband Milky Ways I snuck in my duffel bag."

"Wow, that was . . . ," I started. "Wow."

"Yeah, it was a *wow*, all right. And stupendous. And fabulous. A prodigiously awesome moment in time that I want to repeat as soon as possible."

My mind emptied as I leaned forward again, our lips touching over the dancing candle flame. Whispers, like white noise, floated from the tables around us.

Wait, what was I doing? My emotions, like waves on a beach, dragged me back into the room. Ripples, then bigger swells. Huge boulder-crashing breakers that knocked me off my feet. And then, suddenly, I was drowning. I pulled away, trying to suck in enough air to form words that could explain the panic roiling inside me.

"I'm not sure we should complicate things," I blurted out. My relationship with Sean had been simple. Straightforward and predictable—the way I liked it.

Franklin D.'s face, ebullient seconds ago, seemed to cave in. Why was he looking at me that way?

"But . . . don't you want to be friends?" I said. "I mean, it's not like you ever made a move on me before or anything."

Franklin D. looked stunned. "*You* insisted on that. I've

232

liked you since the day I saw you, Liv. But you told me you had a boyfriend. Maybe I should apologize for losing my high ethical standards in the moment—" He paused. "But damn, I'm glad it happened."

Heat crept up my cheeks. I'd never bothered to clear up the miscommunication—well, lie—over the breakup text that day. "I'm not with Sean anymore," I confessed. "I'm sorry I never said anything. It just kept me from thinking about you . . . you know, in that way."

"You lied to me?" He stabbed a fork into his molten lava cake, which had arrived without me noticing. The chocolate spread like a mudslide across his plate.

I wanted to go home and dive under my pillow. "I'm sorry."

"I felt the world quake when I kissed you, Liv. Are you saying it was different for you?"

I opened my mouth to speak, but nothing came out. I reached for my water glass and took a long sip.

"You know what I think? I think you're afraid," Franklin D. said. "I think you're terrified that someone will get to know you. *Really* get to know you. Because then you might have to *feel* for once in your life."

"What do you mean? I feel. I feel plenty! I feel like I . . . like I just want to be friends, okay?" My frenzied emotions settled to a simmer. I felt calm, in control again.

Franklin D. balled up the napkin in his lap and tossed it on his plate. "Actually I just realized something. It's *not* okay."

He stood up and I did the same, wobbling in my heels. He opened the bill, then dropped Vickie's gift certificate onto the table. I watched helplessly as he pulled out his wallet and slapped another forty down. "That should cover gratuity, too."

My brain turned into a calculator, informing me that the tip was way too generous at 32 percent. At least I had the sense to let it rot in the graveyard of unspoken facts.

We were in front of the restaurant when the waiter came tearing out. "This certificate doesn't work. My manager says it wasn't issued by our establishment." He looked at us the way I imagined security guards did when teenagers walk into Tiffany's.

I looked at Franklin D. and he looked at me. I turned to the waiter, blinking back tears so I could see him clearly. "I'm so sorry. Someone gave it to us, and—"

Franklin D. peeled off some serious cash. "This should make up for the inconvenience."

The waiter counted the bills carefully, muttered, "Thank you, have a nice evening," in a single breath, and went back inside.

We stood in the misty rain as Franklin D., ever the gentleman, tried to hail a cab for us. I started to thank him, but he held up a finger, cutting me off. I mumbled something about taking the bus, which would save the added fare of two separate stops, and took off down the street. I flagged the Number 36, even though I didn't know where it went. The stink of exhaust engulfed me as the bus pulled to the stop. I knew without looking that Franklin D. wouldn't leave until I was safely on board.

"Are you getting on?" the bus driver asked.

I stood there, not answering. Faces peered out the bus windows.

Franklin D. was right. I used facts to keep people away. They helped categorize life, to make sense of the world in a rational way. I used facts like my grandmother used lies. Our methods were different, but they had the same effect. Neither of us dug deeper, revealing what was inside of us. I didn't want to end up alone, like her, because I hadn't let anyone get to know the real me.

Franklin D. wanted to know me, though.

"I said, are you getting on this bus?" the driver asked again.

I shook my head. The door swung shut.

Sure enough, Franklin D. was still there. I limped back in my too-tight shoes.

"I'm not Sean," he said.

"I know that."

"No, I mean, I'm nothing like him. I'm not cool. I'm not popular. I'm not especially hot to look at, or alluringly distant, or hard to get, or . . ."

"How do you know all that about Sean?"

He shrugged. "He's the generic jerk that most girls fall for."

I smiled. At least I was over that stage.

"I'm just me, Franklin D. Schiller," he continued. "I talk too much. I like to debate everything, which I know annoys some people, but I don't care. I stir up trouble because I'm interested in what people will say. Everyone knows all my secrets because I find it impossible to hide anything—"

I raised a finger to his lips. "That's what I like best about you."

"Which one?"

"All of them." I kicked off my heels and stepped onto the tips of his licorice shoes and kissed him without any hesitation at all.

TWENTY-FOUR

I FLOATED UP THE STEPS TO OMA'S PORCH AND turned to face the cab. Franklin D. raised his fingers to the window and mouthed *good-bye*. I waved back, smiling stupidly. When he was gone, I leaned against the door and breathed the cool, damp air into my lungs. The moment of our last kiss washed over me again.

I stayed like that until I began to shiver, my mind straying to darker thoughts. What had happened with the gift certificate? Could Vickie have planned all along to humiliate me in front of Franklin D.? For reasons I didn't understand, my existence ruffled her feathers.

It was cold on the porch, but I didn't want to go inside, knowing that the night was going to end in a fight. No, I couldn't let Vickie punch a hole in my happiness. But I also couldn't risk hypothermia, so I went into the house, kicked off my heels, and took in the odd stillness. The lights were off. Vickie usually left them all on. I padded past Oma's bedroom, listening to her snore. In the kitchen, I whispered, "Vickie?"

She wasn't there. Not in the living room or the library, either. Franklin D. and I had left for the restaurant early.

Vickie wouldn't expect me back yet. She'd taken off. I couldn't believe it.

I went to check on Oma, but her door wouldn't budge. After rattling the knob for a few seconds, I realized the problem. The door wasn't stuck at all. I stared at the new slide lock installed at the top of the frame. It was one thing for Vickie to leave the house for a few minutes—something else to imprison an old woman in her own bedroom. What if there had been an earthquake or a fire?

I fumed all the way to Vickie's apartment and banged on her door. No answer. I pulled out my phone and dialed her number. The call rang several times before going into voice mail. I didn't bother leaving a message.

Back in the house, I unlocked Oma's door and peered into the bedroom. She was sound asleep. I moved in closer, watching the rise and fall of her chest. "Love you, Oma," I whispered.

Her eyes popped open and she murmured my name, getting it right, before her lids closed, weighted by sleep.

The blanket was at the foot of the bed, folded into the square I'd made this morning. I pulled it over her while silently rehearsing the lecture I would give Vickie when she returned. But, really, what was the point? Mom would be back in three days. It wouldn't be hard to convince Mr. Laramie to let us take care of Oma on our own, without Vickie's help.

I marched into the living room, ready to shout into the monitor, "Where are you?" But it wasn't behind the porcelain cat anymore. The laptop was still on the hearth, though. I considered Vickie's "private" e-mails, wondering if they might give a clue where she'd gone.

After typing in her password, I scanned the usual spam until I found an e-mail from Ryan3Gun@google.com—Vickie's love interest. It was a complaint about how bill collectors wouldn't leave him alone, and would Vickie mind helping out with this month's credit card payment? I went back two weeks, but I couldn't find any others.

I was about to log out when I noticed the trash folder. I opened it and started the search again. Up popped an e-mail Ryan had sent Vickie two days ago. My pulse quickened as I read.

We're on for this Tuesday—stop worrying. You said yourself they won't be back until 8:45 or later. I'll call you when they get them. Rex agreed to the terms the first time—probably should've asked for more. How does Kauai at New Year's sound?

I looked at the clock. It was 7:56. I didn't understand some of this, but obviously Ryan was in town, and he and Vickie had planned to sneak off while Franklin D. and I were at the restaurant.

I dialed Vickie's cell again. The ring echoed in the house. I followed the sound to the kitchen. Vickie had left her phone on the table. I swept a hand across the top, sending it flying behind the ficus tree. *What the hell was going on?*

I tried calling Franklin D., but it went directly to voice mail. He probably hadn't turned his phone back on after the restaurant. I slapped my own phone down on the table, and then startled at a noise coming from another part of the house. Oh, great, now I'd woken up Oma. Maybe if I sat beside her in the dark, I could get her back to sleep.

I was almost at her door when I heard something else. A curse, from out on the porch. I strode down the hallway, prepared to face Vickie, and probably her loser boyfriend, too. I wondered what the excuse would be this time. But then I heard more male voices. The words weren't clear, but the agitation couldn't be missed.

I raced down the hall and ducked into my bedroom. A second later, the front door crashed into the wall. Oh my God, they were breaking into the house. We were being robbed. I had to find a hiding spot. There was just enough space to wedge myself between the frame of my futon and the wall. I yanked the comforter over my body and reached in my pocket to call the police.

Oh, no. My phone. I'd left it in the kitchen.

Another crash. Dishes against a wall. *Stay asleep, Oma!*

What was I thinking? I couldn't hide from robbers. My bedroom was near the front door. And though Oma was being quiet right now, it was only a matter of time until they found her, too.

Climbing out of my spot, I scanned the room for a makeshift weapon. When they came in, I'd be ready. Then I'd run out the door and holler until someone called the police. Hopefully the robbers would panic and take off.

From out in the hallway, a single word interrupted my thoughts. No, not a word—a name.

"Text Vickie," a voice grumbled. "Tell her we got in, no thanks to that shitty key."

Oma had insisted that the Nazis had snuck into the house to steal her jewelry. At least three pieces had gone missing.

The gold bracelet, Vickie had found in a Kleenex box. Now I wondered if Vickie had both taken and returned it to shed suspicion. Oma blamed her "lost" jewelry on my mom, but she'd gotten it wrong.

But why would Vickie go so far as to set up a robbery when she could access Oma's jewels every day?

"She thinks it's in here," I heard one of them say. Foot stomps came closer, and then the door to the library slammed shut.

She thinks it's in here. What did they mean? Not jewelry, or they'd go straight to the bedroom. No, these men weren't interested in Oma's jewels. They wanted something else. Something far more important. Something that Vickie knew about, from spying on my conversations with Franklin D. This was a hundred times worse than a robbery. Who were these people? And what would they do to a girl who got in their way?

"Stop making that infernal racket," Oma yelled from her room. "Leave my china alone, you Nazis! You break my good plates and I'll gas you!"

I stiffened. *Stay in your room, Oma. Please, stay in your room!*

Now I wished I'd never unlocked her door. The irony hit me square in the jaw: Maybe Vickie had installed the lock to keep Oma from wandering out. She wanted to keep my grandmother safe, not put her at risk.

I crept out of my room. Books thudded against the library wall. Drawers crashed to the ground. I hoped it had been enough to hide the journal pages in the couch cushion.

I tiptoed down the hallway on a mission to retrieve my phone and call the police, but when a chair skidded across the floor, slamming into the interior of the closed kitchen door, I scrambled for Plan B. Maybe I could keep Oma quiet for long enough to sneak her out of the house.

I found my grandmother in bed, curled on her side like a prodded caterpillar. I put a finger to my lips, hoping she'd understand. If I talked, I knew she would.

"They'll make us go left and take a shower, because we smell so bad!" she yelled, startling me. "We have to escape, Gretchen. We have to catch the last train out. Hurry, grab your yellow star!"

"Oma, please," I whispered. "They'll hear."

Something lodged between my shoulder blades, cutting off my plea. My heart slammed against my chest. I stopped myself from turning around. "Please don't hurt us," I said, as calm as I could. "We haven't seen anything."

Ryan's e-mail came back to me. *I'll call you when they get them.* These men were after the entries, and when they couldn't find them, they'd force me to tell.

"Don't turn around," the man commanded, jamming the gun into my back again as if I needed reminding.

"I'm too sick," Oma wailed. "I'll die on that train without my nurse."

My eyes fell on the glowing green light at the bottom of the baby monitor. "There's a bolt on the outside of the bedroom door. You can lock us in here," I told the man, speaking clearly so if Vickie was hiding out in her apartment, she'd know where we were. If she wanted a way to "rescue" us once the robbers left, to be a hero in Mr. Laramie's eyes, I was game. I didn't care, as long as Oma and I got out of here alive.

"I'm dreadfully sorry," Oma cried. "I've been so bad! You're here to punish me, aren't you?"

"Tell the bitch to shut up or I'll make her," the man said.

The room was spinning. I squeezed my eyes shut. My lungs contracted into twin bullets. I was slipping into panic mode. *Breathe, Livvy. In, out, in, out.* I tried focusing my attention on the tick of the clock, not my pounding heart.

"It's going to be okay. I promise," I told Oma.

You can do this, Liv. You can do this.

She blinked several times like a sleepy child. "Keep me safe?"

I started to nod, but the man yanked me back by my hair. "Move it," he barked. I managed to hook my arm around Oma's and pull her to her feet. The man shoved us out into the hallway.

The men were still in the library, pounding on something metal as if they were beating it into submission. The other person had moved from the kitchen to my bedroom. I heard the tinkle of icicle lights, knocked off their chandelier pins, bouncing on the wood floor.

They had already searched the kitchen. Maybe the man would take us there. By now, I was sure they'd found my phone on the table, but they might've missed Vickie's behind the ficus tree. I'd once heard that emergency operators didn't need a voice to locate a call, but I had to get my hands on a cell first.

My hopes came crashing down as the man pushed us in the wrong direction. Oma stumbled over her feet, smacking her head against the door to the dining room. I screamed, catching her before she crumpled to the ground.

"Be careful!" I shouted at the man, accidentally glimpsing him. He was tall and thin, face obscured by a ski mask. At least I didn't have to worry about them caring if I saw their faces.

In the living room, the man threw us down on the settee. Oma whimpered in my arms. Another man walked in, also wearing a mask.

"It's not in there," the new guy said, his voice deep. I stared at the rope in his hand. He tied it around us three times. The fibers dug into my arms, burning my skin. When they seemed convinced we weren't going anywhere, they took off, leaving us alone.

"I always knew they'd come for me," Oma said.

From out in the hall, someone shouted instructions. Images of sentries in watchtowers, aiming at moving targets, flashed through my head. My back tightened as if the gun was still digging into the knobs of my spine. I tried to lean against Oma to comfort her, but I was tied too tightly.

"They're robbers, Oma. They'll take what they want and leave." I was trying so hard not to cry that my voice was clogged with tears. "They're almost done now."

Oma's mouth froze in a lopsided frown. I hoped she wasn't going into shock.

"I'll call the police as soon as they go. They'll find these men and put them in jail," I promised her.

She didn't say anything. I looked at her more closely. "Adelle?"

That's. Not. My. Name. *Say it, Oma!*

But she didn't. Her arm collapsed to her side, fingers

curling up like the legs of a dead beetle. She fell against me, and her eyes shut. Oh, God, had she fainted?

"Oma? Oma, wake up!" When she didn't open her eyes, I screamed, "Help! Someone help us!"

The deep-voiced man peered into the room.

"Something's wrong with my grandmother. We have to get her to the hospital!" I struggled to free an arm. Oma was a limp weight on my shoulder.

I pleaded with the man, "Please, she needs a doctor!"

"Shut up," he snapped.

I looked at her, willing her to wake up. Half her body was slack, all the way from her drooping eyelid to her right arm, which hung like an anchor at her side.

"She might be having a stroke," I told the man. He looked indifferent. "Please, you don't understand, the longer the blood flow is cut off from her brain, the worse her chances will be."

I couldn't remember where I'd heard the ominous fact, but it didn't matter. I was going to throw all my knowledge at him. "She needs to be treated in the first three hours or the damage can't be reversed. Please, you've got to help."

"Do you think I care?" he asked.

I tried to lunge at him, but the rope kept me moored. "If you don't help us, you could end up in jail for murder."

"Where's the diary?" he said, all business. "We know it's here. You find it, and Grandma lives to slur her words."

If I gave them the entries, they'd leave. I could get Oma the help she needed. But something wouldn't let me do it. There had to be another way. "What diaries?" I said. Beside me, Oma began to move. She moaned. "Please, we're wasting time. Just put her on the street and call 9-1-1. They don't have to know anyone's inside the house."

"Grandma's going to be a vegetable," he said slowly, as if time was a game he was playing. "Do what's right, sweetheart. Be a good granddaughter."

"Okay. Untie me, and I'll get it for you."

The man glanced over his shoulder as a third guy entered the room. He had a tuft of red beard showing under his mask. He aimed his switchblade at my throat and then lowered it to the rope. When it sliced through, Oma slumped back into the bloodred curtains. They swallowed her up, leaving only her eyes to peer from the folds of brocade. Blinking, at least. Still alive.

"I'll give you the diary if you let me call an ambulance," I said, rushing through my words as if they could get Oma to the hospital quicker.

"Get it and we'll leave," Deep Voice said.

I didn't trust him, but I was out of options. Pressing the blade into my arm, the bearded man led me out of the room, the other one right behind. I didn't want to leave Oma, but she'd be safer away from them.

In the library, the cherry bookcase lay tipped onto its side, a lightning-bolt crack running through the third shelf. Both drawers of the file cabinet had been yanked from their sockets and emptied. Old bills carpeted the floor. A painting I'd never paid much attention to—wildflowers in a field— lay on the floor. Someone had stomped a hole through the pastoral scene. My gaze climbed the wall and stopped. Behind the sun-faded imprint where the painting had hung was a metal door that clung to a dented box by a single screw. The safe had been emptied.

"The goddamn diary," the guy with the beard said, as if his knife wasn't enough of a reminder.

"Give me a second," I murmured.

"Ticktock, ticktock, less oxygen to the brain," said the other one. I heard a crash in Oma's bedroom. It sounded like a television flung across the room.

"Do you have scissors?" I asked. One of the guys nodded at the bearded man, who tossed me the knife. I shrunk back as it speared the floor in front of me. Pulling it free with both hands, I crawled toward the cushion, which was under the desk now. I stabbed it, dragging the blade down the middle.

"Ah, clever," the bearded one said.

I stuck my hand into the slit and routed through foam pellets until I touched the folder containing the papers. I peered inside, pulling out what I wanted. The bearded man was beside me in a second, snatching Franklin D.'s handwritten copies from my shaking hands.

"They all there?" the deep-voiced one asked.

The bearded man flipped through them. "Yeah, four."

He knew, because Vickie had told him.

I fixed an outraged look on my face. "Be careful. They're important. A lot of people will want to see them."

I heard the smile in his voice. "Yeah? Well some people will pay a lot of money so *no one* sees them."

So these men—or whoever hired them—didn't intend to sell the diary. They wanted to destroy the words of the most famous Holocaust witness ever. Franklin D. had been right: Some people wanted only a polished version of history.

Goose bumps crawled up my arms. My grandmother had been right to fear the Nazis, but she'd expected Nazis from her day, not mine.

Deep Voice grabbed the cuff of my dress sleeve, tightening it until my wrist throbbed. "This is a copy. It looks new," he growled, his breath hot against my ear. "Where's the original?"

I had no choice but to stick with invented facts as best I could, in case Vickie had told them the story already. "I took the pages to school and someone spilled milk on them, so I threw them away. I didn't think it mattered, because the man who translated them had this copy I made." I pointed to it. "These were his. He gave them back to me."

"Did you tell him who wrote this thing?" Deep Voice asked.

"Of course not," I said quickly. "I didn't even figure it out until we got the translation back. I don't think he had even heard of her."

"Who else has a copy?" he asked. "Don't lie to me."

I kept my eyes on his boots, not trusting my voice.

"Who else?" he repeated, giving my sleeve another wrench.

"No one! I swear! Please, can I call an ambulance now?"

"It's not the original," said the bearded guy.

"Shut up."

"But the deal . . ."

"It's good enough," snapped Deep Voice.

"Yeah? Well maybe she's lying, did you—"

"The story checks out, man. I said leave it!"

To cut off their thought process, I jerked my head toward the door. "Did you hear that?"

Bearded guy took the bait. "I don't like this, man. We gotta go."

A wrinkled corner of a photograph stuck out from under his heel. I'd searched the whole house for pictures and come up empty. Where had it come from? The battered safe?

When the bearded man moved to the door, the crumpled photo stayed behind. I looked at the woman in the black-and-white picture. A teenager, maybe eighteen or nineteen, a little older than me. She wore a white apron over a dress, and a nurse's cap topped her severely combed hair. I squinted at the brooch on her collar. Was that a Red Cross symbol?

The tall man came into the room. The three of them conferred about something, their backs to me. I scooted forward to get a better look at the photograph.

The "cross" had the warped arms of a swastika.

The picture in front of me was more than seventy years old, but I knew the intensity of the woman's gaze. I knew the down-turned mouth, the thrust of the jaw. This woman wasn't a prisoner; she was a nurse. A Nazi nurse. I flipped the photo over. *Lillian Johanna Pfeiffer, February 1945*, it said on the back.

I am Adelle Pfeiffer, Oma had said, the first time I'd met her. Adelle, not Lillian. But Pfeiffer was the name she'd used.

The photo slipped from my shaking fingers.

My sister calls me Lazy Lillian.

I didn't want to accept what I saw. But visual facts were stronger than written ones, or even witness testimony. Visual facts were indisputable. I couldn't deny it.

How could I have been so wrong? I'd thought my grandmother was Anne Frank—an inspiration to many, a symbol of hope that people could live together regardless of their differences. I thought she was a lasting reminder of the horrors of war. In my own story, Oma had sacrificed her identity for a powerful cause, knowing there was more grace in death than in life.

But everything I'd thought had been wrong.

The handwriting on the photograph belonged to the same person who'd written out the shopping list that was now in a desk drawer on the floor.

I'm a secret! she'd told me once. *No one can know I'm here. They'll kill me if they find me alive.*

My eyes pulled back to the photograph. The stubborn frown. The lower lip set in a pout. Oma wasn't a secret to be kept *away* from the Nazis; she was a secret because of her role in the Holocaust.

Oma wasn't Anne Frank.

She was a Nazi.

I'm dreadfully sorry, she'd cried. *I've been so bad.*

It hadn't been fear that plagued her; it was guilt. My grandmother had built a life of lies to escape the justice she deserved.

"Let's go," one of the men said to the other two.

I swallowed hard. "Please, can you call the ambulance? I don't have my phone."

The tall man reached into his Windbreaker and took out two cell phones, Vickie's and mine. With a cursory check, he plucked out the right one and purposefully threw it a few feet behind me. This had to be Ryan. Who else would know the difference between identical iPhones, the only distinction being my teal case?

The three men strode heavy-footed down the hallway. I held my breath until the door slammed behind them, leaving me with my tangled thoughts.

My grandmother was a criminal in the eyes of the world. Some people would say she deserved to die alone, just as the Holocaust victims had. But life wasn't so black and white. It was a gray fog that made it difficult to see more than a few feet ahead.

All I had left was my conscience. It failed my grandmother, but it wouldn't fail me.

I reached for my phone and called for help.

CHAPTER

TWENTY-FIVE

AROUND MIDNIGHT, I SCRAPED MYSELF OFF THE waiting-room couch. I wandered through the urgent-care ward, listening to the bells and beeps of hospital machinery, the suck of blood-pressure cuffs, the squeak of rubber-soled shoes on linoleum, and thinking all the time that the prisoners at Bergen-Belsen hadn't been allowed to leave this world in such luxury.

At one in the morning, the doctor found me at the All-Night Coffee Cart. She gave a no-news update, ending with the cliché "time will tell." She seemed to be waiting for the hail of questions that typically came from concerned family members. I disappointed her.

"Your grandmother's stable," she finally said. "Would you like to see her now?"

"No," I answered. Because I didn't. I couldn't.

She glanced at her watch. "Well unless there's a change, you won't see me until morning. I recommend you go home and get some sleep."

I didn't do that either. I carried my stale coffee back to the waiting room, sat across from a woman immersed in a *People* magazine, and stared at the muted television. I must've dozed, because when I checked next, it was three in the morning and the woman was gone.

A voice jarred me from my zombie-like state. A patrol officer stood in the doorway, pad and pen in hand. "Hello, I'm Officer Nidra. We got a call from the paramedics that your grandmother's stroke happened during a robbery at her home." He gave me a sympathetic smile. "I know it's late, but I'd like to get your statement if you're feeling up to it." My eyes skirted his badge. He wasn't just a cop. He was a detective.

I bit my lip. What could I say? "Yeah, some men broke into my grandmother's house."

"How many?"

"Three."

"Do you know why they were there?"

I couldn't tell him about the diary's existence without explaining why Oma had it in the first place. "To get money or jewelry?"

For all I knew, she'd stolen the diary. Oh, God, what if she, like the robbers, like the revisionists, had wanted to silence Anne's account? She'd had plenty of opportunities to return it to Anne's father, but she hadn't. And something else that didn't make sense: If Oma hadn't wanted anyone to see Anne's diary, then why didn't she destroy it all those years ago?

"Did you hear the robbers say anything?" Officer Nidra asked.

I couldn't mention the diary. It was too dangerous. I couldn't subject Oma, or my family, to that kind of scrutiny. So I told him that I heard the men talk about possible places where my grandmother might keep her jewelry. I fumbled around, tripping over my explanation. From the empathetic expression on his face, he seemed to think that I was incoherent with grief over my grandmother's stroke.

"Did you recognize any of the men?" he asked.

I couldn't even mention Vickie's boyfriend for fear it might lead back to my grandmother's secret. "No."

"Do you know what they took?"

As I tried to come up with an answer that seemed simple, I remembered the jewelry Oma had claimed was stolen by the Nazis. "Maybe her pearl necklace," I said. The other day, Oma had claimed that another necklace went missing, too. I'd checked the house, in case the clasp had snapped, but it hadn't turned up. "Also, my grandmother's Star of David necklace." I felt sick as it hit me that Oma had been hiding behind the same religion she'd once persecuted.

"Who else, besides yourself, might know about your grandmother's jewelry?"

I dug my fingernails into my palm. "Vickie. She's my grandmother's caregiver. The house is a duplex. She lives next door."

"Is it possible she might be involved?"

I don't remember nodding, but Officer Nidra added a note to his report. I knew then that I had.

When he finished with his questions, he asked when he could stop by the house to investigate. I bit the inside of my cheek. Of course the police would want to see the damage for themselves.

"Around one tomorrow?" That would give me time to scour the house for any important clues I might've missed.

He thanked me for my statement and gave me his business card. "I hope your grandmother recovers," he said.

Tears collected in my throat. I smiled, or at least I hoped I did.

When he was gone, I called Mr. Laramie. I left a detailed message, making it clear that with Oma in the hospital, we wouldn't need Vickie's help for the time being. Forever, really, but I didn't say that. Not yet. Next I phoned Mom. I hoped they'd given her phone back by now. Still, it was six twenty in the morning in Vermont, and sometimes she turned her ringer off.

"Hi there," she said groggily. "Wait, what time is it?"

"Mom?"

"Liv?"

"Yeah."

"What's wrong? Are you okay?"

"I'm fine. It's not me. It's Oma."

"Oh," she said, relief coming through loud and clear in one little syllable.

I told her how Oma had whacked her head on the dining room door and ended up in the Intensive Care Unit with a "cerebral vascular attack." I wavered, deciding there was no point in telling her about the robbery right now. She'd find out soon enough. All she'd do was worry about me and fire endless questions my way, questions I didn't know how to answer.

"When can you get here? We're at California Pacific Medical Center, in the ICU."

She hesitated, then said, "My flight's scheduled to get in Friday afternoon. That's only a few days away." She cleared her throat. "I think it would be better if I completed my twenty-eight-day program so I won't have to get into it all with an unsympathetic judge."

I was pretty sure an unyielding judge was a lame excuse. Mom didn't want to put herself out, not for Oma's sake. Forget sparing her the concern. "Actually, Oma's house was robbed. We were both there. They scared her, and she fell," I said. "I think that's what brought on the stroke."

"Oh, Liv! That's terrible. Are you hurt? What happened?"

"I'm fine," I said curtly. "Are you sure you can't come home sooner?"

"I don't think so, hon. They're pretty serious about me fulfilling my obligation here. Could mean jail time otherwise."

She waited for me to agree, but I said nothing.

"Livvy? You there?"

"Yeah."

"Can you handle this until I get there?" Her voice was perky now, sleep driven away, replaced by a familiar optimism in my ability to do everything and anything.

"Did you know that someone in the United States dies from a stroke every four minutes?"

"Liv, you know I—"

"Yeah, Mom, I can handle it." I cut the connection.

It took me a few minutes to realize I wasn't mad at her. Not exactly. Why would I expect a sudden change in behavior just because Oma was in critical condition? The person I was angry at was me. I felt guilty for not going in to see Oma. Didn't she deserve to have one person in the world who cared about her right now?

No, said a voice in my head. *She was a Nazi. She escaped punishment because she lied to everyone she met.*

What Oma *deserved* was a daughter exactly like my mother. Someone who saw her for who she really was. I gasped as the truth hit me. My mother had known. She must have. Why else would she have walked out of Oma's life all those years ago? That had to be the reason for the secrets. It might even be the reason Mom was in rehab at this moment.

I had a sudden, desperate urge to leave the hospital, to get far away from this place where everything I'd thought about my grandmother had already died.

At 4:20 in the morning, the cab pulled up in front of our Fillmore Street apartment. I went straight from the front door to my walk-in closet and lay down, too tired to stay awake and too wired to sleep. The walls, normally comforting in their proximity, seemed to expand and contract with a distant wheeze. I squeezed my eyes shut, trying to shut down the echo of an image: Oma, lying still on the stretcher, a tube down her throat.

I shook off the memory and considered my plan. After calling in sick to school, I would head to Oma's. By the time the police arrived, the original diary would be gone, along with any incriminating evidence. I'd show Officer Nidra the newly installed lock on Oma's bedroom door, and tell him that Vickie hadn't shown up for her shift that night. Finally, I'd hand him the laptop and explain how she'd been on her e-mail right before the break-in. I'd even give him her password.

Hopefully the police would connect Ryan's e-mail to the

break-in. If the men were found, I had a feeling they wouldn't be dumb enough to tell the full story.

Yes, that was my plan.

I wanted them caught.

. . .

You should never tell someone bad news in a text. I'd learned that lesson when Sean dumped me. Still, I couldn't bring myself to tell Franklin D. about Oma's condition in person. He'd take one look at my face and start digging for details, using pointed questions to poke holes in my story. And when he knew it all, every last detail, he'd never look at me the same way.

So I scratched off a text about the robbery and Oma's stroke, assuring him that I was fine, and sent it when he was in class, when there was no way he could call me back, when he wouldn't have the benefit of seeing my face, or hearing my voice, or watching my hands tremble.

When Franklin D. couldn't possibly glimpse the ugly truth about my family.

. . .

Back at Oma's, I forced myself to take stock of the damage, careful not to touch anything. Officer Nidra would be here in a few hours. It couldn't look like I'd cleaned the house.

I found Oma's jewelry box upside down at the foot of her bed. I searched the six tiny drawers for a pearl necklace, but it wasn't there. Had it ever been more than a figment of her imagination? The Star of David with the diamond edging had been real, but that wasn't in there, either. It was as likely to turn up in a box of Cheerios as to have been stolen.

I went into the living room and winced at the porcelain

cat, reduced to rubble. A few seconds later, I realized the laptop was missing. Why hadn't I thought to bring it with me last night? Vickie had the key to the house. I was stupid not to think of that. The only evidence I had linking her to the break-in was now gone.

In the library, the shredded cushion was still on the floor. My fingers burrowed through foam until they found the original pages, safe in their hiding place. I tucked the entries inside my math book and searched for the kind of evidence I *didn't* want Office Nidra to discover.

That included three more photographs. In the first, Oma and a Nazi official were shaking hands. A swastika band snaked around the man's arm. The others were snapshots from her life after she'd come to the United States. Oma and Herbert on their wedding day: her, in a lacy white gown with long sleeves, and him, in a cummerbund and bow tie, shoulders at attention. He looked proud of his bride, and perhaps, I thought, protective. This was not the look of a man who'd knowingly brought the enemy to his homeland.

I read the back of the last photograph before turning it over. *With Gretchen, 1971.* And there was Mom, a wide-eyed toddler with a mess of curls, clinging to Oma's leg and gazing at her mother with fierce adoration. Oma rested one hand on Gretchen's head, while holding a cigarette to her lips with the other. I slid the photograph into the pages of my math book, beside the entries.

I was thinking about whether or not to clean up all of the papers from the file cabinet when I spotted a typewritten page sticking out from under the armchair. I pulled it out, and within a sentence or two, I knew what it was. Page 210 described Oma's mixed feelings when she learned that she was pregnant with my mom.

Crawling around on my knees, I swept aside bills to search for more pages, and there they were, abandoned in the corner, a snapped rubber band lying on top of them like a Christmas ribbon.

The missing memoir.

My grandmother's secrets were right in front of me. Maybe they weren't the ones I'd been hoping for, but they were truths all the same. I skimmed the first fifty pages, which mostly covered her childhood in Germany. Her mother ran off with a shop owner when Oma was six. Her father lived at the office, leaving her and her brother under the care of a housekeeper named Gertrude, who was loving and kind when they were good and beat them with a thorny branch when they weren't.

An hour later, I found what I was looking for. Oma, a nurse, was on her way to her next assignment. A place called Bergen-Belsen. It didn't take long for a familiar name to jump out at me: *Anne Frank*. I closed my eyes for a moment, pressed a hand to my stomach, and turned the page.

I can't forget the day when the girl first came into the infirmary. She looked to be a few years younger than me, slight, with eyes made bigger by her gaunt face. She reminded me of a bird, delicate in her bones, yet she moved with ease and determination. It was something I was unaccustomed to seeing in this place of the walking dead.

She had a child of three or four with her. He

failed to rouse as she carried him in and laid him upon the cot. Having completed her mission, she slipped back out into the morning like an apparition.

Over the next three weeks, the girl returned several more times, always with a new child. One day she arrived with a toddler, his left arm stamped with flea bites. The boy screamed hoarsely as I completed the superficial exam. The girl stayed a few minutes longer that day, inventing a story of water sprites and mermaids that had a hypnotic, calming effect on the boy. This made my job easier, and so the next time I saw her, I requested she stay longer to tell her tales to the youngest patients as I completed my rounds. Of course, she did not object. In such a place, no one ever objected.

I will admit, the exams lengthened as I listened myself. The girl's stories were like a bubble of air at the bottom of a dark ocean, carrying each of us to the surface. It was a welcome respite from this wretched world, where death was a constant companion, where a nurse was forbidden from saving anyone.

Most people were too sick to leave the hospital. Medicine was in short supply, and I had grown stingy over the months, hoarding it in my desk. Still, the girl returned with yet another wisp of a child, despite appearing so weak herself that I feared she'd collapse, doubling my load. The story that day was of a chatterbox duck. I hid my smile behind a cupped hand.

I was mostly by myself in those last weeks of the

261

war. The doctor tended to camp fever in the barracks, and both nurses on my shift fell ill with flu. One day, while delivering a report, I spotted the girl, crouched beside a barrel, scribbling on the back of a can label. Writing was a punishable offense, and I saw the fear flame in her eyes. I strode past her and said only my name. She responded with, "Anne," and then, a moment later, "Anne Frank."

Days later, she came to the hospital with a young boy, a rag doll near death. She recited a poem, though the patient was unable to listen. She herself could barely speak for a dry throat. As I moved past, I dropped a blank sheet of paper onto her lap. She glanced at me with pleasure, but knew better than to show gratitude. I would have taken it away if she had. It was not my job to be kind.

These exchanges happened a few times—five or six, perhaps—establishing an awkward alliance between prisoner and captor. We were worlds apart in circumstance, though close enough in age. It could never be called a friendship—not during wartime, certainly—but it was a connection in the most unlikely of places.

I began to slip her something extra whenever I could. A roll, or turnip or two. Once, an orange . . .

One wet day, Anne flung open the door, her arms empty. I remember thinking she looked more like a chicken plucked down to its bones than a fifteen-year-old girl. I made certain no one was watching before giving thanks to God for her continued strength. It seemed I had not studied her closely enough. Anne's rosy cheeks defied the gloomy weather. Even a feisty girl could not win against the disease.

Oh, how I had looked forward to giving her the three sheets of paper I'd found in Irma's office the day before. A windfall! But even as I shared the news, the sorrow never left her face. Anne couldn't mask her feelings. I'd feared that this would bring her trouble from the likes of Irma and Herta. Still, when her emotions ran full throttle, it served as a reminder that we were not, all of us, dead. I, on the other hand, didn't dare express myself in such free, human ways. Barbed wire surrounded my heart.

"Something horrible has happened," Anne began. "My sister is gone! Why? How could it happen? Margot was so good, so perfect. I want to cry, but I can't! I've lost my tears. Why are my eyes dry, Lillian?" She looked as if her own words failed to make sense. Perhaps, under the cloak of her fever, they did not.

An emotion I hardly recognized cinched my heart. Years later, I would know it as guilt. How many times had I made Anne consume the food I gave her in my presence, despite her pleas about an ill sister? If she'd been caught with extra rations in the barracks, the punishment would have been severe for both of us. I would take the risk for her, but for no other Jew.

Life was dangerous for all as the war drew to a close. Just the previous week, Anne told me how a page of her journal had blown under Herta's boot. My handwriting had been on the reverse side—something

inconsequential, a note to a doctor, perhaps.
Fortunately, Herta had been too busy with roll call
to concern herself with a scrap underfoot. It was
obvious I could not afford another mistake. Not when
guns went off without provocation, aimed in impulsive
frustration. I was not naïve; I could die at the hands
of the SS almost as easily as Anne could.

After that day, I insisted she bring her entries
to me. I stored them in a locked drawer. They would be
safe there, as I was the only one who had the key.

I will never forget what she said next. "If
anything happens to me, you must show these to whoever
will look. Words, not people, last forever."

"Don't talk like that," I told her. "You will live
to write many more things."

Anne ignored my sentiment. Again she demanded
assurance that I would do as she asked. To appease
her, I agreed. Soon I had the four entries she'd given
me, a separate page for each, filled, I assumed then,
with the gibberish musings of a young girl. Words, I
have since learned, are the medicine of the soul.

After a second roll call later that day, Anne
appeared again. She spoke of a rumor—a transport
leaving Belsen in the immediate future. Of course,
I'd heard the same, though my reaction was one of
trepidation, not hope. Days earlier, U.S. forces had
liberated a camp less than 200 miles south. It was
rumored that the train would hold prisoners of value
to be traded for German officials, if such bargaining
became necessary. The prospect of defeat was

overwhelming. I assured myself that we'd heard such things before and nothing had come of it.

"It's for the prisoners of Sternlager camp," I'd said, eyeing the rash on Anne's neck. "The healthiest among them." Anyone could tell that a young girl with twiggy limbs and bloody scratches on her lice-bitten arms would make a poor trade for Axis officers.

"But my father was a businessman in Holland. He had many important connections!"

I felt certain that Anne would not survive such a journey. Her tired body could barely drag her into the hospital. Her chest quivered with effort. She had to stay here, with me, if she wanted to live. Only I could save her.

She fell to her knees, crying, "The train is my last hope."

I pulled her upright, the effort fatiguing me beyond expectation. My stomach gave a cruel twist. I could not upset myself so. I remember thinking this, even as the floor arched beneath me. Despite my training, I denied the signs. Of course, typhus infects all, regardless of religion or status, but back then, I'd told myself it was a disease of the Jews.

"Lillian, what's wrong? You're burning up!"

"You're a fine one to say that . . . you're an oven yourself," I said with a meager smile.

I grabbed the desk edge and struggled to work the lock. My head throbbed. A thin stream of sweat dripped down my spine. Anne had it far worse. I pressed the last of the pills into her palm. "Take them."

She gave them back. "I will be fine. I will get on that train. You can get me on it, can't you? Please, we're friends, despite it all. I know you won't deny it."

That word, *friend*, filled me with unexpected fury. "Shh!" I reprimanded, my eyes sweeping the mostly empty room, save for a comatose boy in the corner. There had been many deaths this morning. The place was near empty.

"Please. Anywhere would be better than here, even if it's on a train heading to nowhere." She looked as if she herself were Saint Peter at the Pearly Gates, weighing the future of my soul.

"I have no say in the matter," I said in a clipped tone. "Now take this food and eat it, or there will be no prayer for you at all." I pushed the scant bowl of limp carrots from my lunch across the desk. I could not eat it now, anyway. It would only come up again.

Anne did not so much as look at it. She turned around and hobbled out of the hospital.

I did not see her again.

TWENTY-SIX

MAYBE MY GRANDMOTHER WOULDN'T ADMIT THAT they'd been friends, but they had—as much as friendship could bloom in such a desolate place. But why couldn't Oma have done more to help Anne? Why hadn't she shared a little food and medicine with Margot? Most of all, I couldn't understand why she hadn't put Anne on that train.

I wiped the tears from my eyes and forced myself to keep reading. Oma, crazed with fever on the day of liberation, had ripped off her clothes and wandered onto the field with a crowd of sick and disoriented victims. The soldiers liberating the camp, without the clue of a uniform, mistook her for a prisoner. They set out to save her life.

Her life, not Anne's.

Anne Frank had already died.

The next chapter was a single paragraph.

It was years later that I contemplated the true reason for keeping Anne with me. I wanted her to live for selfish reasons, as proof of my good heart. If she died, I feared God might inflict on me a horrendous

and prolonged death—an end infinitely worse than any
punishment man could invent. With Anne on my side,
perhaps He would show His mercy. Perhaps I could even
forgive myself one day.

I lay down on the floor, gazing aimlessly at the wall.
Disgust and sympathy knotted in my chest. From the article
on the final transports out of Belsen, I knew that most of the
passengers hadn't survived the trip. Anne probably wouldn't
have, either. Even so, Oma should have put her on that train.
It didn't matter how much time she had left—weeks, days,
hours, minutes—Oma had crushed Anne's hope.

Now, all these years later, the only thing left was a
different disease that had warped Oma's memories until she
didn't know who she was, persecutor or persecuted.

I jumped at a knock on the door. The bruise on my back
throbbed, flooding me with the memory of a barrel jammed
into my spine. Instinctively, I searched for a hiding place,
but when the grandfather clock chimed once, I came to my
senses. It was only Officer Nidra, here to finish his report.

I hid the manuscript behind the poem anthology on the
shelf and went to the door. Officer Nidra followed me into
my bedroom as I described the stolen laptop. I left him to
explore the house on his own. A half hour later, he joined me
in the kitchen. I kept my hands in my lap so he couldn't see
them shake.

"This morning, my partner did what we call a Knock and
Talk at the caregiver's apartment." He glanced at his notes.
"Victoria Gregg."

I already knew what he was going to say. I'd looked through Vickie's glass door this morning. Clothes were scattered on the floor, an open suitcase tossed beside the couch. She was gone.

"I see in the notes that there was a damaged laptop on the floor," he said. "Would you be able to tell if it belonged to your grandmother?"

We headed outside, where I cupped my hands to Vickie's door and peered through the break in the curtain. Finally I spotted Oma's laptop in the trail of destruction that my grandmother's caregiver had left behind.

"That's it," I said, pointing. "Vickie and I were supposed to share it. She wasn't allowed to take it out of my grandmother's house."

"Did your grandmother make that clear?"

"It's in the contract."

I told him about the e-mail I'd read from Vickie's boyfriend that could have bearing on the case. I was relieved when Officer Nidra didn't ask me how I knew Vickie's password. He just wrote down the nine-digit number while I summarized what Ryan had said. His eyebrows shot up when I mentioned the trip to Kauai over New Year's.

"The password might be a phone number, except it's missing a digit," I told him. "It could belong to Ryan. I think the first three digits are an area code from Michigan, which makes sense since Vickie said he lives in the Midwest."

"You're a bit of a detective yourself," he said with a smile.

You don't know the half of it, I thought.

He eyed the dented top of the laptop. "I expect that the

hard drive's been compromised." He gestured for me to follow him to the street, where he pointed to the left side of the garage. "Does that mean anything to you?"

I stared at the graffiti, so small I wouldn't have noticed it if he hadn't shown me. Someone had drawn a fist, surrounded by what looked to be half a wreath.

I shook my head.

"It's an Aryan symbol for white power."

Seeing the Nazi image made everything feel more real, more terrifying. Suddenly I thought of the newspaper article that Franklin D. had shown me that time he'd brought over Dan's translation. "Is this related to the swastikas on the synagogues?" I asked.

"We're investigating the possibility. We found a similar drawing at Temple Beth Sholom on 14th Avenue," he said. "Unfortunately, well-intentioned neighbors covered the swastikas at the other locations before we could get there."

"Why did they target my grandmother's home?" I asked, fishing for his theory.

"We think they're a fringe neo-Nazi group from the Midwest. They probably ran out of money. Senior citizens are prime targets for theft."

A weight slid off my shoulders. He saw this as a robbery, nothing more.

"When we catch them, they'll be prosecuted to the fullest extent of the law," he said. From the bite in his voice, I could tell he took the case personally.

He glanced at the silver Honda Accord parked at the corner. A man sat in the driver's seat, a magazine propped on the steering wheel. "We'll continue to monitor the home for the next few days," he told me. "Do you have somewhere to stay during the investigation? We're going to put lockboxes on both these doors."

"Yeah, I live on Fillmore. With my mom, but she's out of town, so I was taking care of my grandma." Before he could ask anything I didn't want to answer, I said, "Can I get my stuff out of the apartment before you lock it up?"

He took my contact information, then waved me inside. I headed straight for the library and dropped to the floor, rummaging one last time through the scattered bills. This time, I spotted a birth certificate, issued in 1946, with some miscellaneous papers clipped to its back. Figuring it wouldn't be important to the investigation, I took it with me to look at later. I collected my math book with the original journal pages and the photographs inside, along with Oma's memoir, and left my grandmother's house for good.

· · ·

The doctors had weaned Oma from the drugs that put her in a medically induced coma to help her brain heal.

"She's still unconscious, but her vital signs are stable," the nurse said to me later that day in the waiting room, an optimistic lilt in her voice. "You can visit her anytime you want."

I shook my head.

After she left, I pulled the memoir out of my bag. I'd reached the part about Oma's engagement to an American soldier she'd met at the Displaced Persons Camp—my grandfather, Herbert.

I knew that Bergen-Belsen prisoners, those who
arrived via Auschwitz, had identification numbers. I
also knew that after the wedding, I could no longer
hide my arms behind prudish sleeves. The tattoo
declared my love for my husband, while eliminating
the blank slate of my flesh. Herbert was a kind and
accepting man. He never questioned it. We were both
happy to turn our backs on the war and start anew.

But the happiness hadn't lasted. My grandparents had an explosive relationship. Oma was a cold and distant mother. She couldn't make friends. No one ever got to know my grandmother—how could they, when everything she told them was a lie?

I wanted to stop reading. At the same time, I was hungry for the truth. I forced myself to start again at the beginning, combing through every word this time. It was my only chance to rise above the stranger status my grandmother afforded everyone else.

From the start, Oma had turned a blind eye to what was happening to the Jews. She had watched dispassionately as a banker was dragged from his place of employment and shot in front of a crowd. The next day, her unemployed father took over the man's vacant position. The family celebrated as if he'd deserved the new job.

Then came Kristallnacht, "Night of Broken Glass," when more than seven thousand Jewish homes, shops, and synagogues were destroyed. *We thought the Jews had squeezed us,* Oma wrote in the memoir. *We wanted them to return the wealth.* Oma saw to this by making a feast for her brother and father—potatoes, sauerkraut, and boiled chicken that she'd stolen from the back room of a Jewish market, to which her father said, "You see? They keep all the best things for themselves."

Oma never questioned anything, even as she watched her neighbors being carted off in police buses. All she knew was that Hitler promised a better world with the Jews gone. As far as her family was concerned, the proof was immediate and undeniable.

When Oma's brother became a fighter pilot, she wanted to make her family proud, too. She wasn't interested in the traditional role of wife and mother, so she signed up for nurse's training at a women's concentration camp in northern Germany.

My stomach rebelled as I read about the lavish meals my grandmother shared with Nazi officers while the prisoners around her grew more skeletal.

Later, Oma was transferred to Auschwitz, where she worked as an assistant to Dr. Mengele, a notorious criminal famous for his "medical experiments" on live patients. I skipped through gruesome details of sterilization experiments on women. Yes, it took guts for her to admit to such horrors on paper, but in the end, she'd withdrawn the manuscript.

When I got to the part where Oma left Auschwitz for Bergen-Belsen, I put the manuscript down. I needed a break. I walked the two miles back to my apartment, hoping the scenery would stamp out Oma's words. When I reached Fillmore Street, the sun was gone. The apartment was as cold inside as it was outside. I cranked up the heat and burrowed under a blanket on the couch, thinking about the ways Oma and I were similar. We both craved order to feel secure. We both were quick to judge. But Oma had been a Nazi, and that, by itself, made me feel ashamed of every last thing I had in common with her.

My phone chirped. It was another text from Franklin D. to add to the archive of messages he'd sent in the past six hours. I couldn't face him yet. I'd give him an update soon, but for now, I flipped my phone facedown.

The memoir, I urged myself. *Don't stop now or you'll never go back.*

I had reached the part where Oma connected *The Diary of Anne Frank* with the girl she'd known at Bergen-Belsen. She became obsessed with every detail of Anne's short life, attending plays, a movie premiere, even traveling to Ireland to watch the premiere choral performance of *Annelies,* which I hadn't known was Anne's formal birth name.

Ireland, 2005. Something about that trip tugged at my mind, begging for attention. I strolled mindlessly into the kitchen to make a cup of tea, then wandered back to the couch. Finally it came to me. Oma would have needed a passport to get to Ireland. But before she could get a passport, she'd need a birth certificate.

I ran to my math book and flipped through the pages until I found it. A note, clipped to the back of the certificate, stated that Herbert Friedman had served as official witness to the personhood of Mrs. Adelle Friedman, whose records were destroyed in the war. He claimed, under oath, that his new wife had no living relations or neighbors and, that to the best of his knowledge, she'd been born in Holland on June 12, 1926.

Coming from an American soldier, his testimony was golden. Oma got her identification papers with no trouble.

One fact didn't escape me: Anne Frank had received her first diary on June 12, because that was *her* birthday. Even all those years ago, Oma had laid claim to a small piece of Anne's history.

A social security card was paper-clipped to the back of the passport. I fingered the blue paper, thinking about how those nine little numbers were so different from the ones branded on the forearm of Auschwitz prisoners. Numbers that blotted out blame, redefining Adelle Friedman as a victim instead of a bully.

Another number flashed through my head. Vickie's computer password. I took out my phone and began to research. It seemed the first three digits of a social security number were state identifiers. When I typed in the start of Vickie's password, the code for South Carolina popped up.

It's not easy taking a South Carolina drawl out of a girl, Vickie had said.

I'd been wrong. The password wasn't Ryan's phone number.

I reached for the business card on the coffee table and called the number.

"Nidra," he answered, all business.

"Livvy Newman," I said, imitating his tone. He chuckled under his breath. "You know that number I gave you? Vickie's password?" I explained to him that it might be her social security number. He thanked me and hung up.

Next I called the hospital family line to ask about Adelle

Friedman's condition, even though I'd been there only a few hours ago. No change.

"Family visits are a great idea," said the woman who answered the phone, as if I hadn't heard this all before. I imagined the nurses at the desk, chatting about the strange girl who showed up every day but never left the waiting room to see her grandmother.

"My mom can visit her on Friday," I told the nurse, then hung up.

Why should Oma have family at her bedside, stroking her hand, encouraging her to live? The Holocaust victims hadn't died with such love and care.

Those thoughts, as truthful as they were, were a bitch to carry.

I'd just hung up when the doorbell rang, the buzzer going off like an essay in Morse Code. Anne came to mind, terrified as the Nazis incessantly rang the doorbell to her father's business downstairs. I could only imagine what the family felt as the German police charged through the building, heading for the bookcase that concealed the hidden door to the annex.

I stumbled to the window. Franklin D. cranked his head back and peered up at me, squinting past the streetlight that shone in his eyes. A ripple traveled through my stomach, different from the lump of fear that had shared the same space a moment ago. It was great seeing him. Really great. But I couldn't understand what he was saying, so I hoisted the window up.

". . . I went to the hospital, but they said you'd left already, and when I asked them about your grandma, they wouldn't tell me anything, not even if she was still there, so I took an Uber to Oma's house, but it seemed you'd moved out, which I found out when this scary cop drilled me with questions until I thought I was going to wet my pants. I told him I was your friend and not a criminal, and he said you were back at your apartment. Where's that? I asked. So he said it's just a few blocks over that hill, but he couldn't give out personal information. So I hiked over Mount Friggin' Fillmore and stopped at Tully's to see if they knew where a hot blond girl with awesome, shiny hair that smells like coconuts lives, but it turns out they see that kind all day, so I kept going, stopping at every last store, finding nothing, until I asked a homeless guy in front of Tomas's Taqueria if he'd seen a good-looking girl about my age go into any buildings around here, and he pointed to your door. So ready or not, here I am, and I won't stop ringing this bell until you let me in." He stabbed a finger at the buzzer to enforce his point, then shivered, drawing his arms into the puffy sleeves of his green parka. "Take pity on me, would ya? It's arctic cold out here."

I walked to the door and stood there, collecting myself. I was insanely happy to see him. Incredibly terrified, too. In another hour, he might run the other way. Still, Franklin D. deserved the truth—we all did. I buzzed him in.

"Hi," I said, a few seconds later.

"Are you mad at me?"

"At you? Not at all." I didn't like that he felt that way, but I knew it was my fault that he did.

"You haven't been answering my texts."

277

"Oma's not doing well," I started. "The stroke was bad. I needed to be alone with it for a while."

We moved to the couch. "I know, Liv. I'm sorry. I figured as much." He waited expectantly for me to fill in the details.

"Your parents think I'm Jewish," I began. "You told them, and that's why they were so excited about us going out, isn't it?"

His eyes widened as he considered my out-of-the-blue question. "Not exactly. I mean, yeah, I guess that's like icing on the cake and all, but they actually really like you because you're a nice person, and they think that your practical, grounded side is an excellent balance for . . . all that's me." He blinked twice and glanced away. "I was wondering if maybe you'd had second thoughts, and that's why you were putting me off. I mean, the facts are, I talk too much. And I get nosy about people. And sometimes I try to be clever when I should just shut up and listen, and . . . well, I'm fully aware that I might not be everyone's cup of tea."

I fought a smile. Franklin D., insecure? I had to admit, the rare glimpse of humility was charming. "Don't you know that facts aren't everything?" I said.

"Whoa, this from the ferocious fact aficionado."

"Take you and me, for example. It's a fact that you're a nerd, right?"

"I object."

I rolled my eyes but in an affectionate way. "Oh, right, *geek*." He nodded for me to continue. "And fact: You're a major smartass."

"I prefer 'curious.' 'Philosophical' even."

"One might say you have very little fashion sense . . ."

He started to protest. I held up a hand. "But here's the truth: I really like you. For some strange reason, I find those T-shirts you wear with the pithy math and science statements to be incredibly sexy."

He slapped a palm to his forehead. "Pithy! I love a girl with an extensive vocabulary."

"That's because we're all geeks when it comes down to it," I said. "I guess I'd rather have something in common with you than waste time looking at the ways we're different." I glanced away, assailed, all of a sudden, by sadness. "Oma saw the similarities between people, but she couldn't bring herself to act on it." This wasn't going to be easy, but I couldn't let the secret fester inside me the way my grandmother had. "I'm not Jewish," I admitted.

He cocked his head. "You're not?"

I took a breath and explained how the robbers intended to destroy the diary so no one would ever see it. I told him about the safe behind the painting, and how the men had broken into it. He didn't even ask me what they found. He just wanted to know if I was okay.

"I was wrong about my grandmother," I admitted. "She isn't Anne Frank. She knew her, though. Oma promised Anne that one day, she'd share the diary with other people. The thing is, she broke that promise. She couldn't do it, because then everyone would have found out the truth."

"Truth?"

The muscles in my body tensed at that one word that had haunted me for so long. I looked him in the eyes, facing my demons in their reflection. "Oma was a Nazi nurse."

I slowed my breath, hoping the rumblings of panic would

subside. Then I explained everything I knew about Oma's brief friendship with Anne Frank. When I was done, I sat still, waiting. Franklin D. was quiet.

"I don't know how I made that mistake," I said, shaking my head. "Me, of all people. It was like I was blind to some of the facts."

He inched closer. I tensed, fearing his reaction. But all he did was place his hand, firm and steady, over my icy one. "I think we failed to consider all the reasons she might have had the entries in the first place."

He was right. I had wanted to believe that my grandmother was Anne Frank. I wanted her to be the heroine. I wanted it so badly that I dismissed the possibilities that fit a different story.

"What would your parents think, knowing that I was the granddaughter of a Nazi?" I stared at my other hand, which was in my lap. Long, slim fingers. Like Mom's. Like Oma's. "More importantly, I'd like to know what you think."

Franklin D. didn't answer until I found the courage to lift my eyes to his. "I think you're a person who's made all her own decisions, independent of her family," he said. "Let me ask you this, would you go out with me if you knew that my dad smoked weed in college, then got behind the wheel and ran over a homeless woman?"

The unexpected question sparked a glimmer of hope. "That's terrible," I said carefully, "but it doesn't have anything to do with you and me."

"Right. It also doesn't matter what your grandmother did, because that's her *mishegas*. Not your mother's and not yours." He grimaced. "By the way, since we're being honest, I should tell you that I made up that story about the homeless woman to underscore my point."

I smiled. "Yeah, I figured as much." I moved my hand out from under his and brushed a finger across his cheek. "Would you mind terribly if I kissed you right now?"

He grinned. "I was wondering when you would ask."

TWENTY-SEVEN

AFTER FRANKLIN D. LEFT, MY HUNGER, WHICH I'D ignored all day, roared to life. We were deficient in the grocery department, so I had to settle for whole-wheat spaghetti with butter. As I added salt to the boiling water, my phone rang. The hospital? I tensed, fearing the worst. I snatched my cell off the kitchen table. "Hello?"

"Liv?"

"Tom!"

"Hey, I'm a few blocks away. Took me a while to find a parking spot for the rental car."

"You're here? Like, right now?"

"Yeah, I was going to fly in with your mom on Friday, but I decided to come early in case you needed help with your grandmother."

So Mom had told him what was going on. I smiled into the phone, grateful for the company.

"Have you heard of this place I passed a minute ago, Loch Ness Pizza?" he asked. "I was thinking, if you want, we could grab a bite to eat."

"I'd love to! I'll meet you there in ten minutes." I turned

off the stove, abandoning the pasta, and grabbed my coat off the back of a chair.

Tom was sitting on a vinyl stool at the stainless steel counter when I arrived. "I ordered your favorite. Sausage, red bell peppers, and feta," he said.

"You have no idea how amazing that sounds." I looked at him more closely. Something was different. I had a thought: Time could create scars, or heal them, depending on how you lived your life.

"You look good," he said. "I like the new hairstyle."

I touched my curls. I didn't even know where my flat iron was anymore.

"You look good, too," I told him. "Not that you didn't before, but you just seem . . ."

Was it his hair? No, that was the same. Hadn't he said he'd been using the gym as therapy to deal with his breakup with Lynn? "Are you still working out at the YMCA?"

The waiter delivered our pizza, thin crust and loaded with cheese.

"Actually, no. Well, not as much as before." He plucked a piece of sausage off his slice and popped it into his mouth. "I just feel really good these days, because . . . I'm happy, Liv."

I was confused. "Happy because Lynn left you?"

"Not that. It's pretty traumatic when a relationship ends." He kept tapping his fingers on the counter. I waited, giving him the space to say what was on his mind.

"I'm happy because I've met someone," he said at last. "Well, I didn't just meet her, but I just fell in love with her. I fell in love with my best friend."

As the meaning sank in, the words *Oh my God* echoed through my head. It wasn't easy imagining Mom with a man. Even harder with this man, because I'd always thought of Tom as her friend. Her *best* friend, like he'd said. Mom hadn't dated anyone since the divorce. She once joked that her long-range plan was to die a contented old lady with twelve cats. I'd given up on her meeting anyone.

Huh. A slow smile crept across my face. "Really?"

"Really."

"Wow."

"Yeah."

We grinned at each other.

I thought about Franklin D. and how we never ran out of things to say to each other. Best friends, it seemed, made excellent dating material.

Suddenly my excitement took a nose dive. "Are we moving back to Vermont?" I didn't want to leave Franklin D. or his friends, who were now my friends. I liked my high school, at least as well as someone *could* like high school. Not only had the square footage of my town expanded, my world had, too.

"There's a place in the South Bay that needs a rehab counselor," Tom said. "It's designed for working parents. It has an in-house day care to make it easier for clients to get the help they need. It's only a half-hour commute from the city. What do you think?"

I knew what he was asking. He wasn't looking for my opinion on a new job.

"Your mom's going to be here soon, and the thing is . . ."

He raised his eyes from the floor. "The thing is, Liv, I really want your blessing."

I laughed, surprised that he couldn't read the answer in my eyes. I heard Franklin D.'s voice in my head: *Tom doesn't know what you're feeling, because you haven't told him yet.* But then I had a better idea. Why rely on words when you can show someone? I hugged him, pinning his arms to his sides. "Welcome to Casa Crazy," I said.

His body softened under the embrace. "Glad to be here."

CHAPTER
TWENTY-EIGHT

Tom insisted that I return to school, even though it was the last day of the week. During a break between classes, I called the hospital for an update, but there wasn't any.

When the last bell of the day rang, Franklin D. and I blended into the mass of people shuffling toward the exit. My backpack strained at the seams with missed assignments and a new book I had to read for English. Once we were outside, Franklin D. took my backpack and heaved it onto his shoulder next to his own.

"What are you doing?" I asked.

"Haven't you seen reruns of *Little House on the Prairie*? A boy always carries a girl's schoolbag, especially when it weighs almost as much as she does."

"Are you kidding?" I laughed, trying to grab it back, but he dodged me.

There was a honk. My eyes skipped to the blue Kia, double-parked in front of the toy store.

"That's Tom," I told Franklin D. "My mom's here. She came in from the airport an hour ago."

But when I peered through the car window, she wasn't there. Tom popped open the trunk. Franklin D. stuffed my backpack in next to Mom's suitcase. We went around to the front and I made quick introductions, cut short by the line of cars building up behind us. Franklin D. turned down the offer of a ride, kissed me on the cheek, and headed to the bus stop.

I slid into the passenger seat. "Where's Mom?"

Tom glanced into the side mirror, then pulled into the lane. "I took her directly from the airport to the hospital."

"Oh. How's Oma?"

"Nothing new," he said.

"Are we going there now?"

"Later, if that's all right. Your mom finished her visit a half hour ago. She asked me to take you to Ocean Beach so the two of you can catch up."

Mom had always said that the roar of the waves and the smell of sea salt helped clear her head. She hadn't had much time for beach meandering since we'd come to San Francisco.

It didn't take long to get anywhere in a city that was seven miles long and the same wide. Fifteen minutes later, we pulled into the beach parking lot. Funny, San Francisco had felt huge to me just a few months ago.

Tom let me out, made an excuse about getting a newspaper, and drove off. Mom waited by the sand's edge. Our hug was awkward. She launched into stories about Evergreen. I joked that it sounded more like a retreat than a rehab.

"I wish! I had a lot of issues to fix. No time for massages, sadly." The wind lifted her hair. She tilted her head back and closed her eyes.

We talked about Tom next. She filled me in on the girly, romantic parts that he'd left out. Eventually we came to a less comfortable subject.

"The doctors say Oma's in serious but stable condition. Not sure what that means," she said.

I listened for a hint of warmth in her voice but heard nothing. The difference was, Mom seemed stronger and more focused. She pulled a folded paper from her pocket and smoothed it out. "The reason I asked Tom to bring you here is because there's something I have to do," she began. "I've gone through all the steps of AA, except one. Number nine, to make amends. In all my years of meetings, I've managed to glide right past that one. Anyway, I need to admit my past mistakes and acknowledge the pain I've caused others. That I've caused you, Livvy. I need to do it to lead a more honest life." She cleared her throat and read from the paper in her hand, her voice as formal and shaky as a person giving a speech before a packed house. "I regret all the times I hurt you with my drinking, Liv. I'm sorry that my response to the stress of taking care of my mother was to relapse. I wish I could've been the mother you deserved, and more than anything, I apologize for risking your life that night in the car."

I dried my eyes with the sleeve of my jacket. "Thank you," I whispered.

While we were being honest, I knew there was something I had to say. I began in chronological order, from the day she left for rehab to this moment, leaving nothing out. I even told her about Franklin D., though I blushed through the details. When I got to the part about the robbers looking for Anne Frank's concentration camp diary, Mom's hand flew to her mouth, but she kept listening. "I found out the truth when the safe was broken into. There were pictures inside, and a memoir she wrote. Oma wasn't a prisoner,

288

Mom. She was a Nazi."

I watched her face carefully. Her eyes drifted to the Cliff House restaurant, perched on the edge of the bluff beside us. "Yes, she was," she said finally.

Although I'd suspected that she'd known, the hurt, anger, and betrayal dropped like a boulder in my stomach. "How could you keep something like that a secret, especially from me?"

"That's not a simple question to answer." She looked down at the paper that listed her mistakes. It wasn't going to help her with this one. I figured she'd sidestep the question, but she didn't. "You deserve the truth, Livvy. I told you I didn't have an easy time with my mother, but she wasn't as bad as I let on. I exaggerated, because I didn't want you to get to know her."

Mom looked up from the paper, meeting my eyes. Then she folded her notes in half and tucked them into her purse. "When I was in college, I visited her. That's when I found that book she wrote. The memoir. I read half of it, and it made me so sick, I couldn't read another word. My mother was a monster! I told her what I thought, but she didn't care. She kept talking about some big publisher, as if that would fix everything. I was furious. My mother was going to tell everyone that she was a *Nazi*? It was appalling, what she'd done. All the outrageous lies she told us. She let my dad and me think that she was Jewish. I knew if the truth came out, her life wouldn't be the only one ruined." Mom scooped up a handful of sand and let it sift through her fingers. "The last time I saw her, we got into an ugly fight, she dropped me off at the train station, and, well, you know the rest."

"And so you told me that my grandmother was dead." It stung that my mother had transferred her dishonest upbringing to her own daughter.

"I didn't want you to end up hating her as much as I did. It poisoned my life."

I thought about what Franklin D. had said about my grandmother having to carry her own burdens. "If you'd told me, life might've been easier for you. Maybe you wouldn't have an alcohol problem," I said. "Did you talk about this with anyone at Evergreen?"

She shook her head. "Because Tom's my sponsor, they let him help me, privately. I needed someone I really trusted. He's been great, Liv. He helped me see that I was using alcohol as an anesthetic. I realized it was my mother's deal, not mine. It was fair for me to walk away, because she'd hurt me so deeply with her lies and secrets, all her stolen identities."

"It seems like you've figured it all out," I said.

She smiled, taking it as a compliment. Maybe it was, but I couldn't shake the knot in my chest. "I could have handled the truth," I insisted.

She sighed. "I know."

We watched the waves break over a rock, erupting into frothy spray. After a moment, she said, "The lies took on a life of their own. First, between my mother and me, and without my even knowing it, my relationship with you."

"Mom—," I started.

She cut me off. "Please, hear me out. I don't want you to say anything. I need to tell you how sorry I am. I really messed up, Livvy."

I nodded, already understanding why she'd made the

choices she had, even though I didn't agree with them. The sun, breaking through the ceiling of fog, seemed to melt the ice around my heart.

"This isn't part of the ninth step, Liv, but I just want to thank you for all you've done for my mother. Knowing you were in charge gave me permission to focus on myself."

"You're welcome," I said. Then I thought of something. "Mom, have you made amends to Oma?"

"I tried, but she probably couldn't hear me. I told her what I did wrong, but when it comes to forgiving her, I'm not sure I can. I'm not sure I even want to."

I got that. I mean, it would be a nice world if we could all forgive and forget, but I knew that wasn't always realistic. "I have her memoir if you ever want to read the rest of it," I said.

"Maybe one day," she said. "Not now."

Her phone rang. She glanced at the screen and told me it was the hospital. She listened for a moment to the voice at the other end, then said, "Okay. We'll be over soon."

I tensed as she turned toward me. "Oma's had a slight change. The doctor says she groaned in response to stimuli. She's had some eye movement, too. They say she's in a 'light coma' now. They don't know how long it will last, and it could be fleeting. Do you want to go back to the hospital?"

I nodded. Mom typed in a quick text to Tom, asking him to pick us up.

As we walked to the curb, she said, "For the first time in my life, I don't feel so fragile."

I smiled. "That's something. I'll take that."

I felt different, too. I'd become the kind of person who spoon-fed an old woman. I had a best friend who spoke four languages: English, JavaScript, C++, and Perl. I'd discovered that I was attracted to a brand-new type—the typeless type. And I could forgive my mother for messing up my life, because in some ways, it had forced me to make a better one.

Yeah, life was funny that way.

. . .

There was this prayer Mom said at the end of her AA meetings: *God grant me the serenity to accept the things I cannot change; Courage to change the things I can; And wisdom to know the difference.*

My grandmother was a criminal. I could judge her for her part in crimes against countless innocent people. I could turn my back on her, like Mom had. Or I could see Oma as she had been: a girl around my age, who'd sold her soul to believe in a world of Hitler's creation—one that promised jobs, solutions to economic problems, and a shiny new nation. A girl who'd ruined many lives, including her own.

I remember thinking that Franklin D. wouldn't have hidden who he was, even in the face of persecution. His reaction would be highly personal, tied to his life experiences. Without knowing where people came from, it was difficult to judge, or even understand, other people.

So in the end I decided to accept Oma solely for who she was to me—my grandmother. I was her last hope for absolution, the only person who could forgive her when she couldn't even forgive herself.

I looked at the closed hospital door one last time, then went inside. Oma lay on her back, still as a block of wood. The disease had whittled her down, robbing her of memory and agility. The stroke had stolen everything else. I cleared strands of hair from her forehead. Her skin was as soft as suede.

Who was this woman? Not Adelle Friedman, the name she'd taken on through imagination and marriage. Without hearing her truth, the sum of her parts, the essence of her being was lost forever.

I sat down on the edge of her bed and took the last page of the memoir out of my purse. I read it out loud.

"I knew it was treason to help a prisoner of war. During those last months at Bergen-Belsen, I felt more like a traitor to my own people than a good-hearted person. Over time, though, I realized I had done too little, too late. I was, as it turned out, a traitor to my own God."

I placed the page back in my bag and looked at Oma. She showed no signs of having heard. She was a sliver of the powerful, but overwhelming, woman she'd once been.

I weighed the facts one last time. My grandmother had made some horrific choices. But the reality was, I loved her in spite of it. Lifting her papery hand in mine, I bent down and kissed her cheek.

"I know what you did, Oma, and I forgive you."

She didn't nod, or blink, or raise a finger. The room was silent except for the occasional grunt of equipment that worked to keep her alive. Even so, I chose to think she heard me.

That evening, at 7:46 p.m., my grandmother, Lillian Johanna Pfeiffer, passed away.

CHAPTER

TWENTY-NINE

Dear Dad,

 Remember about a month ago when you asked me
to tell you when would be a good time for a visit? I've
changed my mind. I think summer would be great. It will
be nice to see you, Maggie, and the twins, so let me know
the best time for you, okay?
 —Liv

I sent the e-mail and headed out to meet Franklin D. at the Union Square tree lighting. He was going to show me his cardboard holographic glasses that transformed Christmas lights into a thousand Stars of David.

As I passed by the mirror that Tom had hung on the back of my bedroom door in our new Noe Valley apartment, I checked to make sure that I didn't have lip gloss on my teeth. I adjusted my *Statistics Is the Art of Never Having to Say You're Wrong* T-shirt, pulling it down over my hips, and made a face at myself.

Ready or not, I thought, *here I am.*

. . .

The day after New Year's, I got a call from Officer Nidra.

He told me that I'd been right about the password. Mostly. The social security number belonged to a caregiver with a different name: Laura Pratt. Vickie—or Laura, as it turned out—had made quite a business out of stealing from elderly clients. When they died, she moved to a different state and became a new person.

"The bills," I gasped. "Vickie paid a lot of Oma's bills. She had the checkbook."

"These people always find a way to 'help' with financial business. Laura Pratt embezzled over five thousand dollars from your grandmother's bank account."

My feelings about Vickie had been vague and uncomfortable. Why hadn't I gone to Mr. Laramie? Deep down, I knew why. I hadn't had the facts to back my gut. I remembered the Faulkner quote that Oma had shared with me the first day I met her: *Facts and truth really don't have much to do with each other.* Maybe Faulkner hadn't meant that facts were meaningless. Maybe what he'd been saying all along was that truth demanded more than facts.

"Unfortunately we didn't find your grandmother's pearl necklace in Ms. Pratt's apartment," Officer Nidra said. "But I have the Star of David one, and a silver ring with a few rubies that you can see if you recognize. I'll bring them to your home tomorrow."

"Thanks." Mom had mentioned a missing ring. *Probably fell down the sink*, she'd said.

"Laura Pratt has a long rap sheet. In fact, she's been legally prohibited from caregiving. Stolen jewelry, money, an undue-influence charge regarding an estate, and in two cases, elder abuse."

295

I cringed, thinking about all the times she'd been alone with Oma. If something had happened, my grandmother wouldn't have been able to tell anyone.

"I do have some good news to report," Officer Nidra said. "We accessed the e-mail you mentioned, and Ryan Johnson did make an airline reservation for December 28 on Hawaiian Airlines for himself and Laura Pratt. When they arrived in Kauai, we had a greeting committee waiting. They were taken in for questioning and booked for robbery. They didn't even get to see the beach, I hear."

"That's great," I said, relieved for my own reasons, but also because I didn't want them to hurt anyone else. "What about the other charges?"

"That's going to take us a little longer. We're being careful so it's a solid case. We believe a few of them belong to a group of neo-Nazis we've been after for some time. Laura Pratt's boyfriend seems eager to cut a deal with us, so we think he'll turn in the leader."

"The guy with the deep voice?"

"Yes," he said, surprised. "How did you know that?"

"Just a gut feeling."

"Well, your gut's impressive."

I smiled. "Happy New Year, Officer Nidra."

"Happy New Year, Ms. Newman."

EPILOGUE

Mom and I had to wait for forty-five minutes to get into the Anne Frank House and Museum. To keep myself busy, I studied the people around us. Was there a Holocaust survivor in the group? It dawned on me that in another decade or two, there wouldn't be any left on the planet.

The line of tourists curved around the corner, even though it was early in the morning. Americans, Australians, Germans, Italians—more races and ethnicities than I could count. We were almost at the entrance when an Asian man held the door open for the elderly black woman behind him. She nodded and walked inside.

Mom and I were here for our own reasons, though we would follow the crowd through the narrow rooms where the family and their friends lived until the Gestapo stormed their hiding place. At the entrance, we paused at the moveable bookcase that hid the secret stairwell. Mom moved behind me, blocking the view of the visitors in line, while I tucked the four original entries in between two books.

We smiled at each other and mounted the steep stairs. Like millions of people before us, we watched the video clips about concentration camps. We listened to speculation about Anne Frank's time in Westerbork, Auschwitz, and finally Bergen-Belsen. We even saw the original diary encased in a plastic box.

We finished the tour at eleven in the morning, with a brilliant, sunny day in Holland laid out before us. Our plan was to rent purple bikes and trail along the canals of the

Jordaan. Maybe later, we'd stop at a café to have a cappuccino and share some apple pie. At five minutes before closing, someone would call up Prinsengracht 267 and leave an anonymous tip.

And then one of Anne's final wishes would come true.

AUTHOR'S NOTE

Despite heroic attempts to save it, Anne Frank's beloved horse chestnut tree, noted three times in her annex diary, fell over in a windstorm on my birthday in 2010. I had no idea that years later, I would receive an invitation to an event at a nearby university from Professor Elaine Leeder, Dean of the School of Sciences at Sonoma State University. After an arduous application process, the university had been selected as one of only eleven sites in the United States to receive a rare sapling propagated from the majestic original. For three years, the university had nurtured the quarantined tree. Now, at last, it was ready to be moved to the Erna and Arthur Salm Holocaust & Genocide Memorial Grove. Attendees passed shovels around, tossing dirt onto its blossoming roots. (My daughter enjoyed that part very much and returned home a muddy mess.) Four years later, I'm happy to report that the tree thrives, and this symbol of freedom lives on.

The idea for *Stolen Secrets* took root long before, in 1996, when I was eight months pregnant with my first child. As I researched Anne Frank's journey by train to a concentration camp, I stumbled upon her full name on a roster: Annelies Marie Frank. Instant chills. I knew at that moment that I was going to name my newborn after the teenage heroine who hid from the Nazis for two years before being discovered and sent to a concentration camp. Two decades later, my editor-at-home, Annalise, has been made to read every word in this book at least four times. (Ah, the perils of being the offspring of an author.)

Admittedly, twenty years is a long time to cling to an idea. I hesitated about writing it because I knew I didn't have my writer "sea legs" yet. The subject was too big, too important, to do what I felt would be an amateur job. It wasn't until I finished three unrelated manuscripts that I felt ready to tackle the storyline.

At first, I felt uncomfortable altering a story belonging to a sacred, historical figure. I knew it could be challenging and, in some cases, destructive to fictionalize nonfiction. For years, I was the parent who wouldn't let my children watch such films as Walt Disney Pictures' *Pocahontas*, because I'd learned that parts of the plot were historically inaccurate. What if young minds absorbed invented plot points as fact? Parents and teachers should insist that children know the real story. Yet sometimes it's important for authors to fill in the blanks when specific information is unavailable, as long as these fictional details are judiciously evaluated. It's my belief that authors should do their best to honor the authentic character and experiences of any real person. Invention should be duly noted so that it's not mistaken as truth.

It took me some time to figure out how to write *Stolen Secrets* in a way that didn't invent a "new" Anne Frank. I made myself some promises: First, I would do my best to verify the accuracy of all historical information appearing in this book. (See the Acknowledgments page for a list of experts who helped in this regard); and second, I would avoid falsifying Anne or what she might have experienced. As it turned out, I was unable to do this entirely within the context of fiction. In *Stolen Secrets*, I imagined what happened to Anne in the concentration camps and invented the possibility of a

Bergen-Belsen diary. No one truly knows the horrors that the annex residents experienced.

Now that I had come to terms with how to handle the material, I was left with several intriguing questions, such as, *What if Anne Frank hadn't died? What if she had concluded that she would have a more meaningful role in Jewish history as a victim instead of a survivor?* My experience with my stepfather's Alzheimer's made me realize that this heart-wrenching disease that whittles down memory and confuses facts could be the right vehicle for exploring how guilt might rise to the surface after decades of justification and intentional deception. Intertwining these concepts was simultaneously fun, difficult, and heartbreaking.

A note about Anne Frank's annex diary: Most adults remember reading this classic in middle school. While writing *Stolen Secrets*, I learned that this vivid firsthand account of Jewish life during World War II is no longer offered on many school reading lists. As Livvy explains to Franklin D., Anne Frank's story has inspired poems, short stories, novels, operas, ballets, plays, movies, and other art forms. I fear that, without context, art that explores history could grow obsolete. Middle-school teachers, if you are not already doing so, please consider introducing Anne Frank's diary to your students.

My deepest desire is that *Stolen Secrets* will inspire readers to seek out this young woman's thoughts and experiences. Perhaps they will head to the library to check out *Anne Frank: The Diary of a Young Girl.* Maybe they will write me if they do. I would love nothing more than to wallpaper my home office with such letters. And perhaps one day, like Livvy, her mother, and myself, these readers will travel to Amsterdam to experience the Anne Frank House where eight people were forced to live in tight quarters, clinging to their dreams of the future.

While the outcome is tragic, there is undeniable joy in Anne's words, perceptions, and dreams. She became a published writer, her voice reaching sixty nations. She proved that while life can be short, hope is inextinguishable.

L. B. Schulman

ACKNOWLEDGMENTS

An acknowledgment page is a true gift, as nothing gets published without the tireless help of friends and colleagues. When a project takes as long as this one did, the gratitude list can get quite lengthy. I will mention the most major players, but please know that, in my heart, I thank every person who read pages, helped name a character, or answered random research questions.

A big thank you to the team at Boyds Mills Press, and especially my editor, Mary Colgan, who appraised every plot point and polished every word. To Ammi-Joan Paquette for her editorial and agent skills, all of which took tremendous time. And to the experts drummed up by my publishing team: Barbara Krasner, consultant on Jewish books and award-winning author, and Sarah Aronson, author and writing teacher, whose comment that she felt "wrecked" by the ending continues to be one of the best compliments I've ever received. And to Holocaust survivors Lewis and Trudy Schloss, who spoke to me for hours, allowing me to absorb the importance of this project. Though they are no longer with us, I believe that a part of their personal experience lives on in this book.

Much gratitude to my fabulous critique group, M'ladies of the Book, whose members—Alison Berka, Amanda Conran, Shannon Ledger, Darcey Rosenblatt, and Elizabeth Shreeve—have helped me in countless ways to reach this moment. Thanks also to the faculty and attendees of the Better Books workshop for their support and guidance. To my talented and most positive writer friend, Machille

Legoullon, who only deserves the best from the universe. And to those in my family who generously read drafts and offered opinions: my sister, Beryl Vaughan; my father, Martin Hauser; and especially my mother, Kathryn Allan. To my most eager reader, mother-in-law Janice Schulman, whose love of Livvy and Franklin D. helped inspire more pages. I miss her terribly, but will never stop hearing her voice as I write, urging me onward.

Love and thanks to my daughter, Annalise, who never refused to take a look, even though she'd seen the same chapter in multiple disguises before it found its true form. Her encouragement kept me going. And to my youngest daughter, Julia, who served as "Teen Authenticity Board," scouring every word to make sure that none of my stubborn '80s lingo crept in. And finally, a special thank you to my husband, Robert, who not only listened to me read every page out loud, but offered me the time and support to create in the first place.